The Year's Top
Hard Science Fiction Stories

Also Edited by Allan Kaster

The Year's Top Ten Tales of Science Fiction, #1-9

The Year's Top Short SF Novels, #1-6

mini-Masterpieces of Science Fiction

Great Science Fiction Stories

Steampunk Specs

Starship Vectors

We, Robots

Aliens Rule

The Year's Top
Hard Science Fiction Stories

edited by Allan Kaster

These short stories are works of fiction. All of the characters, organizations, and events portrayed in these stories are either products of the authors' imaginations or are used fictitiously.

The Year's Top Hard Science Fiction Stories

Cover art by Maurizio Manzieri

For information, address AudioText, Inc., PO Box 418, Barker, TX 77413

www.audiotexttapes.net

ISBN 978-1976168987 (trade paperback)

First Edition: September 2017

CONTENTS

ACKNOWLEDGEMENTS

"Seven Birthdays" copyright © 2016 by Ken Liu. First published in *Bridging Infinity* (Solaris), edited by Jonathan Strahan. Reprinted by permission of the author.

"Sixteen Questions for Kamala Chatterjee" copyright © 2016 by Alastair Reynolds. First published in *Bridging Infinity* (Solaris), edited by Jonathan Strahan. Reprinted by permission of the author.

"Number Nine Moon" copyright © 2016 by Spilogale, Inc. First published in *The Magazine of Fantasy & Science Fiction*, January/February 2016. Reprinted by permission of the author.

"Chasing Ivory" copyright © 2016 by Dell Magazines. First published in *Asimov's Science Fiction*, January 2016. Reprinted by permission of the author.

"Something Happened Here, But We're Not Quite Sure What It Was" copyright © 2016 by Paul McAuley. First published on *Tor.com*, July 2016. Reprinted by permission of the author.

"Of the Beast in the Belly" copyright © 2016 by Dell Magazines. First published in *Asimov's Science Fiction*, April/May 2016. Reprinted by permission of the author.

"RedKing" copyright © 2016 by Craig DeLancey. First published in *Lightspeed,* March 2016. Reprinted by permission of the author.

"Vortex" copyright © 2016 by Spilogale, Inc. First published in *The Magazine of Fantasy & Science Fiction*, January/February 2016. Reprinted by permission of the author.

"The Visitor from Taured" copyright © 2016 by Dell Magazines. First published in *Asimov's Science Fiction*, September 2016. Reprinted by permission of the author.

"The Seventh Gamer" copyright © 2016 by Gwyneth Jones. First published in *To Shape the Dark* (Candlewick), edited by Athena Andreadis. Reprinted by permission of the author.

"Fieldwork" copyright © 2016 by Shariann Lewitt. First published in *To Shape the Dark* (Candlewick), edited by Athena Andreadis. Reprinted by permission of the author.

Seven Birthdays

Ken Liu

7:

THE WIDE LAWN spreads out before me almost to the golden surf of the sea, separated by the narrow dark tan band of the beach. The setting sun is bright and warm, the breeze a gentle caress against my arms and face.

"I want to wait a little longer," I say.

"It's going to get dark soon," Dad says.

I chew my bottom lip. "Text her again."

He shakes his head. "We've left her enough messages."

I look around. Most people have already left the park. The first hint of the evening chill is in the air.

"All right." I try not to sound disappointed. You shouldn't be disappointed when something happens over and over again, right? "Let's fly," I say.

Dad holds up the kite, a diamond with a painted fairy and two long ribbon tails. I picked it out this morning from the store at the park gate because the fairy's face reminded me of Mom.

"Ready?" Dad asks.

I nod.

"Go!"

I run toward the sea, toward the burning sky and the melting, orange sun. Dad lets go of the kite, and I feel the *fwoomp* as it lifts into the air, pulling the string in my hand taut.

"Don't look back! Keep running and let the string out slowly like I taught you."

I run. Like Snow White through the forest. Like Cinderella as the clock strikes midnight. Like the Monkey King trying to escape the Buddha's hand. Like Aeneas pursued by Juno's stormy rage. I unspool the string as a sudden gust of wind makes me squint, my heart thumping in time with my pumping legs.

"It's up!"

I slow down, stop, and turn to look. The fairy is in the air, tugging at my hands to let go. I hold on to the handles of the spool, imagining the fairy lifting me into the air so that we can soar together over the Pacific, like Mom and Dad used to dangle me by my arms between them.

"Mia!"

I look over and see Mom striding across the lawn, her long black hair streaming in the breeze like the kite's tails. She stops before me, kneels on the grass, wraps me in a hug, squeezing my face against hers. She smells like her shampoo, like summer rain and wildflowers, a fragrance that I get to experience only once every few weeks.

"Sorry I'm late," she says, her voice muffled against my cheek. "Happy birthday!"

I want to give her a kiss, and I don't want to. The kite line slackens, and I give the line a hard jerk like Dad taught me. It's very important for me to keep the kite in the air. I don't know why. Maybe it has to do with the need to kiss her and not kiss her.

Dad jogs up. He doesn't say anything about the time. He doesn't mention that we missed our dinner reservation.

Mom gives me a kiss and pulls her face away, but keeps her arms around me. "Something came up," she says, her voice even, controlled. "Ambassador Chao-Walker's flight was delayed and she managed to squeeze me in for three hours at the airport. I had to walk her through the details of the solar management plan before the Shanghai Forum next week. It was important."

"It always is," Dad says.

Mom's arms tense against me. This has always been their pattern, even when they used to live together. Unasked for explanations. Accusations that don't sound like accusations.

Gently, I wriggle out of her embrace. "Look."

This has always been part of the pattern too: my trying to break their pattern. I can't help but think there's a simple solution, something I can do to make it all better.

I point up at the kite, hoping she'll see how I picked out a fairy whose face looks like hers. But the kite is too high up now for her to notice the resemblance. I've let out all the string. The long line droops gently like a ladder connecting the Earth to heaven, the highest segment glowing golden in the dying rays of the sun.

"It's lovely," she says. "Someday, when things quiet down a little, I'll take you to see the kite festival back where I grew up, on the other side of the Pacific. You'll love it."

"We'll have to fly then," I say.

"Yes," she says. "Don't be afraid to fly. I fly all the time."

I'm not afraid, but I nod anyway to show that I'm assured. I don't ask when "someday" is going to be.

"I wish the kite could fly higher," I say, desperate to keep the words flowing, as though unspooling more conversation will keep something precious aloft. "If I cut the line, will it fly across the Pacific?"

After a moment, Mom says, "Not really…. The kite stays up only because of the line. A kite is just like a plane, and the pulling force from your line acts like thrust. Did you know that the first airplanes the Wright Brothers made were actually kites? They learned how to make wings that way. Someday I'll show you how the kite generates lift—"

"Sure it will," Dad interrupts. "It will fly across the Pacific. It's your birthday. Anything is possible."

Neither of them says anything after that.

I don't tell Dad that I enjoy listening to Mom talk about machines and engineering and history and other things that I don't fully understand. I don't tell her that I already know that the kite wouldn't fly across the ocean—I was just trying to get her to talk to me instead of defending herself. I don't tell him that I'm too old to believe anything is possible on my birthday—I wished for them not to fight, and look how that has turned out. I don't tell her that I know she doesn't mean to break her promises to me, but it still hurts when she does. I don't tell them that I wish I could cut the line that ties me to their wings—the tugging on my heart from their competing winds is too much.

I know they love me even if they no longer love each other; but knowing doesn't make it any easier.

Slowly, the sun sinks into the ocean; slowly, the stars wink to life in the sky. The kite has disappeared among the stars. I imagine the fairy visiting each star to give it a playful kiss.

Mom pulls out her phone and types furiously.

"I'm guessing you haven't had dinner," Dad says.

"No. Not lunch either. Been running around all day," Mom says, not looking up from the screen.

"There is a pretty good vegan place I just discovered a few blocks from the parking lot," Dad says. "Maybe we can pick up a cake from the sweet shop on the way and ask them to serve it after dinner."

"Um-hum."

"Would you put that away?" Dad says. "Please."

Mom takes a deep breath and puts the phone away. "I'm trying to change my flight to a later one so I can spend more time with Mia."

"You can't even stay with us one night?"

"I have to be in D.C. in the morning to meet with Professor Chakrabarti and Senator Frug."

Dad's face hardens. "For someone so concerned about the state of our planet, you certainly fly a lot. If you and your clients didn't always want to move faster and ship more—"

"You know perfectly well my clients aren't the reason I'm doing this—"

"I know it's really easy to deceive yourself. But you're working for the most colossal corporations and autocratic governments—"

"I'm working on a technical solution instead of empty promises! We have an ethical duty to all of humanity. I'm fighting for the eighty percent of the world's population living on under ten dollars—"

Unnoticed by the colossi in my life, I let the kite pull me away. Their arguing voices fade in the wind. Step by step, I walk closer to the pounding surf, the line tugging me toward the stars.

49:

The wheelchair is having trouble making Mom comfortable.

First the chair tries to raise the seat so that her eyes are level with the screen of the ancient computer I found for her. But even with her bent back and hunched-over shoulders, she's having trouble reaching the keyboard on the desk below. As she stretches her trembling fingers toward the keys, the chair descends. She pecks out a few letters and numbers, struggles to look up at the screen, now towering above her. The motors hum as the chair lifts her again. *Ad infinitum.*

Over three thousand robots work under the supervision of three nurses to take care of the needs of some three hundred residents in Sunset Homes. This is how we die now. Out of sight. Dependent on the wisdom of machines. The pinnacle of Western civilization.

I walk over and prop up the keyboard with a stack of old hardcover books taken from her home before I sold it. The motors stop humming. A simple hack for a complicated problem, the sort of thing she would appreciate.

She looks at me, her clouded eyes devoid of recognition.

"Mom, it's me," I say. Then, after a second, I add, "Your daughter, Mia."

She has some good days, I recall the words of the chief nurse. *Doing math seems to calm her down. Thank you for suggesting that.*

She examines my face. "No," she says. She hesitates for a second. "Mia is seven."

Then she turns back to her computer and continues pecking out numbers on the keyboard. "Need to plot the demographic and conflict curves again," she mutters. "Gotta show them this is the only way...."

I sit down on the small bed. I suppose it should sting—the fact that she remembers her outdated computations better than she remembers me. But she is already so far away, a kite barely tethered to this world by the thin strand of her obsession with dimming the Earth's sky, that I cannot summon up the outrage or heartache.

I'm familiar with the patterns of her mind, imprisoned in that Swiss cheesed brain. She doesn't remember what happened yesterday, or the week before, or much of the past few decades. She doesn't remember my face or the names of my two husbands. She doesn't remember Dad's funeral. I don't bother showing her pictures from Abby's graduation or the video of Thomas's wedding.

The only thing left to talk about is my work. There's no expectation that she'll remember the names I bring up or understand the problems I'm trying to solve. I tell her the difficulties of scanning the human mind, the complications of recreating carbon-based computation in silicon, the promise of a hardware upgrade for the fragile human brain that seems so close and yet so far away. It's mostly a monologue. She's comfortable with the flow of technical jargon. It's enough that she's listening, that she's not hurrying to fly somewhere else.

She stops her calculations. "What day is today?" she asks.

"It's my—Mia's birthday," I say.

"I should go see her," she says. "I just need to finish this—"

"Why don't we take a walk together outside?" I ask. "She likes being out in the sun."

"The sun.... It's too bright...." she mutters. Then she pulls her hands away from the keyboard. "All right."

The wheelchair nimbly rolls next to me through the corridors until we're outside. Screaming children are running helter-skelter over the wide lawn like energized electrons while white-haired and wrinkled residents sit in distinct clusters like nuclei scattered in vacuum. Spending time with children is supposed to improve the mood of the aged, and so Sunset Homes tries to recreate the tribal bonfire and the village hearth with busloads of kindergarteners.

She squints against the bright glow of the sun. "Mia is here?"

"We'll look for her."

We walk through the hubbub together, looking for the ghost of her memory. Gradually, she opens up and begins to talk to me about her life.

"Anthropogenic global warming is real," she says. "But the mainstream consensus is far too optimistic. The reality is much worse. For our children's sake, we must solve it in our time."

Thomas and Abby have long stopped accompanying me on these visits to a grandmother who no longer knows who they are. I don't blame them. She's as much a stranger to them as they're to her. They have no memories of her baking cookies for them on lazy summer afternoons or allowing them to stay up way past their bedtime to browse cartoons on tablets. She has always been at best a distant presence in their lives, most felt when she paid for their college tuition with a single check. A fairy godmother as unreal as those tales of how the Earth had once been doomed.

She cares more about the idea of future generations than her actual children and grandchildren. I know I'm being unfair, but the truth is often unfair.

"Left unchecked, much of East Asia will become uninhabitable in a century," she says. "When you plot out a record of little ice ages and mini warm periods in our history, you get a record of mass migrations, wars, genocides. Do you understand?"

A giggling girl dashes in front of us; the wheelchair grinds to a halt. A gaggle of boys and girls run past us, chasing the little girl.

"The rich countries, who did the most polluting, want the poor countries to stop development and stop consuming so much energy," she says. "They think it's equitable to tell the poor to pay for the sins of the rich, to make those with darker skins stop trying to catch up to those with lighter skins."

We've walked all the way to the far edge of the lawn. No sign of Mia. We turn around and again swerve through the crowd of children, tumbling, dancing, laughing, running.

"It's foolish to think the diplomats will work it out. The conflicts are irreconcilable, and the ultimate outcome will not be fair. The poor countries can't and shouldn't stop development, and the rich countries won't pay. But there is a technical solution, a hack. It just takes a few fearless men and women with the resources to do what the rest of the world can't do."

There's a glow in her eyes. This is her favorite subject, pitching her mad scientist answer.

"We must purchase and modify a fleet of commercial jets. In international airspace, away from the jurisdiction of any state, they'll release sprays of sulfuric acid. Mixed with water vapor, the acid will turn into clouds of fine sulfate particles that block sunlight." She tries to snap her fingers but her fingers are shaking too much. "It will be like the global volcanic winters of the 1880s, after Krakatoa erupted. We made the Earth warm, and we can cool it again."

Her hands flutter in front of her, conjuring up a vision of the grandest engineering project in the history of the human race: the construction of a globe-spanning wall to dim the sky. She doesn't remember that she has already succeeded, that decades ago, she had managed to convince enough people as mad as she was to follow her plan. She doesn't remember the protests, the condemnations by environmental groups, the scrambling fighter jets and denunciations by the world's governments, the prison sentence, and then, gradual acceptance.

"... the poor deserve to consume as much of the Earth's resources as the rich...."

I try to imagine what life must be like for her: an eternal day of battle, a battle she has already won.

Her hack has bought us some time, but it has not solved the fundamental problem. The world is still struggling with problems both old and new: the bleaching of corals from the acid rain, the squabbling over whether to cool the Earth even more, the ever-present finger-pointing and blame-assigning. She does not know that borders have been sealed as the rich nations replace the dwindling supply of young workers with machines. She does not know that the gap between the wealthy and the poor has only grown wider, that a tiny portion of the global population still consumes the vast majority of its resources, that colonialism has been revived in the name of progress.

In the middle of her impassioned speech, she stops.

"Where's Mia?" she asks. The defiance has left her voice. She looks through the crowd, anxious that she won't find me on my birthday.

"We'll make another pass," I say.

"We have to find her," she says.

On impulse, I stop the wheelchair and kneel down in front of her.

"I'm working on a technical solution," I say. "There is a way for us to transcend this morass, to achieve a just existence."

I am, after all, my mother's daughter.

She looks at me, her expression uncomprehending.

"I don't know if I'll perfect my technique in time to save you," I blurt out. *Or maybe I can't bear the thought of having to patch together the remnants of your mind.* This is what I have come to tell her.

Is it a plea for forgiveness? Have I forgiven her? Is forgiveness what we want or need?

A group of children run by us, blowing soap bubbles. In the sunlight the bubbles float and drift with a rainbow sheen. A few land against my mother's silvery hair but do not burst immediately. She looks like a queen with a diadem of sunlit jewels, an unelected tribune who claims to speak for those without power, a mother whose love is difficult to understand and even more difficult to misunderstand.

"Please," she says, reaching up to touch my face with her shaking fingers, as dry as the sand in an hourglass. "I'm late. It's her birthday."

And so we wander through the crowd again, under an afternoon sun that glows dimmer than in my childhood.

343:

Abby pops into my process.

"Happy birthday, Mom," she says.

For my benefit she presents as she had looked before her upload, a young woman of forty or so. She looks around at my cluttered space and frowns: simulations of books, furniture, speckled walls, dappled ceiling, a window view of a cityscape that is a digital composite of twenty-first-century San Francisco, my hometown, and all the cities that I had wanted to visit when I still had a body but didn't get to.

"I don't keep that running all the time," I say.

The trendy aesthetic for home processes now is clean, minimalist, mathematically abstract: platonic polyhedra; classic solids of revolution based on conics; finite fields; symmetry groups. Using no more than four dimensions is preferred, and some are advocating flat living. To make my home process a close approximation of the analog world at such a high resolution is considered a wasteful use of computing resources, indulgent.

But I can't help it. Despite having lived digitally for far longer than I did in the flesh, I prefer the simulated world of atoms to the digital reality.

To placate my daughter, I switch the window to a real-time feed from one of the sky rovers. The scene is of a jungle near the mouth of a river, probably where Shanghai used to be. Luxuriant vegetation drape from the skeletal ruins of skyscrapers; flocks of wading birds fill the shore; from time to time, pods of porpoises leap from the water, tracing graceful arcs that land back in the water with gentle splashes.

More than three hundred billion human minds now inhabit this planet, residing in thousands of data centers that collectively take up less space than old Manhattan. The Earth has gone back to being wild, save for a few stubborn holdouts who still insist on living in the flesh in remote settlements.

"It really doesn't look good when you use so much computational resources by yourself," she says. "My application was rejected."

She means the application to have another child.

"I think two thousand six hundred twenty-five children are more than enough," I say. "I feel like I don't know any of them." I don't even know how to pronounce many of the mathematical names the digital natives prefer.

"Another vote is coming," she says. "We need all the help we can get."

"Not even all your current children vote the same way you do," I say.

"It's worth a try," she says. "This planet belongs to all the creatures living on it, not just us."

My daughter and many others think that the greatest achievement of humanity, the re-gifting of Earth back to Nature, is under threat. Other minds, especially those who had uploaded from countries where the universal availability of immortality had been achieved much later, think it isn't fair that those who got to colonize the digital realm first should have more say in the direction of humanity. They would like to expand the human footprint again and build more data centers.

"Why do you love the wilderness so much if you don't even live in it?" I ask.

"It's our ethical duty to be stewards for the Earth," she says. "It's barely starting to heal from all the horrors we've inflicted on it. We must preserve it exactly as it should be."

I don't point out that this smacks to me of a false dichotomy: Human vs. Nature. I don't bring up the sunken continents, the erupting volcanoes, the peaks and valleys in the Earth's climate over billions of years, the advancing and retreating icecaps, and the uncountable species that have come and gone. Why do we hold up this one moment as natural, to be prized above all others?

Some ethical differences are irreconcilable.

Meanwhile, everyone thinks that having more children is the solution, to overwhelm the other side with more votes. And so the hard-fought adjudication of applications to have children, to allocate precious computing resources among competing factions.

But what will the children think of our conflicts? Will they care about the same injustices we do? Being born *in silico*, will they turn away from the physical world, from embodiment, or embrace it even more? Every generation has its own blind spots and obsessions.

I had once thought the Singularity would solve all our problems. Turns out it's just a simple hack for a complicated problem. We do not share the same histories; we do not all want the same things.

I am not so different from my mother after all.

2,401:

The rocky planet beneath me is desolate, lifeless. I'm relieved. That was a condition placed upon me before my departure.

It's impossible for everyone to agree upon a single vision for the future of humanity. Thankfully, we no longer have to share the same planet.

Tiny probes depart from *Matrioshka*, descending toward the spinning planet beneath them. As they enter the atmosphere, they glow like fireflies in the dusk. The dense atmosphere here is so good at trapping heat that at the surface the gas behaves more like a liquid.

I imagine the self-assembling robots landing at the surface. I imagine them replicating and multiplying with material extracted from the crust. I imagine them boring into the rock to place the mini-annihilation charges.

A window pops up next to me: a message from Abby, light-years away and centuries ago.

Happy birthday, Mother. We did it.

What follows are aerial shots of worlds both familiar and strange: the Earth, with its temperate climate carefully regulated to sustain the late Holocene; Venus, whose orbit has been adjusted by repeated gravitational slingshots with asteroids and terraformed to become a lush, warm replica of Earth during the Jurassic; and Mars, whose surface has been pelted with redirected Oort cloud objects and warmed by solar reflectors from space until the climate is a good approximation of the dry, cold conditions of the last glaciation on Earth.

Dinosaurs now roam the jungles of Aphrodite Terra, and mammoths forage over the tundra of Vastitas Borealis. Genetic reconstructions have been pushed back to the limit of the powerful data centers on Earth.

They have recreated what might have been. They have brought the extinct back to life.

Mother, you're right about one thing: We will *be sending out exploration ships again.*

We'll colonize the rest of the galaxy. When we find lifeless worlds, we'll endow them with every form of life, from Earth's distant past to the futures that might have been on Europa. We'll walk down every evolutionary path. We'll shepherd every flock and tend to every garden. We'll give those creatures who never made it onto Noah's Ark another chance, and bring forth the potential of every star in Raphael's conversation with Adam in Eden.

And when we find extraterrestrial life, we'll be just as careful with them as we have been with life on Earth.

It isn't right for one species in the latest stage of a planet's long history to monopolize all its resources. It isn't just for humanity to claim for itself the title of evolution's crowning achievement. Isn't it the duty of every intelligent species to rescue all life, even from the dark abyss of time? There is always a technical solution.

I smile. I do not wonder whether Abby's message is a celebration or a silent rebuke. She is, after all, my daughter.

I have my own problem to solve. I turn my attention back to the robots, to breaking apart the planet beneath my ship.

16,807:

It has taken a long time to fracture the planets orbiting this star, and longer still to reshape the fragments into my vision.

Thin, circular plates a hundred kilometers in diameter are arranged in a lattice of longitudinal rings around the star until it is completely surrounded. The plates do not orbit the star; rather, they are statites, positioned so that the pressure from the sun's high-energy radiation counteracts the pull of gravity.

On the inner surface of this Dyson swarm, trillions of robots have etched channels and gates into the substrate, creating the most massive circuits in the history of the human race.

As the plates absorb the energy from the sun, it is transformed into electric pulses that emerge from cells, flow through canals, commingle in streams, until they gather into lakes and oceans that undulate through a quintillion variations that form the shape of thought.

The backs of the plates glow darkly, like embers after a fierce flame. The lower-energy photons leap outward into space, somewhat drained after powering a civilization. But before they can escape into the endless abyss of space, they strike another set of plates designed to absorb energy from radiation at this dimmer frequency. And once again, the process for thought-creation repeats itself.

The nesting shells, seven in all, form a world that is replete with dense topography. There are smooth areas centimeters across, designed to expand and contract to preserve the integrity of the plates as the computation generates more or less heat—I've dubbed them seas and plains. There are pitted areas where the peaks and craters are measured by microns, intended to facilitate the rapid dance of qubits and bits—I call them forests and coral reefs. There are small studded structures packed with dense circuitry intended to send and receive beams of communication knitting the plates together—I call them cities and towns. Perhaps these are fanciful names, like the Sea of Tranquility and Mare Erythraeum, but the consciousnesses they power are real.

And what will I do with this computing machine powered by a sun? What magic will I conjure with this matrioshka brain?

I have seeded the plains and seas and forests and coral reefs and cities and towns with a million billion minds, some of them modeled on my own, many more pulled from *Matrioshka*'s data banks, and they have multiplied and replicated, evolved in a world larger than any data center confined to a single planet could ever hope to be.

In the eyes of an outside observer, the star's glow dimmed as each shell was constructed. I have succeeded in darkening a sun just as my mother had, albeit at a much grander scale.

There is always a technical solution.

117,649:

History flows like a flash flood in the desert: the water pouring across the parched earth, eddying around rocks and cacti, pooling in depressions, seeking a channel while it's carving the landscape, each chance event shaping what comes after.

There are more ways to rescue lives and redeem what might have been than Abby and others believe.

In the grand matrix of my matrioshka brain, versions of our history are replayed. There isn't a single world in this grand computation, but billions, each of them populated by human consciousnesses, but nudged in small ways to be better.

Most paths lead to less slaughter. Here, Rome and Constantinople are not sacked; there, Cuzco and Vĩnh Long do not fall. Along one timeline, the Mongols and Manchus do not sweep across East Asia; along another, the Westphalian model does not become an all-consuming blueprint for the world. One group of men consumed with murder do not come to power in Europe, and another group worshipping death do not seize the machinery of state in Japan. Instead of the colonial yoke, the inhabitants of Africa, Asia, the Americas, and Australia decide their own fates. Enslavement and genocide are not the handmaidens of discovery and exploration, and the errors of our history are averted.

Small populations do not rise to consume a disproportionate amount of the planet's resources or monopolize the path of its future. History is redeemed.

But not all paths are better. There is a darkness in human nature that makes certain conflicts irreconcilable. I grieve for the lives lost but I can't intervene. These are not simulations. They cannot be if I respect the sanctity of human life.

The billions of consciousnesses who live in these worlds are every bit as real as I am. They deserve as much free will as anyone who has ever lived and must be allowed to make their own choices. Even if we've always suspected that we also live in a grand simulation, we prefer the truth to be otherwise.

Think of these as parallel universes if you will; call them sentimental gestures of a woman looking into the past; dismiss it as a kind of symbolic atonement.

But isn't it the dream of every species to have the chance to do it over? To see if it's possible to prevent the fall from grace that darkens our gaze upon the stars?

823,543:

There is a message.

Someone has plucked the strings that weave together the fabric of space, sending a sequence of pulses down every strand of Indra's web, connecting the farthest exploding nova to the nearest dancing quark.

The galaxy vibrates with a broadcast in languages known, forgotten, and yet to be invented. I parse out a single sentence.

Come to the galactic center. It's reunion time.

Carefully, I instruct the intelligences guiding the plates that make up the Dyson swarms to shift, like ailerons on the wings of ancient aircraft. The plates drift apart, as though the shells in the matrioshka brain are cracking, hatching a new form of life.

Gradually, the statites move away from one side of the sun and assume the configuration of a Shkadov thruster. A single eye opens in the universe, emitting a bright beam of light.

And slowly, the imbalance in the solar radiation begins to move the star, bringing the shell-mirrors with it. We're headed for the center of the galaxy, propelled upon a fiery column of light.

Not every human world will heed the call. There are plenty of planets on which the inhabitants have decided that it is perfectly fine to explore the mathematical worlds of ever-deepening virtual reality in perpetuity, to live out lives of minimal energy consumption in universes hidden within nutshells.

Some, like my daughter Abby, will prefer to leave their lush, life-filled planets in place, like oases in the endless desert that is space. Others will seek the refuge of the galactic edge, where cooler climates will allow more efficient computation. Still others, having recaptured the ancient joy of living in the flesh, will tarry to act out space operas of conquest and glory.

But enough will come.

I imagine thousands, hundreds of thousands of stars moving toward the center of the galaxy. Some are surrounded by space habitats full of people who still look like people. Some are orbited by machines that have but a dim memory of their ancestral form. Some will drag with them planets populated by creatures from our distant past, or by creatures I have never seen. Some will bring guests, aliens who do not share our history but are curious about this self-replicating low-entropy phenomenon that calls itself humanity.

I imagine generations of children on innumerable worlds watching the night sky as constellations shift and transform, as stars move out of alignment, drawing contrails against the empyrean.

I close my eyes. This journey will take a long time. Might as well get some rest.

A very, very long time later:

The wide silvery lawn spreads out before me almost to the golden surf of the sea, separated by the narrow dark band that is the beach. The sun is bright and warm, and I can almost feel the breeze, a gentle caress against my arms and face.

"Mia!"

I look over and see Mom striding across the lawn, her long black hair streaming like a kite's tails.

She wraps me in a fierce hug, squeezing my face against hers. She smells like the glow of new stars being born in the embers of a supernova, like fresh comets emerging from the primeval nebula.

"Sorry I'm late," she says, her voice muffled against my cheek.

"It's okay," I say, and I mean it. I give her a kiss.

"It's a good day to fly a kite," she says.

We look up at the sun.

The perspective shifts vertiginously, and now we're standing upside down on an intricately carved plain, the sun far below us. Gravity tethers the surface above the bottoms of our feet to that fiery orb, stronger than any string. The bright photons we're bathed in strike against the ground, pushing it up. We're standing on the bottom of a kite that is flying higher and higher, tugging us toward the stars.

I want to tell her that I understand her impulse to make one life grand, her need to dim the sun with her love, her striving to solve intractable problems, her faith in a technical solution even though she knew it was imperfect. I want to tell her that I know we're flawed, but that doesn't mean we're not also wondrous.

Instead, I just squeeze her hand; she squeezes back.

"Happy birthday," she says. "Don't be afraid to fly."

I relax my grip, and smile at her. "I'm not. We're almost there."

The world brightens with the light of a million billion suns.

Sixteen Questions for Kamala Chatterjee

Alastair Reynolds

WHAT FIRST DREW you to the problem?

She smiles, looking down at her lap.

She is ready for this. On the day of her thesis defense she has risen early after a good night's sleep, her mind as clean and clear as the blue skies over Ueno Park. She has taken the electric train to Keisei-Ueno station and then walked the rest of the way to the university campus. The weather is pleasantly warm for April, and she has worn a skirt for this first time all year. The time is *hanami*—the shifting, transient festival of the cherry blossom blooms. Strolling under the trees, along the shadow-dappled paths, families and tourists already gathering, she has tried to think of every possible thing she be might asked.

"I like things that don't quite fit," she begins. "Problems that have been sitting around nearly but not quite solved for a long time. Not the big, obvious ones. Keep away from those. But the ones everyone else forgets about because they're not quite glamorous enough. Like the solar p-mode oscillations. I read about them in my undergraduate studies in Mumbai."

She is sitting with her hands clenched together over her skirt, knees tight together, wondering why she felt obliged to dress up for this occasion when her examiners have come to work wearing exactly the same casual outfits as usual. Two she knows well: her supervisor, and another departmental bigwig. The third, the external examiner, arrived in Tokyo from Nagoya University, but even this one is familiar enough from the corridors. They all know each other better than they know her. Her supervisor and the external advisor must have booked a game of tennis for later. They both have sports bags with racket handles sticking out the side.

That's what they're mainly thinking about, she decides. Not her defense, not her thesis, not three years of work, but who will do best at tennis. Old grudges, old rivalries, boiling to the surface like the endless upwelling of solar convection cells.

"Yes," she says, feeling the need to repeat herself. "Things that don't fit. That's where I come in."

When you touched the Chatterjee Anomaly, the object that bore your name, what did you feel, Doctor?

Fear. Exhilaration. Wonder and terror at how far we'd come. How far I'd come. What it had taken to bring me to this point. We'd made one kind of bridge, between the surface of the Sun and the Anomaly, and that was difficult enough. I'd seen every step of it—borne witness to the entire thing, from the moment Kuroshio dropped her sliver of hafnium alloy on my desk. Before that, even, when I glimpsed the thing in the residuals. But what I hadn't realized—not properly—was that I'd become another kind of bridge, just as strange as the one we drilled down into the photosphere. I'd borne witness to myself, so I ought not to have been so surprised. But I was, and just then it hit me like a tidal wave. From the moment they offered me the prolongation I'd allowed myself to become something I couldn't explain, something that had its inception far in the past, in a place called Mumbai, and which reached all the way to the present, anchored to this instant, this point in space and time, inside this blazing white furnace. In that moment I don't think there was anything capable of surprising me more than what I'd turned into. But then I touched the object, and it whispered to me, and I knew I'd been wrong. I still had a capacity for astonishment.

That in itself was astonishing.

It was only later that I realized how much trouble we were in.

Can you express the problem for your doctoral research project in simple terms—reduce it to its basics?

"It's a bit like earthquakes," she says, trying to make it seem as if she is groping for a suitable analogy. "Ripples in the Earth's crust. The way those ripples spread, the timing and shape of their propagation as they bounce around inside the crust, there's information in those patterns that the seismologists can use. They can start mapping things they wouldn't ordinarily be able to see, like deep faults—like the Tōkai fault, out beyond Tokyo Bay. It's the same with the Sun. For about sixty years people have been measuring optical oscillations in the surface of the Sun, then comparing them against mathematical models. Helioseismology—mapping the solar interior using what you can deduce from the surface. Glimpsing hidden structure, density changes, reflective surfaces and so on. It's the only way we can see what's going on."

You mentioned Kuroshio. We have records of this individual. She was an academic scientist at the same institution as you, in the same nation state. This was long before Prometheus Station. Was Kuroshio the first to speculate about the project's feasibility?

Kuroshio was an academic colleague—a friend. We played football together, in the women's squad. Do you know what football was? No, of course you wouldn't. My friend was a solid state physicist, specializing in metallurgy. I knew her a little when I was preparing my thesis, but it was only after I resubmitted it that we got to know each other really well. She showed me around her lab—they had a diamond anvil in there, a tool for producing extremely high pressures, for making materials that didn't exist on Earth, like super-dense hydrogen.

One morning she comes into my office. She had to share one with three postdocs herself, so she envied me having a whole office to myself. I think she's come to talk about training, but instead Kuroshio drops a handkerchief-sized scrap of paper onto my desk, like it's a gift, and invites me to examine the contents. Is any of this making sense to you?

Never mind. All I can see is a tiny sliver of metal, a sort of dirty silver in color. I ask Kuroshio to explain and she says it's a sample of a new alloy, a blend of hafnium, carbon and nitrogen, cooked up in the solid-state physics lab. Like I'm supposed to be impressed. But actually I am, once she starts giving me the background. This is a theoretical material: A substance dreamed up in a computer before anyone worked out how to synthesize it. And the startling thing is, this material could endure two-thirds of the surface temperature of the Sun without melting.

"You know what this means, don't you?" she asked me. "This is only a beginning. We can think about reaching that crazy alien thing you discovered. We can think about drilling a shaft into the Sun."

I laughed at her, but I really shouldn't have.
Kuroshio was right.

What makes you think you might be a suitable candidate for doctoral work? Select one or more answers from the options below. Leave blank if you feel none of the options apply.

- o I am diligent student. I have studied hard for my degree and always completed my coursework on time.

- o I believe that I have a capacity for independent research. I do not need constant supervision or direction to guide my activities. In fact, I work better alone than in a crowd.

- o I look forward to the day when I can call myself "doctor." I will enjoy the prestige that comes from the title.

You felt that the solar heliospheric oscillations would be a fruitful area to explore?

No, an inward voice answers sarcastically. *I thought that it would be an excellent way to waste three years.* But she straightens in her chair and tries to make her hands stop wrestling with each other. It's sweaty and close in this too-small office. The blinds are drawn, but not perfectly, and sunlight is fighting its way through the gaps. Bars of light illuminate dust in the air, dead flies on the window sill, the spines of textbooks on the wall behind the main desk.

"Before I left Mumbai I'd spent a summer working with Sun Dragon, a graphics house working on really tough rendering problems. Light-tracing, real physics, for shoot 'em up games and superhero movies. I took one look at what those guys were already doing, compared it to the models everyone else was using to simulate the solar oscillations, and realized that the graphics stuff was way ahead. So that's where I knew I had an edge, because I'd soaked up all that knowledge and no one in astrophysics had a clue how far behind they were. That gave me a huge head start. I still had to build my simulation, of course, and gather the data, and it was a whole year before I was even close to testing the simulation against observations. Then there was a lot of fine-tuning, debugging...."

They look at graphs and tables, chewing over numbers and interpretation. The colored images of the solar models are very beautiful, with their oddly geometric oscillation modes, like carpets or tapestries wrapped around the Sun.

"P-mode oscillations are the dominant terms," she says, meaning the pressure waves. "G-mode oscillations show up in the models, but they're not nearly as significant."

P for pressure.

G for gravity.

The road to Prometheus Station was arduous. Few of us have direct memories of those early days. But the prolongation has given you an unusual, not to say unique perspective. Do you remember the difficulties?

Difficulty was all we knew. We breathed it like air. Every step was monumental. New materials, new cooling methods, each increment bringing us closer and closer to the photosphere. Our probes skimmed and hovered, dancing closer to that blazing edge. They endured for hours, minutes. Sometimes seconds. But we pushed closer. Decades of constant endeavor. A century gone, then another. Finally the first fixed bridgehead, the first physical outpost on the surface of the Sun. Prometheus Station. A continent-sized raft of black water lilies, floating on a breath of plasma, riding the surge and plunge of cellular convection patterns. Not even a speck on the face of the Sun, but a start, a promise. The lilies existed only to support each other, most of their physical structure dedicated to cooling—threaded with refrigeration channels, pumps as fierce as rocket engines, great vanes and grids turned to space ... each a floating machine the size of a city, and we had to keep building the entire network and throwing it away, whenever there was a storm, a mass ejection, or a granulation supercell too big for our engineering to ride out. We got better at everything, slowly. Learned to read the solar weather, to adjust Prometheus Station's position, dancing around the prominences. Decades and decades of failure and frustration, until we managed to survive two complete turns of the sunspot cycle. Slowly the outpost's complexity increased. To begin with, the only thing we required of it was to endure. That was challenge enough! Then we began to add functionality. Instruments, probes. We drilled down from its underside, pushed feelers into thickening plasma. Down a hundred kilometers, then a thousand. No thought of people ever living on it—that was still considered absurd.

The alignment between your models and the p-mode data is impressive—groundbreaking. It will be of great benefit to those working to gain a better understanding of the energy transport mechanisms inside the Sun. Indeed, you go further than that, speculating that a thorough program of modelling and mapping, extended to a real-time project, could give us vital advance warning of adverse solar weather effects, by linking emergent patterns in the deep convection layers with magnetic reconnection and mass ejection episodes. That seems a bold statement for a doctoral candidate. Do you wish to qualify it?

"No."

But people came, didn't they? Or what we might call people?

Call them what you will. All I know is that we got better at stability. Fifty years without losing Prometheus Station, then a century. I'd have lived to see none of it if they hadn't offered me the prolongation, but by then I was too vital to the project to be allowed the kindness of dying. And I'm not sorry, really, at least not of those early stages. It was marvelous, what we learned to do. I wish Kuroshio had seen it all—I wish she'd been there when the machines constructed a station, a habitable volume on one of the central lilies. Heat wasn't the central problem by then—we could cool any arbitrary part of the station down as low as we liked, provided we accepted a thermal spike elsewhere. Thermodynamics, that's all. Gravity turned out to be the real enemy. Twenty seven gees! No unaugmented person could survive such a thing for more than a few seconds. So they shaped the first occupants. Rebuilt their bodies, their bones and muscles, their circulatory systems. They were slow, lumbering creatures—more like trees or elephants than people. But they could live on the Sun, and to the Sunwalkers it was the rest of us who were strange, ephemeral, easily broken. Pitiable, if you want the truth of it. Of course, I had to become one of them. I don't remember who had the idea first, me or them, but I embraced the transformation like a second birth. They sucked out my soul and poured it back into a better, stronger body. Gave me eyes that could stare into the photosphere without blinking—eyes that could discriminate heat and density and patterns of magnetic force. We strode that bright new world like gods. It's exactly what we were, for a little time. It was glorious.

No, better than that. We were glorious.

Let's turn now to your concluding remarks. You summarize your mathematical principles underpinning your simulations, discuss the complexities involved in comparing the computer model to the observed p-mode data, and highlight the excellent agreement seen across all the comparisons. Or almost all of them. What are we to make of the discrepancies, slight as they are?

"They're just residuals," she says, not wanting to be drawn on this point, but also not wanting to make it too obvious that she would rather be moving into safer waters. The Sun's angle behind the blinds has shifted during the conversation and now a spike of brightness is hitting her dead in the eye, making her squint. There's a migraine pressure swelling up somewhere behind her forehead.

"The worrying thing would be if the model and the data were in too close an agreement, because then you'd conclude that one or the other had been fudged." She squints at them expectantly, hoping for the agreement that never comes. "Besides, the only way to resolve that discrepancy—small as it is—would be to introduce an unrealistic assumption."

What attracts you to the idea of working in Tokyo? Select one or more answers from the options below. Leave blank if you feel none of the options apply.

o   Tokyo is a bustling city with vibrant nightlife. I plan to throw myself into it with abandon. I will never be short of things to do in Tokyo.

o   I have always had a romantic attachment to the idea of living in Japan. I have seen many films and read many comic strips. I am certain that I will not be disappointed by the reality of life in Tokyo.

o   Beyond the university, the city is irrelevant to me. Provided I have somewhere affordable to sleep, and access to colleagues, funds and research equipment, I could live anywhere. I expect to spend most of my time in air-conditioned rooms, staring at computer screens. I could be in Mumbai or Pasadena or Cairo for all the difference it will make.

But to go deeper ... you must have quailed at the challenge ahead of you?

We did, but we also knew no one was better equipped to face it. Slowly we extended our downward reach. Ten thousand kilometers, eventually—feelers tipped with little bubbles of air and cold, in which we could survive. The deep photosphere pressing in like a vice made of light, seeking out the tiniest flaw, the slightest weakness. Beneath three hundred kilometers, you couldn't see the sky any more. Just that furious white furnace, above and below.

But clever alloys and cooling systems had taken us as far as they were capable. Electron-degenerate matter was our next advance—the same material white dwarf stars are made out of. A century before we got anywhere with that. Hard enough to crush matter down to the necessary densities; even harder to coax it into some sort of stability. Only the fact of the Anomaly kept us going. It provided a sort of existence theorem for our enterprise. An alien machine survives inside the Sun, deeper than any layer we've reached. If it can do that, so can we.

Hubris? Perhaps.

But the truth is we might as well have been starting science from scratch. It was like reinventing fire, reinventing basic metallurgy.

We did it, all the same. We sent sounding probes ahead of the main shaft, self-contained machines constructed from shells of sacrificial degenerate matter. Layers of themselves boiled away until all that was left was a hard nugget of cognitive machinery, with just enough processing power to swim around, make observations and signal back to us. They forged a path, tested our new materials and methods. Another century. We pushed our physical presence down to thirty thousand kilometers—a borehole drilled half way to the prize. Conditions were tough—fully murderous. We could send machines to the bottom of the shaft, but not Sunwalkers. So we shaped new explorers, discarding our old attachment to arms and legs, heads and hearts. Sunsprites. Sun Dragons, I called us. A brain, a nervous system, and then nothing else you'd ever recognize as human. Quick, strong, luminous creatures—mermaids of light and fire. I became one, when they asked. There was never the slightest hesitation. I reveled in what they'd made of me. We could swim beyond the shaft, for a little while—layers of sacrificial armor flaking away from us like old skins. But even the degenerate matter was only a step along the way. Our keenest minds were already anticipating the next phase, when we had to learn the brutal alchemy of nuclear degenerate matter. Another two centuries! Creating tools and materials from neutron-star material made our games with white dwarf matter look like child's play. Which it was, from our perspective. We'd come a long way. Too far, some said.

But still we kept going.

What do you mean by unrealistic?

"Look," she says, really feeling that migraine pressure now, her squinting eyes watering at the striped brightness coming through the blinds, a brightness with her name on it. "Everyone knows the Sun is round. A child will tell you that. Your flag says the same thing. But actually the Sun is really quite unreasonably round. It's so round that it's practically impossible to measure any difference between the diameter at the poles and the diameter at the equator. And if a thing's round on the outside, that's a fairly large hint that it's symmetric all the way through to the middle. You could explain away the residuals by adding an asymmetric term into the solar interior, but it really wouldn't make any sense to do so."

And nor, she thinks, would it make sense to introduce that term anyway, then run many simulations springing from it, then compare them against the data, over and over, hoping that the complication—like the cherry blossoms—will fall away at the first strong breeze, a transient business, soon to be forgotten.

They stare at her with a sort of polite anticipation, as if there is something more she ought to have said, something that would clear the air and allow them to proceed. They are concerned for her, she thinks—or at least puzzled. Her gaze slips past theirs, drawn to the pattern behind the blinds, the play of dust and light and shadow, as if there's some encouraging or discouraging signal buried in that information, hers for the reading.

But instead they ask to see a graph of the residuals.

Can you be certain of our fate?

Yes, I'm as sure of it as anyone can be. Obviously there are difficulties of translation. After all the centuries, after all the adaptive changes wrought on me, my mind is very far from that of a baseline human. Having said that, I am still much, much closer to you than I am to the Anomaly. And no matter what you may make of me—no matter how strange you now find me, this being that can swim inside a star, this Sun Dragon of degenerate matter who could crush your ships and stations as easily as she blinks, you must know that I feel a kinship.

I am still human. I am still Kamala Chatterjee, and I remember what I once used to be. I remember Mumbai, I remember my parents, I remember their kindness in helping me follow my education. I remember grazing my shins in football. I remember the burn of grass on my palm. I remember sun-dappled paths, paper lanterns and evening airs. I remember Kuroshio, although you do not. And I call myself one of you, and hope that my account of things is accurate. And if I am correct—and I have no reason to think otherwise—then I am afraid there is very little ambiguity about our fate.

When I touched the Anomaly, I suddenly knew its purpose. It's been waiting for us, primed to respond. Sitting inside the Sun like a bomb. An alien timebomb. Oh, you needn't worry about *that*. The Sun won't explode, and tongues of fire won't lash out against Earth and the other worlds. Nothing so melodramatic.

No; what will happen—what is happening—is subtler. Kinder, you might say. You and I live in the moment. We have come to this point in our history, encountered the Anomaly, and now we ponder the consequences of that event. But the Anomaly's perception isn't like that. Its view of us is atemporal. We're more like a family tree than a species. It sees us as a decision-branch structure frozen in time—a set of histories, radiating out from critical points. An entity that has grown into a particular complex shape, interacted with the Anomaly across multiple contact points, and which must now be pruned. Cut back. Stripped of its petals as the summer winds strip a cherry blossom.

I can feel it happening. I think some of it rubbed off on me, and now I'm a little bit spread out, a little bit smeared, across some of these histories, some of these branches. Becoming atemporal. And I can feel those branches growing thinner, withering back from their point of contact, as if they've touched a poison. Can you feel it too?

No, I didn't think so.

If you were offered a placement, when do you think you would be able to start your research? Select one or more answers from the options below. Leave blank if you feel none of the options apply.

- o I would be able to start within a few months, once I have settled my affairs in my home country.

- o I would like to start immediately. I am eager to begin my doctoral work.

- o I would like time to consider the offer.

We feel that the thesis cannot be considered complete without a thorough treatment of the residual terms. A proper characterization of these terms will lead to a clearer picture of the "anomaly" that seems to be implied by the current analysis. This will entail several more months of work. Are you prepared to accept this commitment?

A moment grows longer, becomes awkward in its attenuation. She feels their eyes on her, willing her to break the silence. But it has already gone on long enough. There can be no way to speak now that will not cast a strange, eccentric light on her behavior. That light coming through the window feels unbearably full of meaning, demanding total commitment to the act of observation.

Her throat moves. She swallows, feeling herself pinned to this moving instant in space and time, paralyzed by it. Her migraine feels less like a migraine and more like a window opening inside her head, letting in futures. Vast possibilities unfold from this moment. Terrifying futures, branching away faster and more numerous than thoughts can track. There is a weight on her that she never asked for, never invited. A pressure, sharpening down to a point like the tip of a diamond anvil.

There's a version of her that did something magnificent and terrible. She traces the contingent branches back in time, until they converge on this office, this moment, this choice.

Agree to their request. Or fail.

She gathers her notes and rises to leave. She smooths her skirt. They watch her without question, faces blank—her actions so far outside the usual parameters that her interrogators have no frame of reference.

"I have to go to the park again," she says, as if that ought to be answer enough, all that was required of her. "It's still *hanami*. There's still time."

They watch as Kamala Chatterjee closes the door behind her. She goes to Ueno Park, wanders the cherry blossom paths, remaining there until the lantern lighters come and an evening cool touches the air.

Number Nine Moon

Alex Irvine

THEY CAME IN low over the abandoned colony near the eastern rim of Hellas Basin, deciding which landing spot gave them the best shot at hitting all the potential motherlodes in the least time. The Lift was just about done, and everything on this side of Mars was emptied out. The only people left were at the original colony site in the caldera of Pavonis Mons, and they would be gone inside twenty-four hours. Steuby, Bridget, and Marco figured they had twelve of those hours to work, leaving enough time to zip back to Pavonis Mons and pay for their passage back in-system on the freighter that was currently docked at the top of the Pavonis space elevator.

"Quick visit," Marco said to no one in particular. "We're just stopping by. Quick trip. Trips end. People go home. That's what we're doing, boys and girls. About to go home, live out our happy lives."

Steuby really wished Marco would shut up.

"That's it right there," Bridget said. She pointed at a landing pad on the edge of the settlement. "Close to the garage, greenhouse, that's a lab complex...."

"Yup," Marco said. "I like it."

He swung the lander in an arc over the settlement, bringing it back toward the pad. Nineteen years of work, people devoting their lives to establishing a human foothold on Mars, and now it was up in smoke because Earth was pulling the plug. It was sad, the way people were withdrawing. Steuby always wanted to think of human civilization like it was an eagle, but maybe it was more like a turtle. Now it was pulling its head in. Someday maybe it would start peering out again, but all this stuff on Mars would be junk by then. Everything would have to start over.

Or humanity would stay on Earth, and in a hundred years no one living would have ever set foot on Mars or the Moon or an asteroid.

"Shame," Bridget said. "All that work for nothing."

"I hate quitters," Marco said.

Steuby didn't mind quitters. He kind of admired people who knew when to quit. Maybe that was a function of age. He was older than both Bridget and Marco by a good twenty years. The older you got, the less interested you were in fighting battles you knew you couldn't win.

But to be agreeable, he said, "Me, too."

"They're not quitting," Bridget pointed out. "Earth quit on them."

"Then I hate Earth," Marco said. "Just kidding. That's where I'll end up, when I'm old."

Nobody knew they were there, since what they were doing was technically illegal. The sun was going down, washing the landscape in that weird Martian blue dusk that made Steuby think he'd had a stroke or something every time he saw it.

"Time to see what the Lift left," Marco said, for maybe the hundredth time since they'd taken off from PM. Steuby was ready to kill him.

Their collective guess was that the Lift had left all kinds of useful things. People always did when they had to get out in a hurry. In the thirty days since the Mid-System Planning Authority announced it was ending logistical support for all human activity beyond the Earth-Moon Lagrange points, everyone on Mars had started lining up to get off-planet and back under the MSPA umbrella. Even the asteroid miners, as antisocial and hardy a group as had existed since Vinland, were pulling back. Things on Earth were bad—refugee crises, regional wars over water and oil and room to breathe. When things on Earth got bad, everyone not on Earth was on their own. That wasn't a big deal for the Moon settlements, which were more or less self-sufficient. Much different story for Mars.

"Are we sure nobody's here?" Steuby wondered out loud. It would be kind of a drag to get arrested in the middle of a planet-wide evacuation.

"I listened to the MSPA comm all night," Marco said. "Last people out of here were on their way to Pavonis before midnight."

Since the easiest way off-planet was the space elevator at Pavonis Mons, that's where the remaining colonists were, hiding out in the caldera until it was their turn to go up. The Hellas Basin settlement, over which they were now circling, was completely deserted. It was newer than PM, so the pickings would probably be better here anyway. Steuby looked out the window. Mars looked different around here. The PM caldera felt like it was already halfway to space because it was so high and you could see so far from the rim, when the storms let you go out on the rim. The Hellas Basin settlement, built just a couple of years ago to take advantage of a huge water supply locked in glaciers on the basin's eastern slope, was about as far from Pavonis Mons as you could get both geographically and environmentally. Practically antipodal. Where Pavonis was high, dry, and cold, Hellas was low, water-rich, and comparatively warm. Stormy during the summers, when the planet neared perihelion.

Which was now. There were dust devils everywhere, the atmosphere in the area was completely scrambled by magnetic auroras, PM was sucking itself up the space elevator as fast as it could get there, and here were Steuby, Marco, and Bridget thousands of klicks away at HB exploring. Well, prospecting. Okay, looting.

"We're just here to plunder the mysteries, Ma'am," Marco said to an imaginary cop, even though the auroras meant they couldn't talk to any authorities whether they wanted to or not. He put the lander into its final descent and ninety seconds later they were parked on the surface of Mars. There was a sharp crack from below as the ship touched down.

"Nice going," Steuby said. "You broke the pad."

Marco shrugged. "Who's gonna know? You find me a concrete slab on Mars that doesn't have a crack in it. Steuby, what was it, ten years since we were here before?"

Steuby nodded. "Give or take." He and Marco had worked a pipeline project on the lower slopes of Pavonis. Then he'd gone back in-system. He preferred the Moon. Real Martians wanted to get away from Earth. Steuby preferred to keep the Earth close by in case he needed it. "Bridget, you've been here before, right?"

"I built some of the solar arrays on the edge of the Pavonis caldera," she said. "Long time ago. But this is my first time coming out to Hellas. And last, looks like."

They suited up and popped the hatch. Bridget went first, Steuby right behind her, and Marco appeared in the hatchway a minute later, after doing a quick post-flight check on the lander's engines. "Good morning, Barsoom!" he sang out.

Marco was three steps down the ladder when they all heard a grinding rumble from under the ground. Steuby felt the pad shift and scrambled backward. The lander started to tip as the concrete pad cracked and collapsed into a sinkhole that opened up right at Steuby's feet. Marco lost his balance and grabbed at the ladder railing. The sinkhole kept opening up and the lander kept tipping. "Marco!" Bridget shouted. "Jump!"

He tried, but he couldn't get his feet under him and instead he slipped, pitching off the ladder and falling into the sinkhole as the lander tipped right over on top of him. The whole scene unfolded in the strange slow motion of falling objects in Martian gravity, dreamlike and all the more frightening because even slowed down, the lander tipped too quickly for Marco to get out of the way. He disappeared beneath it as its hull scraped along the broken concrete slabs.

Before it had completely come to rest, Steuby and Bridget were clambering around the edge of the sinkhole, where large pieces of the concrete pad angled under the toppled lander. Steuby spotted him first, face down and not moving. He slid into the dust-filled space underneath the bulk of the lander, Bridget right next to him. Together they grabbed Marco's legs and tried to drag him out, but he was caught on something. They could pivot him around but not pull him free. "Marco," Bridget said. "Talk to me."

The dust started to clear and Steuby saw why Marco wasn't answering.

The ladder railing had broken off and part of it impaled Marco just inside his right shoulder blade. Blood welled up around the hole in his suit and ran out from under his body down the tilted concrete slab. Now Marco turned his head toward them. Dust covered his faceplate. He was moving his left arm and trying to talk, but his comm was out. His voice was a thin hum and they couldn't understand what he was saying. A minute later it didn't matter anymore because he was dead.

"Marco," Steuby said. He paused, feeling like he ought to say something but not sure what. After a while he added, "Hope it didn't hurt too much when we pulled on you. We were trying to help."

Bridget had been sitting silently since Marco stopped moving. Now she stood up. "Don't talk to him, Jesus, he's dead! Don't talk to him!"

Steuby didn't say anything.

All he could figure was that there had been some kind of gas pocket under the landing pad, frozen hydrates or something. They'd sublimated away gradually from the sporadic heat of a hundred or a thousand landings, creating a soft spot, and when Marco set down their lander, that last little bit of heat had weakened the pad. Crack, tip, disaster.

"What are we going to do?" Bridget asked in a calmer tone. It was a reasonable question to which Steuby had no good answer. He looked around. They were at the edge of a deserted settlement on Mars. The only other people on Mars were thousands of kilometers away, and had neither the resources nor the inclination to help, was Steuby's guess.

He shrugged. "Probably we're going to die."

"Okay," she said. "But let's say we didn't want to die. What would we do then?"

Compared to the Moon, everything on Mars was easy. It had water, it had lots of usable minerals that were easy to get to, synthesizing fuels was no problem, solar power was efficient because the thin atmosphere compensated for the distance to the Sun ... as colonizing projects went, it was a piece of cake. In theory.

In reality, Mars was very good at killing people. Steuby looked at the horizon. The sun was coming up. If he and Bridget couldn't figure something out real soon, Mars would probably add two more people to its tally. Steuby wasn't ready to be a statistic. Marco, well, Marco already was.

Now the question wasn't what the Lift had left, but whether they were going to be able to lift themselves or be left behind for good.

"We'll see," Steuby said.

Bridget looked up. "See what?"

"Nothing."

"You're talking to Marco."

"No, I'm not," Steuby lied.

"Here's a question, since you're thinking about him anyway. What should we do with him?"

"What do you mean, what should we do? It's not like we can strap him to the roof."

She let it go. They started walking toward the main cluster of buildings and domes that made up the Hellas Basin settlement.

Phobos was rising, big and bright. Sometimes sunlight hit Phobos a certain way and the big impact crater on its planet-facing side caught the shadows just right, and for an hour or so there was a giant number

9 in the Martian sky. Steuby wasn't superstitious, but when he saw that, he understood how people got that way.

Number Nine Moon was his favorite thing about Mars. He hoped, if he was going to die in the next few days—and due to recent developments, that seemed more than likely—he would die looking at it.

From behind him Bridget said, "Steuby. Stop looking at the moon."

Marco was the one who had pointed out Number Nine Moon to him, when they'd been on Mars before. "I knew him for a long time, Bridget," Steuby said. "Just give me a minute."

"We don't really have any extra minutes."

This was true. Steuby climbed up out of the sinkhole. "Come on, then," he said.

"Where?"

"We can't walk back to PM," Steuby said. "Can't drive. So we're going to have to fly."

"Fly what?"

Steuby didn't want to tell her what he was thinking until he had a little more than moonshine to go on. "Let's head to the garage over there. I'll show you."

They sealed the garage doors after they went inside. It was warm. Condensation appeared on their faceplates. "Hey," Steuby said. "There's still air in here."

He popped his faceplate and smelled dirt and plants. A passive oxygen system in the garage circulated air from a nearby greenhouse. The plants hadn't had time to freeze and die yet.

With the dirty faceplate off, he could see better in the dim interior. He found a light switch and flicked it on, just in case. "Hey, lights too."

Now for the real test. Along one wall of the garage were a series of spigots and vents, spaced out over underground tanks. Steuby walked along them, saying silent prayers to the gods of chemistry that one of the spigots would be tagged with a particular series of letters.

He stopped at the fourth and pointed out the letters. "MMH," Bridget read. "Monomethylhydrazine, right?"

"Yup," Steuby said. "Also known as jackpot. They must have made it down here for impulse thrusters. Landers would need to tank up on it before they took off again. You know what this means?"

"That we have a whole lot of a fuel that doesn't work in our ship, which is crashed anyway."

"No, it means we have half of a hypergolic fuel combination designed to work in engines just exactly like the one built into that rocket out there." Steuby pointed toward the garage's bank of south-facing windows. Bridget followed the direction of his finger.

"You're kidding," she said. "That thing is a toy."

"*Au contraire, Mademoiselle,*" Steuby said. "I've seen those fly."

When he'd gotten out of the construction business after Walter Navarro's death and spent his next years fleecing tourists, Steuby had briefly worked on an amusement park project. A woman named Veronica Liu wanted to create an homage to classic visions of the Moon from the days before the Space Age. Lots of pointy rockets and gleaming domes. She'd built it over the course of a year, with rides specifically designed for the Moon's gravity, and then at the opening ceremony she had put on a big show of landing a fleet of rockets specifically designed to recall the covers of pulp magazines from the 1940s. They were pointy, finned, gleaming—and when the amusement park went under five years after Liu built it, they were sold off to other concerns. One of them was still on the Moon as far as Steuby knew, because she hadn't been able to sell it for a price that made the deal worth doing.

Another was now standing on a small pad a kilometer from the garage. Steuby had spotted it on their first flyover. He didn't know how it had gotten there, and he didn't care. All he cared about was finding out whether it would fly.

"That's a ridiculous idea. This whole thing was a ridiculous idea. You had to come up with a stupid scheme to get rich and now Marco's dead because you couldn't just get off Mars like everyone else." Bridget was working herself up into a full-on rage. Steuby thought he should do something about it but he didn't know what. His way of dealing with trauma was to pretend he wasn't dealing with it. Hers was apparently to blow off some steam a short time after the traumatic event. "You wanted to come see HB and loot the mysteries! You said we'd be out and back in no time flat, no problem! Now we're going to die because of what you said!"

This was the wrong time to remind her that the whole thing had been Marco's plan, Steuby thought. He wasn't good at dealing with people, or emotions, but since Bridget was the one with the expertise in battery systems and flight control, he needed her help. Maybe a useful task would help her cope and also keep them alive.

"Let's find out if it's ridiculous," he said. "Come with me and we'll do a preflight check." He dropped his faceplate and went to the door.

After a pause, she said, "Why not. If we're going to die anyway."

Bridget didn't really believe him, but given no other option she went along while Steuby climbed up the ladder and poked around in the rocket. From the hiss when he opened the access door he could tell it had been sealed against the Martian dust—as much as anything could be sealed against Martian dust.

She looked at clusters of cables and wires, followed connections, popped open recessed coves in the floor, and eventually said, "We're still going to die, but electronically all of this looks intact."

"Perfect," Steuby said.

"For certain values of perfect," Bridget said. They climbed back down and Steuby checked the thruster assembly, feeling a surge of optimism as he opened panel after panel and found that the rocket had been staged and left. Nobody had stripped it for parts. Probably they'd looked at it and—like Bridget—thought it was just a toy.

But Steuby knew better. All this rocket needed was juice in its batteries to run the control systems, and fuel in its tanks to fire the engine.

"You watch," he said. "We're going to get out of here yet."

Bridget regarded the rocket with open scorn. "If by out of here you mean out of our bodies into the afterlife, I completely agree."

"I will be willing to accept your apology when we reach orbit," Steuby said. "Come on. We need charged batteries and a few tons of dinitrogen tetroxide." He headed for the garage, and she went with him.

They had ammonia, all they wanted, held in another of the underground tanks. It was useful enough that the base had kept a supply. Steuby was willing to bet that one of the machines in the garage either was designed to oxidate ammonia or could be configured to do so. NTO was a standard liquid fuel for all kinds of rocket models. All they had to do was find the right machine.

"We used to do this on the Moon," Steuby said. "You mix the ammonia with regular old air, and as nitrogen oxides form you add nitric acid to catalyze more nitrogen oxides. After that, you cool the mixture down and compress it, and the oxides combine to make NTO. It's just shuffling atoms around. Doesn't even need heat. All you need is compression at the right time and a way to siphon off the NTO. I would bet Marco's last dollar there's an NTO synthesizer somewhere around here."

They went looking for it and found it within ten minutes. There was even a generator, and the generator even still had power left in its fuel cells. For the first time since Marco's death, Steuby started to recover his natural state of irrational optimism.

They ran a hose from the ammonia tank over to the synthesizer, fed it a fair bit, and fired it up. Then they wheeled over a smaller tank of nitric acid and pumped some of it in, Steuby doing the figures in his head. They didn't have to be exact. The reaction, once it got going, just needed continual adjustment of ammonia, air, and nitric acid at the right pressures, and the holding tank on the other end of the synthesizer would fill up with nasty, corrosive, carcinogenic, and in this case life-saving NTO.

The synthesizer rattled to life. Steuby waited for it to explode or fall apart, but it didn't. It appeared to work. He watched the capacity readout on the tank. It stayed at 00 for a very long time ... and then it ticked over to 01. Bridget looked on, and the readout ticked to 02 ... 03 .... "Keep this up and I'll start to believe you know what you're doing."

"Love it," Steuby said. "This is my favorite machine. Now all we need to do is make sure we can fuel up and take off before the storm gets bad and keep the rocket going straight up and escape the gravity well and make the rendezvous and convince the freighter to slow down and take us on board."

"When you put it like that," Bridget said.

Steuby nodded. "Now let's charge the batteries."

The sun was all the way up by the time they found the solar array's charging transfer board and ran cables all the way out to the rocket. Possibly it would have been quicker to pull the batteries and bring them to the charging station, but Steuby was nervous about disturbing anything on the rocket. There were charging ports built into the battery housing, and there was enough power cable lying around to reach Jupiter, so that was the most straightforward way. Still, it took a few hours, and both Bridget and Steuby stood around nervously watching the battery-charging readouts as the morning sky passed through its spooky blue dawn into its normal brownish-yellow.

"Good thing about solar arrays is they're pretty low maintenance," he said, to pass the time.

The charging indicators on the batteries lit up.

"Wonder how the NTO synthesizer is doing," Bridget said. She looked up at the sky. They knew what time it was, but that didn't matter. The only thing that mattered was the position of Phobos, zipping around three times a day. They were practically in Apollo 13 territory. The plan was this: watch until Phobos was in more or less the right place, then touch off the rocket's engines, and if they'd avoided fatal errors they would launch, achieve orbit, and then run out of fuel about when the freighter came along. The freighter's schedule was always the same: wait until the moons passed by, dock with the elevator, split before the moons passed by again. Once the freighter had decoupled from the elevator terminus, it would fire an escape burn. It took about two hours to prep that burn. Bridget knew this because she had worked the Belt before deciding she liked to experience gravity once in a while. Even Martian gravity.

In this case the freighter wouldn't be doing a drop. Instead it would be taking on people and supplies, but the time frame was more or less the same. Counting two hours in Phobos' orbit from when it passed the elevator terminus put the little Number Nine Moon right on the western horizon. They had about an hour from then to fire their rocket so they could be at escape velocity when they got close to the freighter, which would probably make an emergency burn to save them, but maybe not. Everything would be much more certain if they could match the freighter's velocity as closely as possible, which meant putting the rocket in a trans-Earth trajectory.

Problem was, if they did that and the freighter didn't pick them up, they would die long before they got to Earth. The rocket, if it had any fuel left, would do an automated Earth-orbit injection burn and the Orbital Enforcement Patrol would board it to find their desiccated bodies. Steuby hoped he wouldn't die doing something embarrassing.

Actually, he hoped he wouldn't die at all. You had to remind yourself of that once in a while when you were in the middle of doing something that would probably kill you. You got so used to the idea that you were going to die, you started trying to make the best of it. It was a useful corrective to articulate the possibility that you might survive.

The day on Mars was forty minutes longer than the day on Earth. Phobos went around about every eight hours, rising in the west because it orbited so much faster than Mars rotated. They needed to get the rocket up to a little more than five kilometers per second for escape velocity. Steuby liked the way those numbers went together. Forty, eight, five. Factors. Of course they had nothing to do with each other, but given the chaos of recent events, Steuby was willing to take his symmetry where he could find it.

Waiting for the tank to fill again, he looked around at the abandoned settlement. HB seemed nice, more like a real place to live than just a colony outpost. There was even public art, a waist-high

Mount Rushmore of Martian visionaries carved from reddish stone. Wells, Bradbury, Robinson, Zhao. Marco probably would have wanted to take it if he was still alive, and if they could have justified the weight.

"No can do," he said out loud. "We're fighting the math. Man, Marco, when I was a kid, you could get anything. Strawberries in January. We were on our way. Now we're on our way back. Pulling back into our shell."

"Stop talking to him," Bridget said. "He's dead."

"Look." He was crying and hoped it didn't show in his voice. His helmet was so dusty she wouldn't be able to see.

Then she wiped the dust away with her gloved hand and said, "Steuby. I get it. He was an old friend and you're sad. Stop being an ass about it and stop trying to pretend you're not doing it, because if you divide your attention you're going to make a mistake and it will kill us. Okay?"

"Right," he said. "Okay."

He kept an eye on the NTO tank while Bridget did something to the monitors on the solar array, but he kept thinking: I'm millions of miles from Earth waiting for a robot left over from a failed Mars colony to finish refueling my rocket and hoping a dust storm doesn't stop us from making a semi-legal rendezvous with a freighter coming back from the asteroid belt. How had he gotten into this situation?

Steuby was sixty-two years old, born in 2010, and had only ever seen one other person die in front of him. That was back on the Moon, where he'd worked for almost fifteen years. A guy named Walter Navarro, looking the wrong way when someone swung a steel beam around at a construction site. The end of the beam smashed the faceplate of Walter's helmet. The thing Steuby remembered most about it was the way Walter's screams turned into ice fog pouring out and drifting down onto the regolith. By the time they got him inside he was dead, with frozen blood in his eyes from where the shards of the faceplate had cut him. Steuby had gotten out of the construction business as soon as he'd collected his next paycheck. After that he'd run tourist excursions, and seen some weird shit, but nothing weirder than Walter Navarro's dying breaths making him sparkle in the vacuum.

They found a tractor that would run and hooked the tank carriage to it. The tractor's engine whined at the load, but it pulled the tank as long as they kept it in low gear. The rocket's fueling port was high on its flank, on the opposite side from the gantry that reached up to the passenger capsule in the nose. Ordinarily a crew would refuel it with a cherry-picker truck, but neither Steuby nor Bridget could find that particular vehicle in or near the garage and they didn't have time to look anywhere else. So they had to tie two ladders together and lean them against the rocket. They flipped a coin to see who would climb, and Bridget lost. Steuby watched her go. "Hey, if you break your leg you're gonna have a hell of a time getting in the rocket," he said.

Bridget didn't miss a beat. "Better shoot me and leave me, then. Like Marco."

For some reason her tone of voice made Steuby think she was trying to make him feel bad.

"I didn't shoot Marco," he said defensively, even though he wasn't sure what he was defending.

Once the nitrogen tetroxide was topped off, they had to go back and clean the tank out, then fill it with hydrazine. Together the compounds would fuel a rocket via a hypergolic reaction. One of Steuby's favorite words, hypergolic. Like just being golic wasn't enough. Neither chemical would do a thing by itself—well, other than poison and corrode anything they touched. Together, boom.

Usually transfers like this were done in clean rooms, by techs in clean suits. Steuby and Bridget were doing it in a dust-filled garage wearing worn-out spacesuits that probably had a dozen microscopic leaks each. He hoped they wouldn't have to do any maneuvering in hard vacuum anytime soon.

When they cranked the fresh hose onto the nipple and locked it into place, Bridget and Steuby looked at each other. "Just so we're clear," Steuby said, "this will blow up and kill us both if there's any trace of the tetro still in there."

"Yup," Bridget said.

"Okay then." Steuby paused over the dial that would open the synthesizer and start dumping the MMH into the tank. "I'll try not to talk to Marco anymore," he said.

"That's the least of my worries right now."

"It's just ... this is going to sound weird, but I talk to him even though he's dead because if I talk to him, it's like he's not dead, which makes me think I might not die."

"Turn the knob, Steuby," she said.

"I don't want to die."

She put her gloved hand over his, which was still resting on the dial. "I know. Me neither. But let's be honest. If we really wanted to be one hundred percent sure of living, we wouldn't be on Mars."

This was true. Bridget started to move Steuby's hand. The dial turned. Monomethylhydrazine started dumping into the tank. It did not explode.

Riding another spike of optimism, Steuby ran to the door. Phobos was visible. They had about eight hours to get the hydrazine topped off and transferred, and then get themselves aboard the rocket. He checked the batteries. They were still pretty low.

"How much of a charge do we need?" Bridget asked.

"I have no idea," Steuby said. "A few hours at least. It won't take long to reach orbit, but once we're out there we'd better be able to get the freighter's attention and keep pinging them our position until they can get to us."

"Assuming they want to get to us."

"They will. The whole point of the Lift is to evacuate people, right? We're people. We need evacuation."

Bridget spent some time in the rocket's crew capsule testing the electronics, which were in fine shape and included an emergency beacon on a frequency that was still standard. "Should we just set it off?" Steuby wondered. Bridget was against it on the grounds that nobody could get all the way across the planet to them and still make the last ship out, whereas if they sent an SOS from near-Mars space, a rendezvous would be easier. Steuby didn't want to go along with this, but he had to admit it made sense.

Other than that, most of the work they had to do—filling tanks, keeping the solar array focused, monitoring the mix in the synthesizer—was in the shop, away from the omnipresent Martian dust. Most of it, anyway. Humankind had not yet invented the thing capable of keeping Mars dust completely out of an enclosed space. Even so, they couldn't do everything inside. Bridget found some kind of problem with one of the battery terminals in the rocket, and they had to go out and pop the cover to see what was wrong. While she worked on it, Steuby watched the horizon.

A huge dust devil sprouted on the plain out past the edge of the settlement. They were common when Mars was near perihelion and its surface warmed up. Steuby and Bridget watched it grow and spiral up into the sky, kilometers high.

If that dust devil was a sign of a big storm developing, they were going to be in trouble. The rocket's engines themselves wouldn't be affected, but a bad dust storm would slow the recharging of the batteries by, oh, ninety-nine percent or so. That put the full charge of the rocket's batteries, and therefore their departure, on the other side of their teeny-tiny launch window.

They could get into the rocket either way and hope it was charged up enough for its guidance systems not to give out before they achieved orbit, but that was one risk Steuby really didn't want to pile on top of all the others they were already taking.

Steuby knew he was getting tired after a dozen runs back and forth to the rocket, and the hours spent working on machines without eating or sleeping. His ears rang and he was losing patience with Marco, who was saying maybe the rocket's placement was for the best because this way they wouldn't have to worry about the rocket's exhaust pulverizing anything important when they lifted off.

Steuby just looked at him.

Oh, right, Marco said.

"Steuby!" Bridget shouted, and Steuby snapped out of his daydream. "That's freaking me out. I'm alive. You want to talk to someone, talk to me. You want to go crazy and have conversations with dead people, do that after we're on the rocket. Okay?"

He didn't answer. She walked up to him and rapped her glove on his faceplate. "Okay?"

"Okay," he said.

She took a step back. Over their local mic he heard her sigh. "Let's get these batteries covered up."

It only took them a minute, but the dust devil was coming fast, and before they'd started the tractor again, it swallowed them up. Winds of this velocity would have flung them around like palm fronds on Earth, but in Mars' thinner atmosphere it felt like a mild breeze. The sensory disconnect was profound. You saw a powerful storm, but felt a gentle push. Your mind had trouble processing it, had to constantly think about it the way you had to plan for Newton's Second Law whenever you did anything in zero gee. In space, instincts didn't work, and on Mars, they could be pretty confusing, too.

Steuby froze and waited for it to go away. It was only two or three hundred meters across, and passed quickly. But as the day went on, there would be more. Steuby looked at the sky, to the west. Phobos had risen. It was all Steuby could do not to mention it to Marco. He's dead, he told himself. Let him be dead.

"Another hour going to be good enough for those batteries?" he asked. They got on the tractor and headed back toward the shop.

"Do we have more than another hour?"

"Not much."

"Then there's your answer." Bridget paused. She swiped dust away from her faceplate. "Look, Steuby. We're ready, right? There's nothing else we need to do?"

He parked the tractor. "Soon as the last tank of NTO is onboard, that's it. That's all we can do."

Bridget was quiet the whole time Steuby backed the tank into the airlock, closed the outer door, uncoupled the tank and pushed it into the shop, and closed the inner door. Then she said, "While you're filling the tank, I need to borrow the tractor for a minute."

"Borrow it? Why, do we need milk?"

"No, we need Marco."

He dropped the hose coupling with a clang. "Are you nuts?"

"We have to bring him, Steuby. It's the right thing to do."

"Math," Steuby said.

"Fix the math. Throw out what we don't need. You said it yourself. If we don't catch the freighter we're going to die. What's the point of having a month's worth of food for a three-month trip? Or a three-hour trip? That might be all we need."

"How the hell do we know what we're going to need?" Steuby shouted. "Have you done this before? I haven't!"

"I thought you hated quitters," she said.

"I—" Steuby stopped. She had him. He looked up at the sky. Phobos was low on the horizon, maybe ten degrees up. Less than an hour until they needed to fire the engines. He remembered Marco talking about going back to Earth, and he knew Bridget was thinking the same thing.

"All right," Steuby said. "Look. We'll do it this way. You go get him. I'll babysit the synthesizer. But if you're not back by the time Number Nine is overhead, I'm going without you."

"You will not."

"Try me."

She left without saying anything else. Steuby didn't know if he was serious or not. Yes he did. He was serious. If she was going to make a dead body more important than two living people, those were priorities that Henry Caleb Steuben was proud not to share.

On the other hand, he couldn't really climb up into the rocket and leave her to die. That wouldn't be right.

On the other other hand, who the hell did she think she was, endangering their rendezvous with the freighter?

On the ... what was this, the fourth hand? ... it would be pretty ironic if Steuby took off without her and then missed the rendezvous anyway, so both of them got to die cursing the other one out.

There was also the entirely plausible scenario of them taking off on time and still missing the freighter, so they could die together.

While the synthesizer poured NTO into the tank, Steuby suggested to himself that he adopt a more positive outlook. Maybe we'll make the freighter, he thought. It's only six klicks to where Marco is. An hour out there and back, tops. Unless—

He called Bridget up on the line-of-sight frequency. She was just visible. "What?"

"So, um, you have something to cut that piece of the railing, right?" he asked.

"No, Steuby. I survived twenty years working in space by forgetting tools." She broke the connection. Fine, he thought. Be pissed if you want.

Another dust storm rolled in maybe ninety seconds later. Figures, Steuby thought. Right when I have to go outside again.

One human-equivalent amount of mass had to come out of the rocket. Steuby stuck his head in the crew compartment. Dust blew in around him and he clambered in so he could shut the hatch. What could he get rid of? He started to panic. What if he threw something away and they needed it?

"Marco, help me out," he said. Bridget wasn't around. She couldn't give him a hard time. He wished he'd been able to crunch all the launch calculations and see whether they had an extra eighty kilos of payload slack. Maybe he was worrying over nothing.

He wriggled through a tight hatch into the storage space below the cockpit. There were lockers full of crap back here. Five extra helmets and suits. He pushed three of them up into the cockpit. He found spare electronics and computer components. They piled up in the pilot's seat. There were two water tanks. He took a deep breath and vented one of them even though he'd just filled it an hour ago. That saved almost a human's worth of mass right there. Now that he'd started, though, Steuby couldn't stop. What if one more thing thrown out the hatch was the difference between making that five point oh three kilometers per second and making a bright streak in the sky as they burned up on reentry?

He stuck his head into the cockpit and saw that the dust storm had blown through again. The suits, spare gear, and a bunch of other stuff went out the hatch, banging against the gantry before falling to litter the launch pad.

In the west, Phobos was high, nearly forty-five degrees. Steuby pulled empty metal boxes out of the storage compartment and threw them out the hatch. Then he had to head for the shop and make sure the last fuel tank was topped off with NTO, or nothing he'd done in here would matter.

When Bridget got back, Steuby was standing in the open airlock. She backed the tractor in and he hooked up the tank. Marco lay face-up in the small equipment bed behind the tractor's seats. The whole front of his suit was soaked in blood and caked in dust. Steuby climbed onto the tractor and Bridget drove them out to the rocket. "You connect the hose and I'll carry him up," Steuby said.

"This is Mars," Bridget said. "He only weighs about sixty pounds. I'll take him. You know more about the fuel system than I do."

"Whatever," Steuby said. He still had that teetering sensation that panic was right there waiting for him. He started the last fuel transfer and watched Bridget climb the gantry with Marco slung over her back. She pushed him in ahead of her and then climbed in. "Shut the hatch!" Steuby shouted. She couldn't hear him. A few seconds later she came back out, shut the hatch, and climbed down.

They stared at the hose where it was connected to the NTO tank. "Think it's enough?" Bridget asked.

The tank's feeder valve clicked shut. "That's all she'll take," Steuby said. "It'll have to be enough."

He disengaged the hose and backed the tractor away. "So how do we move the gantry?" Bridget asked.

"We don't," Steuby said. "The exhaust will do it for us."

"Not ideal," she commented.

"Neither was holding everything up to go collect a body." Steuby looked around. "Anything else we need? Time is short."

She was already at the base of the gantry ladder again. "Then let's move."

Steuby waited for her to get all the way in, then slid feet-first through the hatch. He turned and tried to push the gantry back, but it didn't move. "Forget about it, Steuby," Bridget said.

"I don't want it to tip against the rocket and tear a hole in us while we're lifting off," he said.

She jammed herself into the hatch next to him and together they shoved at the gantry. It still didn't move. "You think the exhaust will push it far enough away before it starts to tip?" she panted.

"If I thought that, I wouldn't be trying to push it myself," he said.

"I mean is it likely? Can we take the chance?"

"It's the only chance we've got," he said. He backed into the cockpit and Bridget closed the hatch.

They buckled themselves into the pilot's and copilot's seats, lying on their backs and looking at the sky. Old-fashioned, Steuby thought. Like we're off to fight Ming the Merciless or something. By accident he ended up in the pilot's chair. "You want to be the pilot?" he asked.

"There is nothing in the world I care about less," Bridget said. She powered up the onboard flight-control systems and saw that their battery life read about four hours of full operation. Steuby saw it, too.

"Sure hope that freighter answers fast," he said. "Where's Marco?"

Bridget adjusted herself in her seat. "Down in the back. Get us out of here, Captain Steuby."

"Blastoff," Steuby said. He flipped the fail-safes on the fuel-mixing system, took a deep breath, and pressed the rectangular button labeled IGNITION.

Liftoff was like nothing Steuby had ever felt. He'd never actually been in an old-fashioned rocket before. Every time he'd gone from Earth to space he'd used the space elevators out of Quito or Kismaayo. This was multiple gees, what the old astronauts had called eyeballs-in, sitting on top of a bomb and riding it into orbit. Steuby was terrified. He couldn't breathe, he couldn't see very well, he didn't know if they were going in a straight line or curving off into a fatal parabola ... he wanted to start screaming but he was afraid if he did he wouldn't be able to get a breath again. As it was he could only gasp in little sips of air that felt like they weren't making it all the way down into his lungs. Bridget wasn't making any noise either, which on the one hand comforted Steuby because it meant she wasn't giving him a hard time but on the other hand upset him because she was solid and reliable and he wanted to hear her say something reassuring.

At first the sound was loud, overwhelming, but as the atmosphere thinned out it modulated down into a rumble they felt more than heard. The rocket didn't shake itself apart. It didn't shred from a hole caused by the gantry. It went straight up like it had been made to do, and if Steuby had been able to speak he thought he might have cheered. They'd done it. If they managed to live long enough to rendezvous with the freighter, people would be telling this story for decades. Also they might end up in jail, but at the moment that was fine with Steuby. Jails had air and food and water.

The thruster cut out. Their velocity was five point seven kilometers per second, plenty for escape velocity. They were nine hundred and sixty-one kilometers from Phobos, which arced away from them toward the horizon. They rose through its orbital plane. The rocket started to tip sideways, aligning its long axis with the direction of Mars' rotation. They were curving up and out of its gravity well, and now they could see the vast reddish emptiness of the southern highlands. Storms tore across the eastern limb, where it had been daylight the longest. Olympus Mons peeked over the horizon far to the northwest, its summit high above the weather.

"We did it," Bridget said.

"We sure did. There's a little fuel left," Steuby said. "Trans-Earth burn, or do we park here and wait for help?"

Bridget leaned over and activated the rocket's emergency beacon. "Park it here," she said. "We don't really have anywhere to go."

Steuby slowed them a little, right down to the edge of escape velocity. He didn't want to get into a parking orbit in case the freighter wanted them to do a rendezvous burn. He looked toward the Tharsis plateau, now visible as their silver museum piece of a rocket rose higher and arced west, following Number Nine Moon. They would be coming up on the freighter if they were lucky. They'd already had a lot of luck, and just needed a little more.

"Hope somebody comes back," Bridget said. "It would be a shame to let all this go to waste."

"Somebody will," Steuby said.

But it wasn't going to be him. No, sir. He was done with everything that didn't obey the gravity of planet Earth. I might go back to the moon, Steuby thought.

"You were right," he said to Bridget.

"About what?"

"Bringing Marco. I gave you a hard time about it."

She shrugged in her harness. "Doesn't matter."

The ship's comm crackled. "This is Captain Lucinda Nieto of the freighter *Mary Godwin*. We are responding to a distress call. Over."

Steuby toggled his mic. "This is ... well, I don't know what the ship is called. But we sure are glad to hear from you."

"We have a fix on your location. If you are able, stabilize your altitude and stand by for rendezvous. How many on board?"

"Two," Steuby said.

"Three," Bridget said at the same time.

He looked at her. Then he leaned into the mic. "Sorry, three," he said.

"And what the hell are you doing out there, exactly?" Captain Nieto asked.

"Not quitting, Captain," Steuby said. "We sure appreciate you giving us a lift."

Chasing Ivory

Ted Kosmatka

THE HELICOPTER PIVOTED suddenly and Adia grabbed the ceiling strap to keep her balance.

"Spotted them," came the pilot's voice through her headset.

The chopper thrummed around her. She craned her neck, staring out through the curve of glass. Scanning the horizon. *There.*

Her heart rose up in her chest. Even now, after all these years— the countless hours in the field—it still happened. That feeling she got when she first saw them.

The mammoths formed a dark line in the distance.

As a young researcher, she'd followed them on their annual migrations. North to the Arctic Ocean in the summer; then South, to central Quebec in the winters. A migration of hundreds of miles. But this was the newer, Western herd. British Columbia. Milder winters. A better location for what they hoped to accomplish.

The helicopter pivoted again, and Adia felt her stomach flutter. The dark line seemed to spread itself out. Became distinct blots. A dozen animals now; she could count them. Their red-brown forms lumbering slowly across the wide open landscape. As the helicopter flew over the flat terrain, it bled altitude and banked away from the herd, keeping to the mandated distance.

"Wind direction?" She asked.

"From the northeast."

"Set it down over there." She pointed to a distant spot in the taiga. The trees here were sparse, stunted things, scattered randomly across the open grassland.

"Copy that. Putting down."

☼   ☼   ☼

The blades spun overhead as she gathered her gear. She pulled her pack from the rear door and set it on the soft ground. Then the gun. Even at quarter power, the blade noise was deafening. There was a reason helicopters had to keep their distance from the herds. Mammoths spooked easily. Get too close, and she'd be chasing them for days.

"Eight hours," she shouted.

A nod through the glass bubble. The pilot mouthed, "Be careful."

"Always am," she said, mostly to herself.

And it was true. She'd seen what happened to those who weren't.

Researchers had died doing what she was doing. Well, not *exactly* what she was doing. No one had done that before, not precisely. But researchers had died facing the mammoths.

It was one of the risks you took.

Woolies were not pets. The training hammered that home. They were wild creatures from a harsher time. Far more aggressive than elephants had ever been. Mammoths killed humans who were careless, or unlucky.

She gave the pilot a thumbs up, and the helicopter lifted off—rising like a huge wasp, straight up into the blue sky, then curling back to the south, ascending until even the sound had faded to a faint ratcheting. Then gone.

The sudden solitude struck her.

There was no one. Just the moan of the wind. The feel of the soft ground beneath her boots. She was hundreds of miles from the nearest settlement. More than sixty miles from the nearest road. There'd be no one to help her if she needed it.

She turned and scanned the grasslands in the distance. She could just make out the wavy line. The distinct double humps—back and skull. Like low, red-brown hills. From here they didn't look so huge. They'd be a lot bigger before she was done. She shouldered her rifle and set out.

☼   ☼   ☼

Mammoths were the last of the Elephantidae. Sole survivors of a taxonomic family that dated back millions of years. *Primelephas, Mammuthus, Elephas, Loxodonta.* You could tick off the clades.

In the early part of the last century, the program had used Asian elephants to bring them back—implantation, gestation. Years of nursing and enculturation. The elephant herd watching over, guiding the young mammoths to maturity. But now those elephants were gone.

Only the mammoths remained.

She crossed the mushy ground, moving as efficiently as possible. It would be a long eight hours. She'd need to conserve her energy. Pace herself. Mammoths could usually outrun humans, but not these mammoths. Not now. Not unless they were spooked. They'd be moving slow, covering ground at the speed of their slowest member.

It took her almost three hours to close the distance. An exhausting march across rolling swales of northern prairie. A scatter of low, twisted trees broke up the profile of the horizon, providing some cover for her advance. Mammoths, for all their size and grandeur, had weak eyes, so she had to use that to her advantage.

When she was still half a mile out, the herd slowed. She dropped to the mushy ground and pulled the binoculars from her pack. The eyepieces were cold on her bare skin. She adjusted the focus and the animals zoomed into existence, close enough to touch. Huge and hairy—their pelts a dull, rust red. All except Masha, who was a shade darker. Part of the natural variation in coat pigment, scientists had discovered, when the first specimens were cloned all those years ago. Mammoths were born shaggy and dark, and their coats tended to lighten with age. Some more than others.

She watched them for a full minute, noting every detail. The small, triangular ears. Their backs like sloping hillocks. White tusks marking out space in front of them—a tool meant to sweep away snow so they could browse in the winter. Everything about these animals was designed for the cold. Here in British Columbia, it was almost too warm for them. A borderline case. A good test for the warming world, perhaps. A future when no north might be north enough.

Through the binoculars, she could see but not hear them, and that was a thing you had to get used to when you watched them this way. The stomp of their feet, silent. The sound of their breathing missing from the scenes, like one of your senses had been ripped away. A TV with its sound turned off.

She counted them. Eight, nine, ten, and *there*. She saw it. Or imagined she saw it. Just a hint of movement—a dark shape, seen but not seen. Something smaller, hiding beneath the long, wooly overhang of Masha's pelt.

She unfolded her rifle and slammed a load into the chamber. A single silver cartridge as long as her middle finger.

She could still remember the arguments against the mammoths—all the moral equivocating. Elephants weren't lab creatures after all, their precious fertility easily disbursable to more deserving species. They were perceptive beasts, with their own rudimentary language. Research dollars could more safely be spent on the living, rather than on zygotes of those long dead.

All true, she supposed. Or possibly true.

All the arguments. All the justifications *not* to do something. The ethicists could go on and on.

Too risky. Too dangerous.

But in the end, immaterial.

You might as well ask why mountains need to be climbed. Why the moon, why Mars.

An answer so simple, always, that you either understand it intuitively, or you never will.

Because it's in us to do.

She slid the bolt of her rifle home and rose to one knee. Eyes on the herd. She watched them as they grazed, waiting for them to turn.

Working with the mammoths had given her a new respect for ancient hunters. The mammoths were wary, not easily stalked. Even with a rifle, in the open plain, it was difficult to get within range. Yet somehow, twelve thousand years ago, they'd been hunted with spears. The thought amazed her. What a strong people those must have been.

How fast and fearless.

Sticks and stones brought to bear against all that meat and muscle and will to live.

The mammoths swayed while they grazed, their huge bodies slowly turning back to the north. Back to the wind.

When they were faced away from her, she set out again, keeping low. She ran hunched over, until her back muscles burned, and her quads began to shake.

She closed the distance in bursts. Moving quickly, then pausing. Then quickly again.

Twenty minutes later, it began to rain. A cold, steady drizzle that beaded her Gore-tex.

When she was still a hundred yards out, the mammoths stopped suddenly.

She dropped to the ground.

Something had caught their attention. Some scent in the air, or some movement. Perhaps a sixth sense. She was coming at them downwind, so they shouldn't have been able to smell her, but who knew how sensitive their noses might be. Even sixty years on, there was much about them that had never been tested.

It was one of the lessons they'd learned from elephants. Elephantidae did best when left alone. Cage them in, treat them like lab rats, and things go badly. The tighter you hold them, the more they slide out between your fingers.

In captivity, elephants had produced approximately two deaths for every live birth. A demographic death spiral that could only be halted by procurements from the wild.

For the mammoths, there had never been an option to put them in zoos. Instead there were parks, protected and watched. Safe in the north. Sanctuaries where they lived and migrated and mated.

The big females pivoted, circling around, shifting their weight on their long front legs. They formed gradually into a ring. Protecting the center. They sensed something wasn't right, something out there in the dim gray rain.

She watched them. Beasts the size of buses. You couldn't describe it, though you might try. Asked at a faculty party: *What's it like?*

And what can you say? How do you speak the truth?

It was one thing to see them from a distance, or on high-def-holo, but it's another to experience them up close.

The mammoths were to her what religion was to some people.

How do you *say* that?

She looked from beast to beast, counting off their names in her head. *Masha, Roya, Wolla.* She knew them by sight, and by haplotype sequence. Not clones, but the offspring of clones. Or the offspring of those offspring. And *Mito,* the herd's single male. A gigantic bull sixteen feet at the shoulder. The natural born get of forebears conjured into existence from DNA found on opposite sides of a continent, opposite sides of a millennium. As large as any mammoth ever dug from the ground. A head like a crane as he pivoted. Tusks massive enough to cradle an automobile and fling it into the air.

Even the smallest of them were bigger than Asian elephants, to whom their species had been most closely related. Those old pictures seemed strange now. Images on a screen, dating to the original experiments. The original implantations. She'd seen all the old files— the herd of females, their gray skin strangely naked.

A sound brought her back.

The savage snort of their breathing—then a sudden low frequency rumble. A pattern studied, but not understood, most of it beyond the range of human hearing. If mammoths had once had their own language it was lost forever, for this was the language of elephants—a series of clicks and rumblings passed down within the social group.

The mammoths swayed and stomped their feet. She could smell them now. Wet fur, and something wilder.

How many do you plan to bring back? The question came up often.

And her answer, always the same: As many as it takes.

She'd never liked zoos. Even as a kid. The last of the elephants had died there when she was six years old. A zoo in California. Her father had seen it once, when he was a child, and he often spoke of it while she was growing up. The world's last elephant. "It's skin as bare as yours or mine," he said.

By then there were already a dozen mammoths roaming the taiga.

But elephants couldn't live in the arctic. Couldn't handle the cold. Trapped by their physiology. All the places warm enough for them to range free were overrun with people. With wars. With poaching. Once the population in the wild was driven to extinction, those in captivity could only circle the drain. Two deaths for every birth, until finally, in a dismal zoo decades later, behind steel bars, the last elephant died.

She put the gun to her cheek. She stared through the sight, and the mammoths zoomed close.

Red-brown fur. Long guard hairs, with a woolly undercoat. She could make out the individual strands.

This was the risky part. The part where she succeeded or failed.

There was no better way to do it. No safer way. The helicopter drop off. The single shot, from her position in the grass. The risk was on her, which is how she wanted it.

A shuffle of movement, and she saw it then. The calf. Saw it clearly for the first time. Moving beside the mother.

A week old perhaps and already two hundred pounds. The gray skin, bare and smooth.

Skin as naked as yours or mine.

Her breath hitched in her throat, and she felt tears in her eyes. She wiped them away.

She was the first person to see an elephant in forty years.

A clone of one of the last zoo animals. Though this one would never see captivity.

She followed the calf with her scope, bringing the crosshairs into position. The medical dart loaded and ready. She concentrated on her breathing. Exhaled, squeezed the trigger.

There was a puff of air, and the baby startled. It squealed and rose up on its hind legs—the silver dart protruding from its haunch. Three seconds later, the dart fell away, ejected by timer. A cocktail of vaccines now safely injected.

The baby elephant calmed after a few moments.

She watched through the scope—its small gray trunk, its enormous ears. She smiled, thinking of her father.

He'd seen the last elephant.

Now she'd seen the first.

"As many as it takes," she said.

They'd questioned bringing back the mammoth all those years ago. But in saving the mammoth, they'd saved the elephant. Buying time, until the time was right.

A three-hundred square mile sanctuary in Texas now ready and waiting.

And one day elephant herds would roam the panhandle, like mammoths now roamed the north. And if the world continued to warm—well, she could imagine the two trading places down through the ages. An artful dance. The same rumbling language passed from one species to another and then back again.

There came another stomp of feet then, and the big animals turned away, rounding back to the north. The wind had changed. The rain came harder, though the beasts seemed not to notice. The little elephant moved against its mother, disappearing from sight.

Adia laid her gun on the grass and watched them go, until they again grew small and remote. Red-brown hillocks. She did not follow.

And still the herd lumbered on, as perhaps it always would, in one form or another, heading for the horizon, carrying with it a new beginning.

Something Happened Here, But We're Not Quite Sure What It Was

Paul McAuley

THE ORIGIN STORY we like to tell ourselves is that our little town was founded by a grumpy loner name of Joe Gordon, who one day parked his RV at the spot where a ceramic road left by an unknown long-lost Elder Culture cut across the new two-lane blacktop between Port of Plenty and the open-cast iron mine at Red Rocks. He named his crossroads campsite Joe's Corner, set up a couple of picnic tables, and commenced to sell coffee, hot dogs, candy bars, and e-cigarettes and rolling tobacco to the passing trade and the first explorers of the City of the Dead.

Joe Gordon had come up and out three years after people first set foot on First Foot. A lanky, morose man from Hoboken, New Jersey, he peers with narrow suspicion out of the only known photograph of him and his makeshift truck stop, as if wondering how much he should charge for the liberty of having his picture taken. By then, the shuttle cycling between Earth and First Foot was bringing up ten thousand people every three weeks. Too many people for Joe's liking: He'd spent just two months in Port of Plenty before striking out into the backcountry, and when other people started to make themselves at home around his crossroads he moved on again, heading deeper into the dry heart of the planet's largest continent. We know that he worked for a time at the copper mine at Mount Why Not, but after that his trail goes cold. One story has it that he burned his ID and joined a group of homesteading Sovereign Citizens; another claims that he set up a road tavern on the far side of the Badlands and was shot dead in a brawl or a robbery. He left behind his name, a story slowly fading to myth, and the photograph which—enlarged, retouched, and printed on canvas—hangs in the reception area of our community center, a steel-framed glass box erected just last year next door to the ragstone bunker of the Unitarian church whose spire, three steel I-beams welded into a skinny pyramid and topped by an aluminum weather vane burnished by sun and sandstorms, is visible for miles around in our flat desert territory.

Joe's Corner is approaching its thirtieth anniversary now. We are some three thousand souls, with a school and a small clinic; a strip mall anchored by a Rexall's; a sheriff's office and a volunteer fire department; two charge stations (one of them a Toyota franchise); three churches; six motels; a dozen bars, coffeehouses, and restaurants; a solar farm and a nine-hole golf course; a small factory that fabricates mining equipment; and a workshop turning out handmade souvenirs of the City of the Dead, mostly for the export trade. The community center houses a small library and a cinema club that just closed a season of classic Westerns with Quentin Tarantino's *The Hateful Eight*. At a lodge run by a couple from New Mexico, guests pay six hundred bucks a night to sleep in tar-paper shacks, wallow in black mud baths, and eat vegan Mexican-Chinese food. They come here for the silence, panoramic views of alien constellations in night skies untainted by light pollution, and, of course, to explore the tombs of the City of the Dead.

There are several million tombs scattered across fifty thousand square kilometers, built from small, round-edged clay bricks that some believe to have been excreted by the creatures that constructed them, the so-called Ghostkeepers. We call them tombs because they appear to memorialize the dead of the Ghostkeepers, although no bodies have ever been found. They may be houses, works of art, the by-product of some kind of mating ritual, or something beyond the grasp of human imagination. Once upon a time, tomb raiders made fortunes by finding Elder Culture artifacts that kick-started new industries. Our last sheriff played an instrumental role in the discovery of navigation code that had migrated from a fragment of a crashed Ghajar spaceship into a nest of hive rats, and pointed toward the wormhole network of the New Frontier. Although it's generally agreed that the glory days of mining the City of the Dead are long gone, tomb raiders still dig up various trinkets—sympathy stones, ceramic shards containing entangled electrons used in q-phone manufacture, tesserae doped with algorithms that generate scraps of Ghostkeeper memories as well as, sometimes, actual ghosts—and people still come out here hoping to hit the jackpot. Most leave broke and disappointed after a year or so, but a few stay on, and others drift out here and set up homesteads or little businesses. Living the good old American dream on an alien planet, at the edge of a vast alien ruin.

Leah Bright was one such incomer, moving to our little town after a divorce and a business failure in Port of Plenty. She rented a single wide in the trailer park, used eBay to sell inert tesserae that she claimed to have activated by a secret psychic process, gave lessons in dowsing for artifacts and consultations with her familiar, which she said was the ghost of a Byzantine priest whose spirit had transmigrated to First Foot a thousand years ago. She was a handsome woman in her late thirties who wore boho scarves, denim jackets and jeans, and tooled leather boots, and mostly kept herself to herself. She gave the impression that residence in Joe's Corner was a temporary setback, but we grew used to seeing her sitting at an outside table in the Old Bean Café and poking with furious concentration at her iPhone, or leading a gaggle of tourists on a dowsing expedition amongst the tells and dust heaps at the northern edge of the City of the Dead. It was general knowledge that she and the town clerk were an item. We told ourselves that because neither party was married it was no business of ours that they liked to pretend that they were no more than casual acquaintances, but we sometimes wondered what they had in common. Leah Bright with her glamour and flair; Troy Wagner a mild, pedantic guy ten years younger than her, so straight-laced he was the only person in town who went to work every day in a suit.

Someone suggested that Leah kept him around to remind herself of a road not taken, and everyone pretty much agreed that Troy must have told her about the planning application for a radio telescope array. At the town meeting where it was due to be heard, Leah sat in the center of the front row with half a dozen allies flanking her, a solid block of defiance in a hall otherwise sparsely occupied by the usual professional busybodies, people who had a planning or licensing matter they wanted to see through, and a few cantankerous cranks who at every meeting aired old grievances that everyone else had long ago laid to rest.

The planning application came at the end of business, a seemingly innocuous statement that a company named Universal Communications had been granted a license to erect radio communications equipment on a four hundred acre patch of land they had acquired several months ago, plans available upon request at the library or to view on the town's website, and so forth. After Troy Wagner dryly read this out, the mayor, Joel Jumonville, said that if there were no comments he would declare the meeting closed. But before Joel could bang his gavel, Leah Bright reared up and said that as a matter of fact she did have something to say.

"It's my understanding that the 'radio communications equipment' is in fact an array of radio telescopes," she said. "And I also understand that Universal Communications is planning to establish communication with extraterrestrial intelligences."

"I believe those might be more in the nature of unfounded assertions rather than comments," Joel Jumonville said in his Texas good-old-boy drawl. "As Mr. Wagner explained, there'll be a copy of the plans lodged in the library. Anyone who wants is free to check them out."

Joel was a former astronaut, one of the Fortunate Fifty who had come up and out on the very first shuttle trip from Earth, back when it seemed very likely that the Jackaroo's gift of fifteen worlds and the means to reach them was some kind of trick or trap. He had been mayor of Joe's Corner for a quarter of a century. Although his majority had been considerably reduced at the last election, he had lost none of his God-given authority, looking at Leah over the top of his old-fashioned gold-rimmed bifocals like a teacher humoring a difficult pupil.

But Leah wasn't the least bit intimidated, saying firmly, "If you want facts, Mr. Mayor, then it's a fact that Universal Communications is owned by the Omega Point Foundation, which once upon a time funded a company called Outland Archaeological Services. A company that caused some considerable trouble here twelve years ago, as I'm sure many of you will recall."

She was referring to the breakout of a harmful eidolon that had gotten into the heads of people who had dug up a second fragment of the crashed Ghajar spaceship, causing them to attack and kill each other with their teeth and bare hands. The last person standing had run repeatedly at a boulder until she'd split her skull open. At the mention of Outland's name, a couple of old-timers sat up and started to pay attention.

"I can assure you that the application is in order," Joel Jumonville said, with a trace of exasperation. "Universal Communications doesn't have anything to do with archaeology. And it has no plans to do any digging, apart from a few trenches when it lays foundations for its equipment."

Troy Wagner had the look of man trying to become invisible by the power of thought alone. Everyone else was following the conversation as if it were a tennis match.

Leah said, "This equipment being radio telescopes."

"Something like that may be mentioned in the plans," Joel said. "Which, as I've said, anyone can go check out."

"Radio telescopes which Universal Communications wants to use to talk with extraterrestrials," Leah said, with her supporters nodding and saying *exactly* and *there it is* like a gospel chorus.

"I believe that they may be planning to search the sky for signals or suchlike," Joel said, clearly on the back foot now.

"And if they find a signal, they'll want to talk," Leah said.

Joel tried to turn it into a joke. "Is this about the planning application, or are you making a criticism of their scientific methods?"

"It's about the harmful effect this project will have on the City of the Dead," Leah said. "And the very real possibility that the Jackaroo may not approve of it."

"The approval of the Jackaroo has nothing to do with our planning process. And in any case, the application is merely a formality. The site is on federal land outside town limits. I can no more stop it going ahead than I could stop a sandstorm," Joel said, and when several of Leah's supporters stood up to shout objections he banged his gavel so hard the head flew off the handle.

That was the end of the meeting and the beginning of Leah Bright's campaign. Her most prominent supporters were dealers and assayers in the artifact trade, merchants whose business depended on tourism, and a number of tomb raiders, including Jayla and Shelley Griffith-Fontcuberta, who had been in the biz more or less from the discovery of the City of the Dead. All had good reason to worry about possible disruptions to their livelihoods. Despite decades of research, no one could claim any authoritative knowledge about the revenants left by the Ghostkeepers. They were rooted in algorithms that ran deep inside the quantum properties of the tesserae, projecting fleeting emotions, glimpses of exotic landscapes, and actual eidolons or ghosts. Harmless scraps like tattered bats or the animated shadows of warped dwarves; rare potent spirits that got inside people's heads, as in the breakout that had killed the crew employed by Outland Archaeological Services. Which is why the association between Outland and the outfit that wanted to build the radio telescope array was enough to give even the hardened rationalists amongst us pause for thought.

In an interview with Sally Backlund, the owner, editor, and sole reporter of our town's newspaper, Leah announced that she intended to hold an open meeting about what she called the reckless and outrageous intrusion. It was a riotous affair at which everyone with a crank to turn or an ax to grind held forth, everyone talking over everyone else and fierce little arguments breaking out everywhere; people had to drag Ben Lamb and Aidan Fletcher apart when raised voices and finger poking threatened to escalate into a fistfight. Leah struggled to keep any kind of order, and her keynote speech was shouted down by people who felt that their own opinions were equally important. As Sally wrote in her story about it, although the meeting ended with a unanimous condemnation of the project, everyone appeared to have a different objection.

Universal Communications set up a public event to explain its plans, with a free buffet and a lecture by a tame scientist about SETI, the search for extraterrestrial intelligence, but after Leah and her supporters declared that they would picket the event, it was canceled by our sheriff, Van Diaz, on the grounds of public safety. Van had good reason. The ranks of Leah's supporters had been swollen by out-of-towners, and there was a discordant mood in the air. Rival street preachers set up at opposite corners of the crossroads, one ranting about an upcoming Rapture that would transmigrate our souls to permanent servitude in an alien hell world, the other warning about the dangers of what she called cargo-cult culture and colonization by alien memes. An outfit that called itself the Brotherhood of Human Saints marched down Main Street, dressed in monk's habits and spraying onlookers with what they claimed was magnetized water, to ward off unsympathetic eidolons; Hoke Williford objected to being sprayed and punched out one of the monks and was promptly arrested. And a group of earnest young people held a be-in outside the community center, with banners, drumming, and chants, and consciousness-raising exercises that some of us worried would brainwash our children. The jamboree went on for three days, long after Universal Communications' PR people had folded their tents, and none of it did a thing to stop the construction work that started up two weeks later.

Sally Backlund did her best to be evenhanded in her coverage. She published an editorial supporting the view of Leah and her supporters that science did not have all the answers. A hundred years ago, she wrote, we thought that we would soon know everything worth knowing. Now, after the arrival of the Jackaroo and colonization of the fifteen habitable planets they gave us, we are equally certain that the universe is more complex than we can possibly imagine, and if there are fundamental questions that science can't answer, then perhaps other ways of addressing them are equally valid. She also interviewed Darryl Hancock who owned the hardware store and with the twenty inch reflecting telescope in his backyard had spotted more than two dozen comets and discovered one of the tiny moons that orbited Godzilla, the biggest of our system's three gas giants.

Darryl explained that SETI was still a valid enterprise long after the Jackaroo had first revealed themselves. We know now that we are not alone, he said, but we still do not know if we are the only clients of the Jackaroo, or if there are other alien civilizations as advanced as theirs. The bedrock of SETI research is a famous equation written by the astronomer Frank Drake, which gives an estimate of the number of active, technologically advanced extraterrestrial civilizations in the galaxy by multiplying together estimates of relevant parameters—the percentage of stars with life-bearing planets, the proportion of those planets on which communicative technological civilizations arose, the life span of those civilizations, and so forth. After the Jackaroo made contact, we acquired real numbers for parameters that previously had been hypothetical; we know, for instance, that the Elder Cultures, clients of the Jackaroo who previously inhabited the gift worlds, flourished for an average of approximately five centuries. Plugging hard data into the Drake equation suggests that between one and twelve civilizations are presently active in the Milky Way, which raises all kinds of interesting questions. Do the Jackaroo currently have other clients besides ourselves? Are there alien civilizations they are watching but have not yet contacted, or alien civilizations more advanced than theirs, which have refused their offer of help? Are all the Jackaroo gift worlds more or less habitable by humans, like First Foot and the others, and those worlds previously inhabited by Elder Cultures that we've discovered out in the New Frontier? Or are there more exotic gift worlds, for more exotic clients? Gas giants where intelligent blimps ride frigid poison winds, worlds that are wrapped in ocean from pole to pole, or baking at furnace temperatures and inhabited by life-forms whose biochemistries are based on sulfur or silicon rather than carbon, and half a hundred other possibilities.

The Jackaroo have been asked these and other questions many times, of course. But their answers are always about as much use as fortune cookie sayings. "It's an interesting question," they'll say. Or: "The universe is very large and very old, and contains many possibilities." Or: "Many of our previous clients asked similar questions. Each found their own answers, in their own way."

This was why Universal Communications was building radio telescope arrays on the fifteen gift worlds, whose stars were scattered across the Milky Way. The galaxy is huge, some four hundred billion stars, so there is only a vanishingly small chance that an active, communicative alien civilization will be orbiting a star close enough to one of those arrays for easy detection. Even so, according to Darryl, the implications of success were so staggeringly profound that it was worth the gamble. Suppose we could get answers to all the questions that the Jackaroo so skillfully and charmingly evade? Suppose we could get a different perspective about the Jackaroo, or even discover their history and origin?

The interview didn't endear Darryl to Leah Bright and her supporters. There were anonymous threats, and an attempt at swatting. Someone spray-painted ALIEN LOVER across the window of Darryl's store. A small group gathered outside his home and banged saucepans and blew whistles and chanted insults until he came out with his 12 gauge and fired a double load of bird shot into the air. He was arrested for that, but Van Diaz, whose patience was being sorely tried by the protestors' antics, released him without charge a couple of hours later.

Leah denounced the threats and vandalism, but also accused Darryl of being in Universal Communications' pocket. And some of us accused her of being in the pay of outside parties who had a financial interest in sabotaging Universal Communications' plans. The whole town was divided. You couldn't not have an opinion, for or against. Meanwhile, heavy trucks brought in the prefabricated parts for the radio telescopes, big white parabolic reflectors set on skeletal support structures that allowed them to point at any part of the sky, assembled in a twenty-by-ten grid. Construction took six months, and all the while Leah Bright and her crew of protestors camped outside. They held up traffic, locked themselves to construction machinery, tied banners and balloons to the mesh security fences, leafleted traffic and people in town, sat around campfires in the cold desert evenings, and sang old songs from Earth.

Most were out-of-towners, and most were young. They had not volunteered to come up and out to First Foot after winning a shuttle ticket in the UN lottery or buying a ticket on one of the repurposed Ghajar ships. They had been born here. It was not a wonder, for them, to be living on another planet. As far as they were concerned, First Foot was home and Earth the alien planet. A hundred years ago, they would have been protesting about the Vietnam War and the Man. Now they were campaigning against the colonial attitudes of off-world companies, and the alliance between scientists and big business that was exploiting Elder Culture artifacts they believed to be theirs by right of birth.

Some of us sympathized with them. A large part of our town's income derived from the City of the Dead and the artifact business, and we'd chosen to live there because it was remote from central government and gave us the space to express our lives as we saw fit. So although we had businesses to run and families to feed, many of us visited the camp, donating food and water, sitting and talking with the kids, and participating in sing-alongs, an attempt to encircle the camp with a chain of people holding hands, and an attempt to levitate the radio telescopes as a demonstration of human will triumphing over science (some swore it actually happened). Elmer Peters, the Unitarian minister, held a nondenominational service at the camp every Sunday. Ram Narayan supplied daily meals of vegetable curry and bread; the New Mexico couple from the yoga retreat brought macrobiotic food and said that the camp had a beautiful air of spirituality; Jeff James sold pot he grew in his hydroponic greenhouse. Sally Backlund was often to be seen interviewing someone, an external microphone clad in a furry windshield attached to her iPhone like a dead hive rat soldier. She was writing a series of stories about individual protestors and uploading her interviews to SoundCloud. Craig and Jody Mudgett brought their kids as part of their homeschooling. And other kids visited, of course, because of the excitement and transgression. It was the biggest thing to have happened in our town since that unfortunate breakout. A carnival. A freak show.

Leah was there from beginning to end, holding daily séances to consult her Byzantine priest, chairing interminable camp meetings, giving interviews to TV and net journalists from Port of Plenty, and leading every protest action. She said that the presence of the camp was a shield between the black energy of the radio telescopes and the fragile noosphere of the City of the Dead. She was arrested twice, but although Joel Jumonville wanted to keep her ass in jail until things cooled off, she was quickly released both times, thanks to supporters who paid her fines and a sympathetic lawyer from Port of Plenty who was doing pro bono work for the protesters. She was dogged, determined, and, most of us agreed, very happy.

She'd broken up with Troy Wagner soon after she'd begun her campaign. He sourly confided to the bartender at Don's Joint that it wasn't so much that she'd found a cause, but a cause had found her. She had become the lightning rod for the discontent of well-to-do kids who joined protests because it was the hip thing to do, or because they were rebelling against their parents. He felt badly treated by his former lover—Joel had investigated him over the leak about the planning application, and although nothing implicated him, bad blood remained—and we weren't surprised when, two months later, he took a job with the UN in Port of Plenty.

By then, construction was nearing an end. The garden of radio telescopes sat behind a double wire fence topped with razor wire, bowls turned to the sky like giant albino sunflowers. There were ranks of solar panels to provide power, a short string of flat-roofed, single-story prefabs where security guards and technicians would live and work. Q-phone circuits linked it directly and instantaneously to a facility in Paris, France, and to the headquarters of Universal Communications' parent company at Terminus.

Several of us were invited to the facility's inauguration, including Joel Jumonville, Sally Backlund, and Darryl Hancock. As was Leah Bright, in what was either a spirit of reconciliation or a sneaky PR move. She formally burned the invitation in front of a crowd of her supporters and a couple of reporters (Sally and a stringer from NBC First Foot) and announced that there would be an intervention, but refused to divulge any details.

"It will be nonviolent but potent," she said, adding that testing of the equipment had already caused significant agitation amongst eidolons and other potencies in the City of the Dead.

"She felt a great disturbance in the Force," more than one of us wisecracked, but many had a sense of foreboding. We were remembering that breakout, and all the tomb raiders and explorers who had been to one degree or another driven crazy by exposure to eidolons and other manifestations of Ghostkeeper algorithms. People who had invisible friends, or believed that they were dead, rotting corpses, or had caught counting syndrome or spent half of every day scrubbing themselves down with industrial bleach in the shower because they believed that the pores in their skin were infested with alien bugs. And all of us were affected to some extent, living as we did in the penumbra of a vast alien necropolis, where alien ghosts infested alien tombs and scenes from long-lost alien lives were replayed to any sentient creature that strayed close to the tesserae that contained them. All of us were changed.

A couple of years ago, a PR company hired by Joel Jumonville to boost the tourist trade came up with a cute cartoon mascot, a fat green-skinned elf with puppy-dog eyes, a goofy grin, sparkly antennae, and a slogan: *Experience Ten Thousand Years Of Alien History!* But that history wasn't cute, wasn't amenable to Disneyfication. It was the background hum of our lives, a psychic weather acknowledged by the amulets or tattoos some of us wore to ward off bad luck and bad eidolons, jokes stolen from corny old horror movies, and the little rituals tomb raiders performed before entering a tomb. I guess you could say that our love of gossip and stories was part of our coping mechanism: a way of reassuring ourselves that we were still human. Even visiting scientists and archaeologists talked about bad spots and weird feelings. That psychic weather, those weird feelings, were what Leah and her protestors had tapped into. And it turned out that they were right, although in the end it wasn't the radio telescopes that blew everything up. It was Leah's attempt at sabotage.

The company and the government took her talk of an intervention seriously. There was heavy security around the radio telescope array on the day of its inauguration. Two hundred state troopers were on standby and a small army of private goons checked the IDs of VIPs, patrolled the perimeter, and flew drones above the protestors' little encampment. According to Van Diaz, they weren't so much worried about Leah and her friends, but that some lone crackpot might use them as cover.

"Still, none of us has any idea about their plans," he said. "The company tried to infiltrate the camp with a couple of undercover guys, but they were spotted and turfed out. Leah is playing everything very close. But man, really, what can she do?"

Many of us resented the intrusive security, the closure of Main Street while a convoy of press and guests rolled through, the noise of helicopter traffic that brought the VIPs, the journalists stopping us on the street or knocking at our doors or coming into our places of business, asking us for our opinions. And while we wouldn't admit it, we were anxious that there might be an outbreak of some kind of stupid violence, or that Leah might turn out to be right, and the radio telescopes really would trigger something incomprehensible and catastrophic out in the City of the Dead. So although we tried to go about our normal business, we were secretly watching the skies. And at four P.M., when the radio telescopes were due to be switched on, most of us found excuses to hunker down at home.

But nothing happened. Despite all the rumors, Ada Morange, the billionaire who bankrolled the Omega Point Foundation, did not appear at the inauguration. Instead, a colorless executive read out a short message from her, and an astronomer who had helmed a TV series about the gift worlds and the New Frontier, brought from Earth especially for the occasion, gave a short speech before pressing the button that activated the dishes. All swung ponderously towards a spot high in the day sky, aiming towards a G2 star eleven light years away. It was the twin of Earth's sun, but it wasn't known if it possessed any planets, let alone one that could support life. As Darryl Hancock said, the project was in many ways a symbolic gesture, making the point that the human species wasn't going to stop asking big questions just because the Jackaroo had happened along with their gift worlds and shuttles, and their offer to help.

The protestors built a huge bonfire that night and held a cross between a séance, a prayer meeting, and a free concert. Leah didn't appear; she was in conversation with her Byzantine priest. We didn't know then that her plan to disrupt the inauguration had been foiled by a failed comms link.

That link went live two days later.

The first most of us knew about it, the power went off in the town. It was just after seven in the morning. The municipal grid, solar power, generators, and LEAF batteries: everything cut out. Vehicles drifted to a halt, broadband fell over, TVs and radios and phones howled like wolves. Some people say they saw an arc of pale sun dogs in the sky; others that a host of eidolons rose up from tombs and sinkholes across the City of the Dead and formed a thickening haze that poured north, towards the radio telescope facility. Esther Aldrich, the manager of the Shop 'n Save, claimed that she saw beings like glowing balloons drift through the plate glass window, head down the liquor aisle, and vanish, leaving behind an odor like burnt plastic. Several people suffered fits. Kyra Calliste, a former tomb raider who for three years had panhandled around town, haunted by an eidolon fragment that had robbed her of her voice, suddenly stood up in the church hall where she was eating her customary breakfast with other transients and started talking about everything that had happened to her out in the City of the Dead. She hasn't stopped talking yet. On the other hand, Monica Nielsen, eating breakfast with her husband in Denny's, was struck blind. Hysterical blindness is the opinion of specialists who have examined her, nothing organically wrong, but she hasn't seen a spark of light since.

Others spoke of hearing the voices of dead relatives, or a vast lonely roar like a jet plane passing low above the roofs of the town, although the sky was cloudless and empty that morning. And at the radio telescope array, the dishes began to move under a command fed through a clandestine link which a sympathetic IT worker had installed in the control system, overriding the program that until that moment had kept them tracking the G2 star.

The technicians had not yet started their shift; by the time they responded to a q-phone call from the actual controllers, on Earth, it was too late. The dishes locked onto a new target and their dormant transmission system came online, linked to a qube in the protestors' camp that was running algorithms extracted from several hundred tesserae. At least one of which, it turned out, had been contaminated or overwritten by code extracted from a fragment of that crashed Ghajar spaceship. The ship code took control of the telescopes, and began to send a complex powerful signal towards a distant star.

After the technicians tried and failed to regain control of the array, they shut everything down. It's still shut down three years later, so I suppose you could say Leah Bright and her followers scored some kind of a victory. Trouble is, they also helped Universal Communications discover something new.

Leah was arrested by the UN geek police and charged with sabotage, interference with telecommunications transmissions, and a ragbag of lesser crimes. She and several of her supporters, along with the technician who had installed the clandestine link, were released on bail put up by an anonymous supporter, and all charges were eventually dropped. Partly because a trial would have been a PR disaster; partly because Universal Communications discovered that the transmission had been aimed at a red dwarf star more than twenty thousand light years away—a star with, it turned out, a single wormhole orbiting it.

An expedition was promptly dispatched, taking more than a month to make its way from wormhole to wormhole, star to star. It discovered a vast debris disc circling close to that cool, dim star, a churning mass of organic and metallic fragments twelve million miles across and just thirty feet deep, with about half the mass of the Earth's moon. The remains of millions of Ghajar ships, perhaps. Or the wreckage of some huge structure, a space metropolis or moon-sized orbital fort, ground small by innumerable collisions and time.

Five companies have purchased licenses to map and explore the debris disc, searching for artifacts and scraps that contain active algorithms. So far no one has found anything useful—or if they have, they aren't talking about it—but one thing is clear. Radioactivity, chemical changes, and stress marks show that the debris was subjected to energies so immense they would have caused serious deformations in local spacetime.

It seems, the experts say, that the Ghajar were divided against themselves. The spaceship that crashed in the City of Dead did not crash by accident, but was shot down while fleeing from an enemy; the debris disc was created by some unimaginable battle, part of a war that ended with the Ghajar's extinction. And in their fate we may glimpse our own future, because the human race is already split into opposing factions by the influence of artifacts or technologies. By ideas not our own. By the ravings of mad alien ghosts.

The Jackaroo have said nothing at all about this theory. They will neither confirm nor deny our speculations about what happened to the Ghajar, saying only that they are "interesting." There is a rumor that three of their gold-skinned avatars visited the radio telescope array while the geek police were making the qube safe. Van says neither he nor any of his deputies were informed about their presence, but one night in the Green Ale Inn one of the facility's technicians said the avatars stood there for an hour, facing each other like gunfighters in some old Western, then walked off to a town car without saying a word and were driven away.

Perhaps someone will find something immensely valuable in the debris disc. Or perhaps it will drive those trying to understand it insane, or infect them with some kind of combat eidolon. But despite those risks the prospect of reward is too great to stop exploring.

Meanwhile, although the radio telescopes remain offline, Leah Bright is still camped at the gate. Like our founder, Joe Gordon, she lives in an RV. She supports herself with royalties from a self-published e-book about her campaign, by charging tourists for taking selfies with her, and by holding consultations about the Ghajar message that, she claims, passed through her. Unlike Joe, she loves to talk. She'll talk to anyone who'll listen. And with her garrulous eccentricity, and her obsession with the inscrutable alien dead, she has finally become one of us.

Of the Beast in the Belly

C. W. Johnson

A KILOMETER DOWN, the weight of the water squeezed Nawiz. It was balanced by the dense oxygenated liquid inside her suit, filling Nawiz's lungs and throat and every cavity. But the real pressure came from herself. She was close, so close to her vengeance. It would burst her heart, she thought, were not it strapped with titanium bands of will.

Where the continental shelf fell away into the deep ocean they had come upon a pod of cetiphants drifting over the benthic ooze, heads down, tails up, searching for mollusks with supple, sensitive trunks. The scene was rendered by passive interferometry, exploiting the cetiphants' own clicks and whistling songs. In another twenty minutes or so the cetiphants would stop feeding and ascend to the surface to breathe. But at that moment the sound-painted sight was breathtaking.

Tonight, she thought. *Tonight I will finish this.*

"Janum," she said aloud over the sonar communicator. *Janum.* As if she hadn't brushed aside his thin disguise as easily as wet paper.

The boy floated nearby—though he wasn't a boy any longer; he was a young man. And he wasn't spoiled and superrich anymore, either, but had given up wealth, family, connections, power. Given it up for "love." She might have admired his choice, too, if it hadn't selfishly destroyed her own hopes.

Janum's voice in her ear hushed her. "They're not normally skittish but—"

The cetiphants had been moving around nervously, when suddenly they spiraled away from the ocean floor. Janum switched to active pings.

Something was wrong. At first she thought a pack of sea-jackals were attacking the cetiphants, but they were too deep for that. Then she thought the shelf had collapsed, until she realized she had it backwards: A wall had risen from just beyond the edge of the shelf. No volcanic activity was that fast, and there was no heat, no seismic shuddering, just squeals of terror from the cetiphants. A fissure in the wall opened, the cetiphant pod tumbled into the resulting vortex, and Nawiz was dragged by the current, sucked past massive boulders—no, not boulders, nothing geologic at all—

Teeth.

And she and Janum were swallowed up.

After years of searching dozens of planets, she had found her quarry sleeping on a beach illuminated by brittle shards of stars scattered across the sky, while the ocean pulsed against the sand in long, slow sighs. He was curled up with that girl, the two of them tucked under a tree like a pair of ripe fruit. Nawiz had been afraid of this moment, because she had poured her entire life into the search, and when the deed was done and she had sold him back to his father, would she just be a husk emptied of purpose? Would her reward be tasteless in her mouth, the riches bitter on her tongue?

But upon seeing them asleep, innocent as babes, Nawiz felt a bolus of poison rise inside her, and she was glad. "Hey," she said, nudging him awake with her toe. "I want to hire you."

Nawiz had forged her own identity, of course. She called herself Orfiiju Aleata, picking a minor superrich clan with little contact with the Samraatjus. Since they had never met, she had only changed her appearance a little. He might not have bothered to look at her image.

Soon after a lilac dawn they had been out on the ocean, the tang of salt in her nose and the sting of sun on her skin. "Janum" and "Zoka" had a small trimaran that skittered insect-like across the glassy waves. Nawiz—now "Aleata"—felt the wind burnish her face to a high sheen. Once, she had dreamed of owning a world like this. The reward she would garner from Old Samraatju wouldn't come close to that, but she would live comfortably.

First, though, she paid Janum and Zoka to be her guides.

As a child, Nawiz had been privileged to many sights. She thought herself immunized against wonder. But each day, as they swam downward, the abalone light of the surface faded, giving way to a darkness as subtle and shifting as a whisper. Constellations of luminescent fish swirled around them, and shoals of phytokrill danced in the saline currents. From far off the siren songs of the cetiphants called. Nawiz had heard recordings, but here, in the belly of the ocean, it seemed different, more alluring, a narcotic, and each day she looked forward to putting on a balrog suit.

It was the suits that had tipped off Nawiz. She had nearly run into her quarry on Choel, a furnace-like venusiform world in a distant system, though he had worn yet another identity there, not yet Janum. The biomechanical balrog suits afforded protection against the immense pressure and sulfuric acidity of the surface, while batlike wings radiated away heat. Learning of his masquerade as a local bandit, she had plotted to insert herself into his gang, reshaped her body, and started martial training. But then he disappeared abruptly, and it was two years before Nawiz, sifting through exabytes of rumor, caught a sniff of tour guides using balrog suits to dive the deep oceans of Tazhatanka, their thermoregulating wings now flying in salt water. She was afraid he would slip away again, and when she found him asleep on the beach with an arm around Zoka, the wave of relief had nearly knocked Nawiz to her knees.

Zoka was compact and tough and, frankly, not all that pretty, and when she spoke her words were as straight and unadorned as the ocean horizon. Maybe he liked that in her. Zoka came from a family of lowly guides, which is how she slid her way into Janum's heart, and she seemed insulated against Aleata's brusque indifference.

Aleata's flirtation with Janum was another thing entirely. When she stood next to Janum, letting the rocking of the ship bump her up against him every so often, out of the corner of her eye she saw Zoka stiffen. Janum seemed uncomfortable, too, leaning a few millimeters away from Aleata.

Nawiz wanted to laugh. It took all her enhanced strength to concentrate on her mission.

Mostly she acted as if Zoka were invisible, just a wisp of breeze on her face. And when Zoka led the dives Nawiz-as-Aleata made deliberate mistakes, feigned confusion, broke down into panic. At last Janum took over. She became a star pupil, praised him as a guide and teacher. "I was so distracted I didn't see that school of sea-jackals," she said. "You saved me."

Janum flushed and turned his head away. "You only have to worry about sea-jackals near the surface," he murmured.

After a few days she was rewarded by a low-voiced argument between the two of them. She had to hide her grin, as if it were something stolen, something she kept hidden in a pocket.

Nawiz planned to seduce Janum, of course, and had special erodisiacs from a brothel on Choel for the purpose. It wasn't just enough to sell him back to his vengeful father. Nawiz wanted to split Janum and Zoka, ruin them the way they had ruined her. Then her mission could be completed.

"There's a pod of cetiphants below," Zoka had called from the sonar hut. "You can probably catch them feeding."

Tonight, Nawiz had thought. She silently repeated her daily promise to her dead mother, her promise of vengeance. *After one last dive.* She did find the cetiphants fascinating....

Nawiz tumbled and spun. The cetiphants screamed in panic. It sounded like metal being torn in two. Her sonar goggles showed only flashes and incoherent static.

"... eata? Aleata?" Janum's voice came over the sonar comm, staticky and broken.

"I thought I saw," she whispered, but couldn't finish: *Teeth.* It would sound crazy.

"... n't contact the surface. Let me ... frequency."

The tug of current had slowed. Around them swirled the cetiphants, some broken and dead, others calling out to their family, their mates, their friends. She felt the buzz of their ultrasonic bursts. They churned in the water, battered against her. She tried to swim out of the stampede, but something grabbed her.

She turned, and it was Janum. "One of my wings is broken," he told her. "Caught between two cetiphants."

She dragged them both down, her balrog's wings taking in big scoops of water. The irony of her rescuing him from injury and death was not lost, not even in the adrenaline-soaked moment.

They didn't get far. A soft floor blocked their way. Not stone, but not mud and ooze, either. She could still hear the screams and whistles of the cetiphants. She felt woozy, and her balrog tightened around her.

"Pressure is dropping," Janum said, "fast." Yet they seemed to be floating motionless, just above the spongy bottom.

"Where are we?"

"I think," Janum said, "I think it's an arcthant."

She had heard tales of arcthants, inconceivably giant creatures of this planet's oceans. His statement startled her.

"We're on the back of one?"

"*Inside* one," Janum said. "In its stomach." Her own stomach did a little flip. "They get five kilometers long. They're reputed to swallow ships."

"I've heard that, too. I thought it was a myth."

"They're supposed to have twelve stomachs, so this must be the first one. Twelve or more stomachs." He paused. "I tried sending a distress signal, but I don't think it can get out. They'll think...."

"They'll think we're dead," she finished for him. The words tasted like ashes in her mouth, and it wasn't just the oxygenated fluid.

Half an hour later, the cetiphants began to drown. Nawiz saw a mother cetiphant try to urge her limb baby upward. Her own guts twisted like wet cloth.

A booming bass twanging sounded through the water. A sudden, new current dragged at them and the cetiphants, swept them through a hole, a valve, and into another stomach.

The pressure was much less here. Dead cetiphants drifted at broken angles in the water, while the ones still alive swam upward. And with her sonar Nawiz saw something else move among them.

An ultrasonic squeal knifed through her as the things slashed at the cetiphants. They were small, only a couple of meters long, but there were dozens of them. Her balrog tasted cetiphant blood in the water. One of the things swerved towards them, all teeth and clawed fins: a sea-jackal.

She grabbed Janum and swam down. Sea-jackals seldom dove deeper than fifty or sixty meters. But then she saw the sunken ship twenty meters below, corroded and encrusted with sea life. They pulled themselves among the spars and beams, just as jaws snapped behind them. The sea-jackal could not reach them, and the metal in the ships confused its electric sense, so it turned away for easier prey. Up above the massacre of cetiphants continued.

"How did sea-jackals get in here?" Nawiz asked. "There weren't any with us when we got swallowed. We were too deep for them."

Janum didn't answer. The booming bass twanging began again. The next valve opened and current swept them through.

☼   ☼   ☼

The next stomach was even bigger, over a hundred meters across, the floor littered with the wreckage of ships and the fallen scaffolding of skeletons of cetiphants and other creatures, covered with thousands of small, wriggling eel-like creatures. "Another valve," Janum said when they reached the far side, pushing at the tense muscles of the stomach wall.

"Doesn't that lead the wrong way?"

There were sea-jackals in this stomach, too, but fewer, and swimming close to the wrecks they escaped their attention. Nawiz used her balrog's thick paw to grip a taut steel cable leading upward. "Where does this go?" she asked.

Janum pinged. "That's a surface ... there's something up there," he said.

"I see it." Rendered in passive sonar, the surface was a flickering, shimmering barrier. The cable stretched up toward something big. "Would the air be breathable?"

"I hadn't really thought about it, but it must be. Sea-jackals, hmm, sea-jackals *are* air breathers, so there must be oxygen."

The balrog suits were oxygenated for several days, so, unlike the cetiphants, they wouldn't drown. But, *like* the cetiphants, even their balrog suits could be torn to bits if ganged up on by sea-jackals. The balrog's sulfur-based metabolism would make them taste awful, but sea-jackals bit first and never bothered with questions.

"Let's go up," she said, and before Janum could say anything she rose. The surface was a slaughterhouse, ragged cetiphant carcasses everywhere and the water thick with torn flesh.

The cable led to a big object bobbing on the surface. Nawiz broke the surface first and grabbed the edge. It was a ship or a raft. As she hoisted herself up she felt her body vibrate. The stomach walls were twanging again.

As Janum joined her, she turned and saw the puckered valve open. Water sluiced through it, and the current tugged at the raft. They both almost lost their footing as it swayed beneath them.

She turned to face Janum. "I guess it's good we weren't in the water. I guess—" But she stopped.

They were surrounded by people. *People in the air.* And though their outlines were blurred in sonar view, the nastiness of their weapons was very easy to see.

☼   ☼   ☼

Only later did Nawiz think of how they must have looked: monstrous trolls twice the height and three times the breadth of a person, dripping slimy water, with hideous echolocating faces and demonic bat wings.

No wonder the inhabitants of the raft jabbed lances at them. Janum took a step back, fumbled with the opening of his suit.

"We mean you no harm!" he shouted. "Can you read sonar comm?" He added something in a dialect Nawiz didn't understand.

"I think the answer is 'no,' " Nawiz said.

The raft swayed as the valve opened up, in sonar a black, gaping maw. The uneven deck shifted and slid beneath their feet. Lances darted in their faces. Though she thought herself brave, Nawiz flinched and backpedaled.

She bumped hard against Janum, felt it inside her suit, and turned to see him tip over the side of the raft and splash into the water. The current grabbed him, and she had a last glimpse of his balrog with its broken wing as it was swept into the next stomach.

Getting out of a balrog suit is a messy business. It was even harder with half a dozen blades pressed against her. She considered fighting, but if her balrog was badly injured she wouldn't get far. So she knelt and tugged at the seals.

Nawiz found herself in humid air saturated with salt and decay, coughing heavy liquid out of her lungs. Six men and one woman surrounded her. In the sweltering heat and slimy humidity they were naked. Though someone had torn her sonar goggles from her face, the scene was still lit a sickly yellowish green, the light coming from luminescent algae growing on the upper folds of the stomach. A small, scrawny man with a snail-like snub of a nose growled in a dialect she couldn't follow.

Nawiz retched the last of the oxygenated fluid and slowly stood up. The valve to the next stomach had closed. Still unsteady on her own feet, she followed the scrawny man—he looked like a shaved monkey, and even in the dim light was as pale as an oyster pried from its shell—as he hopped over a short stretch of water to the next raft, or ship, or wrecked hull, lashed to the first one with cables. Above them curved the vault of the stomach of the arcthant.

They brought her to the largest raft. In the center of the raft, nailed to a crooked antenna mast, was a star. No, not a star: a single electric light, its sterile whiteness so bright it felt like a dagger to the eye. Nawiz could barely look at it.

About a dozen people stood around in a loose arc, gaunt and gray in the electric light, and three or four children crawled underfoot, also naked in the steaming humidity. They looked with fear and hostility at Nawiz as, a blade at her back, she was pushed to her knees.

The man who stepped forward wasn't the tallest or the broadest, but even in the poor illumination, his wiry arms and legs, his outsized hands and feet, looked as hard and dense as iron, and he had a head as bald and ugly as a piece of broken stone. One of the men who had captured Nawiz spoke to him. Then the man said something in the same dialect.

Nawiz shook her head. "I don't understand," she said. She shivered, even though she was roasting in the heat. When she came to Tazhatanka, she'd had edit-lessons, but only the dialect of the planet's wealthy elite, of course.

The man slapped himself on the chest with his large hands. "Peshi," he declared. "I a'boss in Wakangshi's belly." His lower-class accent, one she'd heard among the laborers at the spaceport when she made planetfall, was breathy, sibilant: *Hai ha'bhosss hin Wakhangsshi's bhellhy*.... He stepped forward. "You a'huh...?"

"Aleata," she said. By habit she gave her pseudonym, even though Janum was dead and gone. "Orfiiju Aleata."

"Expensive names a'not needed here," Peshi said.

"Expensive names can buy much," she said.

Peshi laughed, a cold and bitter laugh. "You think huh Wakangshi craves money? Wakangshi c'buy what with your money? More ocean huh?" He turned his face upward and cupped his hands around his mouth. "Hey, Wakangshi, she wants to give some bribe at you! You demand how much?" He cocked his head as if listening for an answer, and then shrugged.

"You see huh? Wakangshi takes no bribes, unless you h'maybe some whole sea of fish." The people snickered at this joke.

Peshi gestured to the shaved-monkey man with the snail-like nose. "You a'wife-mate of Chehupa now. Those cannibals ate up his last wife-mate, he needs some new one."

As Nawiz stood up straight, Chehupa stepped forward, his gaze in the bright white light of the single bulb scything up and down her body as cool as a farmer looking at his fields. He reached out a hand.

When she had been hunting Janum—call him by his real name, Samraatju Majnu—and had tracked him down as a bandit on the planet Choel, Nawiz had had her strength and reflexes enhanced, had trained in martial sparring, the better to infiltrate his gang. Now she unleashed that training.

She wanted to smash that snub snail nose of Chehupa, but she reined in that impulse. Instead she took a step forward, put a heel behind his calf. A shove to his chest, simple leverage, and he smacked down on the deck, and she had her bare foot on his throat.

Another man, tall and lean with a big beak of a nose and wide, floppy lips, rushed forward. Nawiz flipped him over her hip, heard the wet smack of his flesh against the uneven deck and his grunt as air was knocked out of his lungs. A third man started to sweep his lance around, but it was long and clumsy and she easily stepped inside, grabbed the haft, and jabbed its owner in the stomach with the butt.

Peshi stepped forward, whistling his admiration. "You a'some fighter," he said, waving a broad hand. "You a'fighting for us, not against us." Although Nawiz tensed, he stood next to her, so close she could smell his musky sweat over the stink of the stomach, and placed a calloused palm on her shoulder. "I declare you a'some honorary man among us Salties, here in Wakangshi's belly." A wire-thin smile crept up on his face. "You a'taking some wife-mate," he said, and as he snapped his finger a small group, mostly of children and a couple of underfed women came forward, staring at the deck of the raft.

"I don't need a wife, uh, a wife-mate," Nawiz said.

"Boy, girl, woman, no matter," Peshi said. "Sex or not, no matter. Wife-mate serves you."

Nawiz was going to protest, then thought better of it. Looking over at the huddled group, she crouched down and crooked a finger at the smallest and dirtiest girlchild. The girl looked away, and only flinched when one of the women nudged her. Peshi pursed his lips and uttered a screeching three-note trill. The girl leaped forward as if electrified.

Nawiz ran her finger through the girl's tangled, matted hair. "What's your name?" she whispered. The girl repeated the three-note whistle. Nawiz looked around helplessly. Some of the men snickered, and a woman sang out, "She i'called Whew-wheew-wheeew," echoing the trill. It sounded a little like the distress call of the cetiphants. It sounded like the song of loss in her heart.

The girl led Nawiz to a bed of rags, where she threw herself down. Sleep took her immediately.

When she awoke she felt dizzy, disoriented by the darkness and the bobbing of the raft. At first she thought she was still on the trimaran, still with Janum and Zoka. Then she became aware of Whew-wheew-wheeew's, warm, damp body nestled up against her own, and of the stink filling her nose and mouth. For a moment, gagging, panicking, she thought she would be unable to breathe. She sat up and slowly sipped the air, as if through a straw. Her head remained fuzzy, but the panic subsided.

Seeing she was awake, Whew-wheew-wheeew took Nawiz by the hand and led her across the rafts—which were indeed wrecks of ships, lashed together with cables and anchored to wrecks on the bottom of the stomach. They stopped in front of one of the great valves, a muscled gate fit for an emperor.

Disoriented, Nawiz said to Whew-wheew-wheeew, "Where are we? Where are we going?" When the girl looked puzzled, Nawiz tried to imitate the dialect. "We a'where? We go where?"

"We a'in Big-Stomach," Whew-wheew-wheeew replied. "We go at Stink-Stomach." With some questions, gestures, and no small amount of exasperation, Nawiz learned that Big-Stomach was stomach three, and Stink-Stomach was stomach four. Stomach two, it turned out, the killing ground for the sea-jackals, was a kind of gulag for those who dared defy Peshi.

The valve began to twitch and twang, and others gathered at the edge of the raft. When the valve opened, a black maw, one of the men pulled at a cable leading into the water. On makeshift coracles they pulled themselves through the valve. The air in Stink-Stomach was hotter and indeed stank worse, like rotting garbage in old vinegar, but there were fewer sea-jackals.

Along the side of the raft, fishers pulled up traps and tipped the contents into baskets. Nawiz's job was to watch the fishers to make sure no one stole a bit of food. Scrawny Chehupa was there, too, no doubt to watch the watcher; Nawiz herself was not to eat anything on her own but receive her food from the bosses. As soon as they arrived, Chehupa whistled Whew-wheew-wheeew and the girl obediently cocked her head to him. He said something in dialect, and off ran Whew-wheew-wheeew.

Several women pulled up traps containing fish or wriggling eels. "Are the eels good?" Nawiz asked one woman.

"Peshi-boss and his friends eat bone-eels," the woman said. She crouched down and poked at a squirming bone-eel with a finger. "We eat nibblers," she said, pointing to the basket full of dull-colored, fist-sized fish.

"What do they nibble?" Nawiz asked. "Toes?"

"Sea-jackal shit. Taste like shit, too."

After a few hours, or maybe a thousand years, Peshi's lieutenants gathered up the baskets and distributed food. Nawiz's share was disappointingly small, just scraps of raw eel and a gruel of briny algae.

Out of the brown darkness Whew-wheew-wheeew ran up, her bare feet slapping on the raft. "Where have you been?" Nawiz asked.

The girl stared at her for a moment, then curled up her arms and said, "I carry messages for Peshi-boss and his friends. They need some message, they Whew-wheew-wheeew." She looked around at everyone gobbling down their food. She tugged at Nawiz's hand and said, "Aleata-husband, I a'hungry."

Nawiz squeezed shut her eyes at being called "husband," then said to Chehupa. "Hey, you forgot, uh, Whew-wheew-wheeew here." She managed a credible whistle.

He shrugged. "Whew-wheew-wheeew i'your wife-mate, so she i'your responsibility now. You a'sharing."

But Nawiz, famished, had already gobbled down her portion.

"I'm sorry," she whispered.

The girl looked down. "Peshi-boss says you a'going at him," she said in little more than a whisper.

They worked their way back to the valve, and when it boomed and opened, they quickly punted through to Big-Stomach, sea-jackals trailing in their wake. The third stomach seemed darker than Nawiz remembered. As they crossed from raft to raft, she realized Peshi's solitary light, a beacon in the dimness before, had gone out.

At the crooked antenna mast, a man was replacing the light. He gave it a final twist as Nawiz walked up, and the light ignited; the sudden stab of brightness made her turn her face away. When her eyes had adjusted, she saw the repairman's face was shining with sweat, his eyes pools of light.

Then she blinked and realized he was wearing corrective glass lenses, mismatched, propped in front of his eyes. She also saw that his right leg, scarred and twisted like a cable, ended in a stump, strapped to a crude peg. The man was speaking to Whew-wheew-wheeew, and when he turned to Nawiz he continued in dialect. Seeing Nawiz's puzzled expression, he switched fluently, with a much lighter accent than the others. "I a'Kaga," he said, slapping himself on his chest.

"Uh, I am Aleata," Nawiz said, attempting to imitate the gesture.

"I know. Peshi wants me to ask about that strange beast who carried you in his belly."

"Oh, the balrog suit," Nawiz said. "It's kind of hard to explain."

"Kaga i'our fix-it wallah," Whew-wheew-wheeew said.

"I w'only some lowly machinist, but good enough for these Salties," Kaga said.

Whew-wheew-wheeew darted off and returned with a flask and lifted it to Nawiz. "Kaga made," she said.

Nawiz sniffed the liquid and gingerly tasted it. It was water, warm but clear and clean. She gulped several mouthfuls, then remembered to give the girl some. "You made it?" she asked.

"Distilled it," the fix-it wallah said.

From the wrecks of ships Kaga had salvaged electric motors and turned them into dynamos. The natural wave motion which pushed the rafts together and apart drove the dynamos and provided some electric current; not much, but enough to distill water, cook algae into a thick gruel, and to grill eel for Peshi and his men.

He shifted on his feet. "D'you mind if I sit? Some sea-jackal," he said, tapping his peg, "tried to make lunch of me long time ago. Peshi fished me out before it c'get some second course."

"How did the sea-jackals get in here, anyway?"

Kaga smiled. "They help Wakangshi's digestion. Sea-jackals, they kill and tear apart creatures swallowed by Wakangshi. Other fish, they eat these remnants. Bone-eels, they eat bones, of course, while nibblers, they eat sea-jackal shit. Algae, they make oxygen for these sea-jackals and for us. And algae feed on nibbler shit."

"You know a lot about the stomach of an arcthant."

"Before I w'swallowed up, I w'machinist aboard some Ministry of Fisheries trawler."

Kaga looked out over the surface of the water. "Aboard that trawler, I overheard these scientists talk about what happened in digestive tracts of arcthants. They knew, for instance, sea-jackal reproduction i'tied up with these arcthants. Sea-jackal eggs a'very tough. You see huh sea-jackals d'not like so much Stinky-Stomach? It i'more acidic there, and it i'worse further on. But sea-jackal eggs must go through some heavy acid bath in some arcthant stomach before they hatch. And these arcthants evolved to make some hospitable home for sea-jackals—oxygen, low pressure in stomachs, everything."

He paused, then said, "Now about this ... balrog suit?"

She didn't really want to talk about it, but didn't see how she could wriggle away. So she told him: It was a biomechanical suit, originally developed for the intense pressure and heat of hothouse worlds, but adapted for deep ocean going.

"The inner cavity is filled with oxygenated fluid," she said, "that fills your lungs, protects you against pressure. Nasty taste," she added.

"This fluid i'made how?"

She explained the balrog exuded it. Supply it with fresh water and organics with a high sulfur content, and it would create its own. "Takes a few days," she said.

Kaga nodded and lumbered upright.

"Can you take me to the balrog suit?" Nawiz asked. "I could—"

"It belongs to Peshi, now." He turned to go.

"You've been here a long time?" she asked. "Many years?"

"No sun or stars down here," he said over his shoulder as he limped away. "Just valves open, close, open, close, open, close."

Nawiz settled into a routine, and with nothing but valves marking time it soon seemed as if she had lived in the stomach all her life. She tried to keep count: open, close, open, close. She soon gave up.

She did her duty, strolling among the fishers, but duty didn't keep her single stomach from gurgling and twisting, and the few scraps of raw eel and algal porridge did not tamp down her hunger pangs. She resented sharing with Whew-wheew-wheeew. The resentment burned bright when she heard Peshi's lieutenants roar with laughter, saw the grease on their faces from the grilled eel stuffed in their mouths and the way they did nothing but stroll up and down the rafts, the lords of the hell that was Wakangshi's stomach.

She took her resentment out on the fishers, slap and hit and spit at them, even when they did nothing wrong; not just a slap but really hard, so that she could hear the crack of bone and gristle, and she realized this was not the first time she had hit a fisher like this, and not the second, and not the third. She was just a nub of anger, and hunger, and resentment.

She went to Peshi and offered to fight any of his men, any of the Salties. Peshi snorted and waved her away. "You d'not choose," he said. He slapped himself on the chest. "*I* choose."

Crossing his arms, he added, "Kaga says, that beast who carried you, i'ready to carry me. You a'coming."

He gestured, and she followed him across the rafts to a small one, guarded by one of Peshi's burlier men. There Kaga crouched by a small pool. In the dim light Nawiz could not see much, but the liquid was thick and nacreous and at the bottom of the pool was a massive, monstrous shape.

"It i'some fascinating thing, this balrog," Kaga said. "It really protects you from pressure? Just like Wakangshi's ribs?"

Nawiz said, "In a way. The fluid counters the pressure, but the arcthant's ribs seem to keep the digestive tract at low pressure for the sea-jackals...." She felt her heart banging against her own ribs. She knelt down to touch the surface of the oxygenated fluid.

"And you say I c'breathe this water huh like some fish?" said Peshi, who had come up behind her. "Or it i'some trick huh to get me to drown?"

Nawiz looked up and over her shoulder. "I'll show you, if you like," she said.

Peshi smirked and stroked his chin, as if considering. "I w'risk it."

With her heart burning black, Nawiz put the sonar goggles over Peshi's eyes, told him how to breathe in the oxygenated fluid and to wait out the gag reflex, how to slip inside the balrog and move its limbs like a puppeteer.

He couldn't wait out the gag reflex on his first try, and his head shot up out of the pool as he coughed and sprayed liquid. His lieutenants exchanged smirking glances but were careful not to say anything aloud.

On the second try Peshi stayed submerged, and Nawiz and Kaga slipped into the liquid and helped him into the suit. At last, dripping with oxygenated fluid he rose from the pool a monstrous creature of legend, the balrog's hideous, instrument-studded face frozen in an evil grin. He slipped while trying to stand and tumbled backward into the pool with a splash. Chehupa snorted aloud at that.

But an hour later Peshi had more or less mastered the balrog suit, and they all stood on the small outpost raft in the second stomach, where sea-jackals circled and stalked.

The stomach walls began twanging. The sea-jackals immediately abandoned circling the raft and headed for the valve, greedy for the flood of food they were about to receive. And Peshi in the balrog suit crouched and tensed, an athlete just before a race.

The puckered muscle of the valve split open and a wall of water rushed in, the dark gray bodies of cetiphants tumbling in the foam. The sea-jackals jostled with each other, as if they had bets as to who could take the first bite, and soon the water was dark with cetiphant blood.

And Peshi dove in, like an arrow shot from a bow, and swam for the valve. The valve that lead toward the mouth, and freedom.

☼   ☼   ☼

But the next time the valve opened, the current flushed through only the balrog.

Kaga and Nawiz helped Peshi to climb aboard the raft and to free him. The boss of Wakangshi's stomachs lay on the raft and vomited fluid.

At last he lifted his head and said, "That current w'too strong." Slowly he got to his feet, kicked at the now empty balrog suit, a monster deflated. "You a'taking it back to that pool."

The valve closed.

Open, close.

Open, close.

Sometimes Nawiz was too exhausted to sleep, and she listened to the boom and twang of the valves as they opened, then closed.

Open, close.

Lying awake she thought, not for the first time, there was no one left above to mourn her. She had lost her mother, her position, her wealth. Even her name had been swallowed up. But was there a greater monster than uncountable, unstoppable time?

Off duty, she stepped from raft to raft, until she found herself at the last valve, staring at the pink-gray maw that had swallowed up Janum. Roasting in the heat, she couldn't remember how many times she had come here.

Is he dead now, finally dead? she wondered again. Even if he was, she was a failure. She had wanted him dead, but he hadn't died at her hand, and she didn't get to watch him die, didn't watch him suffer. Another thing stolen from her: He, in his selfishness, had made her and her family suffer, and above all else she had wanted to watch him suffer. Without that, she felt empty, trapped. She would have felt that way even if she weren't in the belly of an arcthant.

"I wonder if he is being digested in there," she mused aloud.

"Who?" Whew-wheew-wheeew asked.

"My, uh, friend. He fell in the water and got swept into the next stomach. Not many sea-jackals, there, I suppose."

Whew-wheew-wheeew peered at the valve. "No, husband," she said at last. "Cannibals live there." She took Nawiz's hand and looked up at her. "Cannibals ate him up. They eat everyone up." And she turned back to the valve and waved her hand in front of her face, some sign of warding Nawiz supposed.

Nawiz looked down and saw the girl was crying. "What's wrong?" she asked.

Whew-wheew-wheeew lifted her tear-streaked face. "He throws people at those cannibals."

"Who?"

"Peshi-boss." Together they stared at the puckered valve. "He threw my mama at those cannibals," the girl said, and Nawiz felt a little earthquake strike her heart. "I w'little, but I remember. He threw her in this water and this current took her at those cannibals." She sobbed aloud and pressed her face to Nawiz's body. Nawiz could feel the girl's whole body shaking. "Egg," the girl whispered. "That i'what she called me. Not Whew-wheew-wheeew, but Egg. That w'my name, before Peshi threw my mama to those cannibals."

Then one of Peshi's men whistled for the girl. Nawiz surprised herself by clutching the girl tight, but Whew-wheew-wheeew slipped away. "I m'go," she whispered.

Nawiz was still staring in the direction where Whew-wheew-wheeew had gone when Kaga limped up to her on his peg leg.

"You take good care of her," Kaga said. "I h'watched you. And you a'kind with those fishers, or at least no more cruel than any other Salty." Nawiz would have laughed aloud, but she didn't have the energy.

The fix-it wallah nodded toward the last valve. "You miss your friend, that one who fell," he said. Of course that wasn't it at all. But she was too tired to explain and had no reason to. She said nothing, which Kaga took as assent. "You have some good heart," he added, and she did snort, and she thought his line of talk so comical she was about to confess everything, when he leaned in close and said, "Your friend 's'alive."

Her heart almost stopped. The shock must have shown on her face, for Kaga gently touched her on the wrist, and inclined his head toward the last valve.

"The cannibals?" she asked.

Kaga shook his head. "Not cannibals. They follow this cannibal *religion*." He made the sign of warding, and the faint yellow-green algal light glinted off his crude lenses.

Not understanding, Nawiz asked, "How do you know he is alive, and not drowned or eaten by sea-jackals—"

"Sea-jackals d'not go into other stomachs. Those stomachs get more and more acidic, which grown sea-jackals c'not stand. As for your friend—" He paused, searching her face, as if he would find some answer written there. "This i'some secret, you a'not telling anyone. But I h'seen your friend, I h'spoken with him. He i'relieved you a'alive." He couldn't help but grin. "I have some machine, I, I, I c'travel into this next stomach. I a'one of them. I belong to that cannibal religion." And he made the sign of warding again, only Nawiz saw now it wasn't a sign of warding at all.

Kaga had a small submersible, he told Nawiz, one of the many ships swallowed over centuries by the arcthant Wakangshi. "I c'not take you at him," he said, "but I c'pass on messages."

After a long pause she realized he was waiting. But she stood there like a dull, fishy beast, while a net of thoughts whirled in her head. *What should I say? I'm so glad you aren't dead so I can still get my revenge?*

Instead, she said, "Why didn't you leave?"

He blinked at her. "You mean leave huh Wakangshi?" He shook his head. The submersible was too damaged and leaky to do more than traverse between two stomachs, he said, and beyond his abilities to repair. The motors were not strong enough to swim out the mouth, and further along the digestive system the acidity was too much. His face sagged as he explained all this.

And in a way, she understood. She was weary. She felt old. Her mother had been old, old and weary, and for most of her life Nawiz hadn't understood her mother's weariness. When Samraatju Majnu had died, or faked his death, and there was to be no marriage between Parvaanthju and Samraatju, and the Parvaanthju family would fade into cold, dark insignificance, like a dying star, her mother had turned her face from everyone and everything. Nawiz hadn't understood then; she had burned with anger and a thirst for vengeance and a hunger to get something, *anything*, for her family and for herself. And when her mother had exhaled her last breath, a wisp of carbon dioxide and water vapor, Nawiz had burned and not understood why her mother had not burned with her.

But now, weary to her creaking bones, she understood. And maybe she would have spent the rest of her days like that, like Kaga and like her mother, weary and gray with hopelessness, a bit of flesh called "human" but in reality little more than an automaton, eating cold eel and beating up fishers.

Coming from her shift watching the fishers, she wandered into the third stomach, where Peshi and his lieutenants were eating grilled eel, and the smell of charred, cooked flesh made her mouth water and her stomach churn. *I want*, her own flesh said. *I want. I want to have the worlds promised my family, if I had been married. I want to have what I lost, even just a small portion. I want to not be hungry. I want.*

So she walked up to Peshi. His face gleamed with eel fat even in the dim, yellow-green light from the algae on the stomach walls.

"I want," she started, and her words stumbled, and Chehupa snickered, and Peshi leaned forward, wiping his mouth with the back of his hand. She looked at his arm, tried to imagine the enhanced fast-twitch muscle in it, wondered how the physicians who had enhanced him compared with those who had enhanced her.

"I want to tell you something," she said finally. "I want to tell you about Kaga."

She tried not to hear Kaga plead and cry out as she ate her grilled eel. She gobbled it down greedily. Egg danced around her, her mouth opening like a chick in a nest. Nawiz glanced over at Peshi and his lieutenants. They were occupied with Kaga, so she slid a morsel into Egg's mouth.

The grease tasted good on her own tongue, but her stomach flopped around and threatened to toss it back. "Don't you dare," she whispered to her gut. "Not after what I had to do to get this. Don't you *dare*."

Peshi had not seemed surprised Kaga was in league with the cannibals, only angry. It did not take long for Kaga to break down and confess. He told them the submersible was tethered at the far end of Stink-Stomach. "You a'showing me," Peshi said.

As they stood before the puckered muscle of the last valve Kaga, his face slick with blood, pointed into the water. Chehupa stuck the butt end of a lance down and hit something. Metal.

Boom, went the stomach, and the valve shuddered and twitched.

Peshi gestured at Kaga and said something in dialect. At first Nawiz thought he was saying to kill him. Her heart fluttered in her chest like an insect in a jar. But then her brain caught up and she realized Peshi had ordered Kaga taken to the gulag stomach. A wave of sick relief washed over her.

Boom, the stomach walls twanged.

Peshi turned to Nawiz. "You understand huh?" he asked. "Kaga i'too valuable to throw away, even if he i'treacherous." He paused, with his ponderous head tucked down, as if checking a list, and then raised his face again.

Boooom.

"But you," Peshi said, "you a'not so valuable. If you betray Kaga so easily—"

And he pushed her over the side.

Nawiz fell. The wet slap as she hit the surface stung, and the water was warm as blood. She sank, but two kicks of her legs pushed her head into air. The raft was dwindling, shrinking: The current was pulling her into the next stomach.

Egg screamed, "*Husband!*" Peshi picked up the girl and threw her in after Nawiz.

The flow picked up speed. Nawiz spun in a vortex. When she had turned full circle she saw Egg, splashing and sputtering, crying out in fear. Many Salties didn't even know how to swim.

Nawiz scanned the water for sea-jackals as she was swept through the arch of the valve, the pillars of striated muscles twitching and trembling. When she looked back, she couldn't see Egg. She shouted, she whistled, but the twang of valve muscles and the gurgle of sour water was the only reply.

She dove. The acid water stung her eyes, and in the dim algal light it was nearly impossible to see more than a few feet. With strong strokes she swam in the direction she thought Egg had been. Her heart raced with panic. She might have taken on a sea-jackal, maybe, with her enhanced strength. But now she fought ticking seconds. How do you break the bones of time?

Nawiz swam to the surface, sucked in air, dove again. The thought of Egg's terror beat against her imagination, drove her deeper as she searched for shadows of movement, bubbles, listened underwater.

And then she felt something with the tips of her fingers. She lunged, slid her hand along skin, grabbed a limb. And now, now, where was the surface? She was disoriented, her lungs desperate for air. With one hand she gripped the girl, with the other she clawed in the direction she thought was air and life, but what if she was going the wrong way, what if she had been going the wrong way for years now? Her mouth opened and bitterness overwhelmed her tongue and poured down her throat and something grabbed her, pulled at her, but she was just fooling herself again, the way she had over and over again. Her last thought, before all went black, was to wonder what had impelled her to try to save the girl.

Dimly Nawiz floated to awareness. She was surrounded by roasting heat but her skin felt cold and clammy.

She sat up. She swung in a crude hammock. A single small light lit the interior of a tent. In the next hammock lay Egg, her damp hair sprawled out, and a woman like a column of smoke bent over her. Hearing Nawiz stir, the woman turned and murmured something in dialect. Nawiz's eyes burned and she felt drained, so she lay back down. The woman lifted Nawiz's hand and kissed it, then left the tent.

She must have fallen back asleep because when she opened them she saw Janum. "You're with us again," he said soberly. She sat up, glanced over at the empty hammock next to her. "There's someone who wants to meet you."

Nawiz thought he meant Egg, but when he stepped back and opened a flap in the tent, a small stooped woman entered. Her face was hard and lined, her hair the color of steel.

"This is Bhulna," Janum said. "She's the leader of the Bitters."

"Bitters? Is that what the cannibals call themselves?"

"Not cannibals," Janum said. "Theophages."

"We eat this devoured god," said Bhulna, making the same gesture Egg and Kaga had made, "this god who gifts his body to us that we may live."

Nawiz pointed to the now-empty hammock next to her. Bhulna smiled. "That girl i'fine. She babbles so quick none of us c'make out quite what happened. You c'tell us huh?"

"Peshi," Nawiz said. "The boss in the other stomachs—"

"I know Peshi, yes."

"He threw me over. Threw us over."

"And Kaga?" Both Bhulna and Janum were looking intently at her.

"He fixes machines that keep the Bitters alive," Janum said.

Nawiz took a deep breath. "He is alive, but ... Peshi knows he was helping you, I think."

Bhulna and Janum exchanged glances. "You a'strong now huh? You a'coming. It may take some while for you to tell your story."

The flaps led into a larger tent. The rafts were like those of the Salties, Nawiz learned, only smaller, and tented over. They had machines set up by Kaga to filter the air, to strip out carbon dioxide, and to bubble oxygen out of the water. Oxygen leaked out of the tents, of course, and the sour hot stench of the stomach leaked in, but the air, while so saturated with water vapor the sides of the tenting dripped with condensation as if sweating, remained breathable.

And while Peshi had only his one light, Nawiz noted a constellation of lights strung across the rafts in stomachs five and six.

People in the tent—the cannibals, the theophages, the Bitters—smiled at Bhulna, but stared hollow-eyed at Nawiz as they passed. At the far end of the tent the older woman invited Nawiz to sit. She produced a pair of small, sharp knives, and began to nimbly shuck a pile of gut-oysters.

They sat in silence while Nawiz fumbled with the knife. "You're very good at oysters," was all she could think to say.

"I grew up on this sea," Bhulna said, popping a shucked oyster into her mouth. "My family w'fishers. When I w'small, I shucked beach oyster and turtle barnacles all day long."

When Nawiz was young, she was schooled not only in letters and numbers but also in politics and family interests and her role as the family scion. Now she had lost all that, but it seemed selfish to say so to Bhulna, so she keep silent and popped a shucked oyster into her mouth. It had an oily taste.

"Kaga 's'alive huh?" Bhulna said quietly.

"I heard Peshi say he was too valuable to kill. But he is being held in stomach two, which they use as a kind of gulag."

Bhulna nodded. "And Peshi, how d'he learn about Kaga?"

Nawiz shrugged. "They found his submersible vessel," she said, which was true enough.

The older woman blew out a long, slow breath. "Without Kaga it i'bad for us." She shucked a few more oysters. "And then Peshi threw you at us. Little Egg only seems to know part of this story. She says you w'good for her."

Nawiz blinked. She remembered slapping Egg on the back of the head, hard enough to make Egg cry, when the girl had pestered her for food, or whined about pulling up traps for nibblers.

Then she shook her head. "Peshi saw me as a threat, I suppose," she said, picking out the words carefully the way she might select sweet berries from a bush with bitter leaves.

Bhulna nodded. "He feels this same way about me." She sighed. "He i'my younger brother." Of all the things Bhulna might have said, this hit Nawiz like a punch to the stomach. "We w'raised in this cannibal religion," the older woman continued. "But he never quite fit. He signed up for this interior defense league and w'gifted strength. We a'pacifists, of course, and our family w'not happy with him. But his flesh 's'our flesh, his blood our blood.

"Our family w'fishers, and one day when he visited us on leave, some arcthant swallowed up our boat. He and I and some aunt w'all who survived. She sleeps now, our aunt, in this flesh of Wakangshi. But we found these people who live here in this belly of Wakangshi.

"Peshi, he turned against our god when he realized there w'no way out. He worshipped strength by then. And I think my presence w'some thorn for his heart. My presence, and my worship of this devoured god. When he caught us in this feast, he would kick and scatter our feast, and us. These others, they worshipped Peshi's strength. Eventually, he banished us into these stomachs here.

"But Kaga saved us. These machines he fixed kept us alive. I believe he w'sent at Wakangshi's belly to save us." The old woman ran her finger along the surface of the raft, then looked up. "You c'save him huh?"

Someone knelt down next to Nawiz: Janum. "Yes, yes I c'save him," he said. Switching his accent, he said to Nawiz, "Can you draw me a map, show me where he is?"

As she sketched out a map, her stomach tightened like a wet rag. Kaga, of course, would tell them all how she had betrayed him. But she saw no way to refuse.

"And the other balrog suit? Where is it kept?" He had already explained how his balrog's wing had healed; he would use it to rescue Kaga.

Nawiz frowned. "Peshi barely knows how to work it. No point to sabotage."

"No," said Janum. "We could escape with the balrog suits."

"Peshi tried." Nawiz shook her head. "He took mine and tried to swim out the mouth, but the current was too strong."

"Not out the mouth."

Nawiz stared at him. "Kaga said the other stomachs get increasingly acidic—"

"Kaga's submersible is leaky," Janum said, rolling over her words like a boulder, "and built for a saltwater sea. The balrog suits were designed for runaway greenhouse worlds, for atmospheres saturated with sulfuric acid." He grinned.

Nawiz was still processing this news when Egg ran up and flung herself at her. "Husband!" cried Egg. Nawiz couldn't help but smile and stroke the girl's hair. Egg leaned in close and whispered, "I like it here, husband. No one hits me. I eat as much as I want. We stay huh?"

I am not your husband, she wanted to tell Egg.

The girl grabbed Nawiz's hand and tugged. "And you a'looking who i'here!" She stood and pointed at the smoky woman, who hid a smile full of broken teeth behind her hand. "My mama! These cannibals d'not eat her up!"

Egg's mama bowed before Nawiz, murmuring something. Meanwhile, Egg spoke rapidly to Janum in the same thick dialect.

"Another air machine broke down," he told Nawiz. "The Bitters overestimate me and hope I am another Kaga. But, they need this, so I will give it a try before I go. Are you any good with machines?" Nawiz could only shake her head.

Egg alternated between clinging to her mama and to Nawiz, chattering so fast she could not follow. Egg's mama said something from time to time, and Nawiz could only nod her head in feigned understanding.

After a few hours she managed to extract herself, and found Janum working, screwdriver in hand, sweat pouring down his bare back.

"Still fixing that air machine?"

"Huh? No, that's beyond me. I could fiddle with the engine on the trimaran, but Kaga's machines, well, we really need him back. This," he said, tapping a metal cylinder with the screwdriver, "this is compressed air. Kaga rigged it up so he could go underwater, fix his submersible the best he could, maintain the underside of the raft. Crude compared to a balrog suit, but it seems to do the job." He stood up. "I need it so Kaga can breathe underwater on the way back, avoid the Salties. But I'm exhausted now. I'll sleep, go when I wake up." He splashed some water on his face and yawned. "After I get Kaga back, we can take the balrog suits and leave."

Nawiz laid down in a hammock at the far end of the rafts, as far away from everyone as she could get. But she couldn't sleep: Her eyes still burned from the acid in the air. Her heart burned too. *After I get Kaga*

back, he had said. When Kaga came back, he would denounce her. Even if they were truly the pacifists Bhulna claimed, they would never let her go. They might throw her to the next stomach. They might send her back to Peshi. She sat up. Whatever her fate, she could not stay here.

She found the opalescent pool with the balrog suit. *One last task*, she thought, *before you carry me away.*

On the deck, she found an oyster knife, short but sharp enough to do the job. Everyone was asleep. And Janum's hammock—no, she reminded herself, remember his real name, the name under which he betrayed her: Majnu. She had trouble hating *Janum*, but no trouble at all hating Samraatju Majnu—*Majnu's* hammock was right by a stuttering air machine. If he struggled, the machine would mask the noise and allow her to get away.

In her mind she rehearsed her movements. One hand over his mouth, the other hand to press down and break his larynx. Majnu's larynx. Then slit the arteries in his neck. She had dreamed of making him suffer, but she didn't have time, and she had lost that dream. Even the desire to kill him didn't burn as brightly anymore. It had dwindled to a compunction, an itch she had to scratch.

She took a step closer, stared at him, willed herself to burn this last look into her mind. Without proof she would get no reward from the father. This would have to be her only reward. She passed the knife from one hand to the other, wiped her sweaty palms on her thighs. Her heart drummed in her chest. *Now*, she told herself. *Do it.*

She sensed movement just behind her.

Nawiz swiveled reflexively, swifter than thought, and her left fist swung hard. It connected with soft flesh—she heard a cracking sound—and a small body flew across the deck.

Oh please, she begged, though she believed in no gods, though she knew the universe to be uncaring and indifferent to entreaties, but still she thought, *please don't let it be* but of course it was what, and who, she feared.

She ran and knelt by Egg. The girl lay limp on the deck, dark blood gushing from her nose and mouth, a bruise blooming on her face. Nawiz's mouth opened, and for a few moments nothing came out. And then her shouts woke everyone.

A squall of anguish and confusion swept through the Bitters. Nawiz retreated to the corner of a tent and curled up into a ball. Bhulna knelt by her and stroked her head and her arms, but Nawiz was too distraught to focus on her words.

"Bhulna says she has seen this before," Janum, or Majnu, said, squatting next to her. "Those who escape or are banished from the Salties, are so traumatized, beaten, starved, raped, they lash out violently." He paused, lowered his head and his voice. "And you've had training, haven't you? Like a lot of the superrich. Afraid of being kidnapped or assassinated. Trained to react defensive, automatically. I explained it to Bhulna."

But Nawiz sat saying nothing, a stone.

A couple of valve cycles later Bhulna returned and gestured to her. Reluctantly Nawiz followed. Within a semicircle of the Bitters, who crouched at a respectful distance, Egg lay cradled in her mama's arms, while her mama tenderly stroked her face with a wet rag.

Majnu gestured to her, and she sat cross-legged next to him. Perspiration trickled down Nawiz's back and breasts in rivulets.

For a long while they said nothing. Watching Egg in her mama's arms, Nawiz felt as if she were sitting on the edge of a precipice, her feet dangling over a void into which she might fall at any moment. Her chest felt constricted with a chaos of emotions she couldn't begin to name or count.

At last Majnu spoke: "She has Unina with her," which Nawiz took to be the name of Egg's mama. When he talked, some of her old hatred lifted its head. She felt rubbed raw, or worse, as if her skin had been peeled off and her body was nothing but exposed muscle and sinews and arteries. Janum-Majnu scratched at his face for a while. "I never really knew my mother."

"I don't want to hear about your *mother*," Nawiz found herself saying. The savagery in her voice startled even her.

Majnu looked at her. She could imagine the wheels turning in his head. He knew what superrich families were like, but calling himself Janum, he couldn't admit that. At last he said softly, "I was just sad, looking at them." He tilted his head toward Egg and Unina. "I never had that."

"Am I supposed to feel sorry for you?" she hissed, and then, unable to contain herself any longer, blurted out, "Spoiled superrich boy!"

Majnu-Janum stared at her with open mouth. His mouth moving like a dying fish, he managed to stutter, "Why, why, why did you say that?"

Rage boiled up inside her, a geyser she could no longer contain. She cried out, "You are Samraatju Majnu," so loud everyone looked at them. She stood up and said, "I am Parvaanthju Nawiz," adding with all the sarcasm she could muster, "I suppose you forgot you were supposed to marry me."

Bhulna ran up to see what was the matter. "You feel bad," she said, putting a hand on Nawiz's shoulder. "About Egg. We understand. You d'not mean any harm."

"But I *did*," Nawiz said, the words torn from her throat. She turned toward Majnu. "I meant harm to you."

"I was so careful," Majnu said after a long silence. "And what do you mean—"

"I was going to betray you to your father, sell you to him," Nawiz said. The words felt like a knife in her mouth. "You ruined my family."

"I did nothing to dishonor you. Or your family."

"My marriage to you was to be our salvation."

"I'm just the last of many sons," Majnu said. "I was just a boy, twenty years younger than you."

"My family's finances were falling apart. But we had once, long ago, been business partners with your father. My mother pinned her last hopes to my marriage. When you died, or faked your death in the supernova, it was over. Our family's resources were exhausted. My mother died from the shame."

Majnu shifted from one foot to another, agitated, his nostrils flaring as if snorting fire. "But why did you hunt me down? Hunt us down? What were you planning?"

"Your father wanted revenge," she told him, her heart racing, "wanted revenge worse than I did. But he thought you were dead. Dead and beyond the reach of his hand. Do you know what he did? He found young men who looked like you. Paid them and their families enormous sums of money, though they didn't know what for. Had them surgically altered to look even more like you. Had them trained to walk and talk like you.

"And then he had them tortured. He listened to them scream and beg for mercy. He had them tortured and...." She broke off, shook herself. "He had agents throughout the galaxy searching for look-alikes. It was easy to piggy-back on those rumors. I heard of a new, young warlord on Choel...."

"So you went to sell me out," Majnu said sharply.

Bhulna touched him on the upper arm. "We all d'things we regret."

"Do you?" Majnu demanded of Nawiz. "Do you regret wanting to betray me?"

Nawiz hung her head. "I was about to kill you when Egg surprised me," she said. "Kill you and take the balrog suit to escape." She took pleasures in the gasps.

Bhulna reached out to her. Nawiz felt a black clot of hate for the older woman's pity, her compassion. Like a reflex she snarled, "I betrayed Kaga, too. I was the one who told Peshi."

The older woman's face tightened with anger. Crying out, she slapped Nawiz across the face. Bhulna clutched her hand to her chest, as if to keep it from flying again on its own accord, and dashed away.

Nawiz wandered to the far end of the rafts. She could hear the booming of the next valve as it opened, then closed. It cycled twice before Bhulna came and found her.

Nawiz said dully, "I was thinking to throw myself into the water."

Bhulna's brow furrowed. "You tempt me to strike you again! I 'm'ashamed I hit you, and you make me want to hit you once more!" She spat onto the floor.

Nawiz hung her head. "And I am ashamed for ... for so much."

"As you deserve." Bhulna sighed. "You betrayed Kaga why?"

Nawiz closed her eyes. "I was hungry."

"You w'not fed?"

"Not with grilled eel." It sounded so childish when she said it aloud. "Not what Peshi and his friends ate."

Bhulna was silent for a while. She didn't look at Nawiz, just down at her fingers. It felt to Nawiz as if a heavy curtain had been drawn between them.

They were silent for a long time. Nawiz felt a hot pressure in her eyes. But then the words bubbled up inside her, from inside her chest (which right then, exhausted as she was, felt as thick and stiff as chitin, felt like an insect's thorax), and up her throat, and then into her mouth, and she could no more restrain them than she could a mouthful of helium. "And it gnawed at me." She closed her hot, dry eyes and wished she could cry. "Like a mouthful of teeth, gripping my guts. You don't understand, I was raised to lead my family, to govern over worlds, planets, and we lost it all. Majnu, Janum, I don't know what name he told you, but he was my family's hope, my hope, and he took it away. And I saw him with that girl and they *were happy* asleep there on that beach and I ... I ... I ... if I couldn't have that happiness, I wanted to smash it, and if I couldn't have a piece of grilled eel I had to smash something, someone, anyone...." She rubbed her hands over her face. "That's why I betrayed Kaga. I know it was selfish. That's why I should just throw myself into the stomach."

"W'your mother want huh you to throw yourself away?" Bhulna asked.

"My mother," Nawiz said, and then stopped. Her jaw shook so bad she could barely speak. "M-mother," she stammered. She couldn't breathe. She closed her eyes. It was like drowning. In her mind's eye she saw Unina cradling Egg. She leaned forward, gasping, desperate for air. Tears flooded her eyes and she began sobbing in great gusts, bawling, howling.

When she had cried herself out, she whispered, "My mother wouldn't have stopped me. My family," she sucked in air, "my family was as bad as Majnu's." How could she explain? Her mother's example and expectations had dominated her life, curved her life like the gravity well of a massive planet. Her mother had talked of planets Nawiz would rule over, but had never stroked her, never even fed her. That had been servant's work. To her mother, Nawiz had been a means for continuation of the family's greatness. It had been her prospective marriage to Majnu that was important, not Nawiz herself.

So why should this woman, these people, these *cannibals* swallowed by a fish feel sorry for her? Why should she feel so sorry for herself?

Nawiz felt a warm, calloused touch on her arm and raised her wet face. "This world eats us up, swallows us and shits us out," Bhulna said. "There i'no way out of it, but this devoured god gave himself for us to eat, so that we d'not hunger, so we a'not alone. Whether in Wakangshi's belly or digesting in some other sorrows, you d'not need to stand alone." She gestured toward the center of the rafts. "You a'coming. We share this feast of this devoured god."

The entire colony of Bitters crowded under an oxygenated tent. Everyone except Majnu, who put on the balrog suit to go rescue Kaga. Nawiz wanted him to succeed, but doubted he would believe her, so she said nothing.

Bhulna distributed a cracker made from dried algae and a thick, green fermented liquor tasting faintly of fish. If it wasn't the worst meal Nawiz had ever had, it was close. "This universe i'some desert," Bhulna said, as the food and drink were passed around, "and those who rule this universe gave us grudgingly only some few, tiny planets to inhabit. We a'but specks on some filthy floor in this shadow cast by this table of heaven, far far above us.

"This devoured god saw us starve. He swept crumbs from this table of heaven for us. Those other rulers, they hated him for his compassion, and they threw him down from that table and broke his body upon this floor of this universe. But he thwarted their malice, and gave his body at us as some feast.

"Those rulers believe to have life, you must take life. But that hunger i'never satisfied, and w'only devour itself, devour *you*. If you hunger, feed another. If you weep, comfort another. If you tire, give another your bed. If you bleed, stitch another's wounds."

The so-called cannibals leaned against each other, placing morsels in their neighbor's mouths and lifting small bowls of the fishy liquor to each other's lips. Watching them, Nawiz felt again like she was drowning. She had been drowning all her life.

And then someone pressed a small bit of algal cracker to her lips. It was a small morsel, but she was fed, fed by a stranger's hand. And she wept once more.

The theophages whooped with joy when Kaga, still dripping stomach water, ducked through a tent flap and made his appearance. Bhulna hugged him, and one after another of the cannibals. Finally Kaga shrugged them off, clasping his hands in apology. "I sh'fix these machines," he said.

Within a handful of valve cycles the slosh-driven dynamos were humming again, and a wave of fresh, carbon-dioxide-scrubbed and oxygen-enhanced air filled the tents on the rafts.

Majnu came up to Nawiz. "There's enough oxygenated fluid for both balrogs. We can leave anytime." He looked over his shoulder. "Egg's breathing better," he said, his voice softer. "I think she'll be okay."

Nawiz was listening as the valve thrummed and opened, and as a river of effluent poured into the stomach. "I thought you would leave without me."

Majnu frowned and shuffled from one foot to the other. "Look, it's not that I actually want to forgive you, but, well, I guess Bhulna has had an influence on me. Please don't try to make me regret that."

The valve groaned and squeezed shut. Nawiz opened her mouth, but before she would say anything, the raft shuddered. "Is the arcthant diving?" Nawiz said.

"I don't know," said Majnu. "Uh, I don't think so. That feels different."

The raft shuddered again. There was a cry from the far side. Majnu and Nawiz ran over. One of the Bitters pointed down. The water was thick, almost opaque, and the yellow-green light from fluorescent algae was faint, but even so they could see a mass just beneath the surface.

The submersible.

The raft shook again. Kaga ran to the side and peered into the water. When he turned around, Nawiz could see the fear in his face.

"It has some claw," he said, and he pantomimed with his hand. "I used it to repair these rafts here, but he—it i'Peshi, I a'sure—he...."

He didn't have to finish. With a terrible shriek of metal, the submersible tore off one of the raft's crude pontoons. The pontoon spun away on the surface, and the raft listed in the water. The submersible lurched to the next pontoon. People began jabbing poles and lances into the water at the submersible, but they were useless against its metal carapace.

Majnu asked Kaga, "Does the submersible have any weak points? Any way we can sink it, damage it, stop it?"

"There i'some ballast valve on this underside, it h'always given me trouble. But how ... oh. These balrog suits." Majnu began to walk quickly, with Kaga and Nawiz trailing.

They crossed over the little cable bridge to the next raft, where the balrog suits had just recently been laid in their pool of opalescent, oxygenated fluid. Behind them the raft shuddered and listed even more, and screams floated up over the groans of metal twisting.

Nawiz sprinted the rest of the way to the pool, where Majnu was already up to his waist in the fluid. Others of the Bitters followed them. Bhulna pushed her way through the crowd. "You a'waiting!" She puffed. "He i'my brother." She spread her hands. "Please. You c'not talk to him huh?"

"I don't think he would listen," Nawiz said, "even if he could."

Majnu lifted a small black box from the pool and turned to Kaga as he was limping up. "Does the submersible have sonar comms?"

Perhaps the devoured god was smiling on them: Peshi answered the sonar comms. His voice came over the speaker metallic and distorted. "I w'give you some few minutes to pray," he gloated, "before I sink these rafts."

"You want to see us dead huh, little brother?" Bhulna leaned forward to ask. "Even me?"

Peshi was silent for a moment. "Kaga d'not tell me you a'still alive," he said finally.

The fix-it wallah cleared his throat. "You d'not ask."

"I sh'not need to ask! I a'boss in this belly of Wakangshi. You 'm'obeying *me*! And I say, you a'handing Kaga back to me."

"You w'not hurt him huh?" Bhulna asked.

"I w'not *kill* him, that I promise." He paused. "But that woman, Aleata—I make no such promise for her."

"And I make no promise not to kill *you*," Nawiz said. "I am not of the cannibal religion."

Peshi laughed. "Good! You a'putting on your suit, and we wrestle!" The encrusted claw of the submersible broke the surface and clacked open and closed at them.

Bhulna looked at Nawiz and Majnu. She said quietly, "Perhaps you and Majnu sh'take these suits and go. You a'living again in that world above."

Majnu shook his head. "I want to go back to Kazo, more than anything. But your brother—"

Nawiz picked up the thought. "He won't let it go. He'll persecute you, or kill you, or just let you die without Kaga."

"It i'better to die than to kill," Bhulna said.

Nawiz shook her head. "See, there I disagree."

The submersible moved forward and banged against the raft. "Aleata! We h'something to settle! I know you a'no coward. Bhulna-sister! You a'not thinking you c'protect that woman."

"You h'forgotten mercy?" Bhulna asked.

Peshi laughed. "Wakangshi, he h'forgotten mercy." Nawiz heard Peshi say, "While we live in his belly, there i'no mercy."

Majnu started to splash into the pool of the balrog's oxygenated fluid. "I guess there's nothing for it then," he said to Nawiz. "Shall we?"

But Peshi's words had set her chest ringing like a bell. She leapt into the fluid and grabbed Majnu. She knew what she wanted to do. What she had to do—no, not that. All those years chasing Majnu had felt like a compulsion, like something infecting her brain. But now, she chose a different path, and it was her choice. It was easier than she would have thought.

"Wait," she told Majnu. Wading out of the pool, she leaned toward the sonar comm and said, "Then you a'going. You a'leaving Wakangshi. We know a way—we know some way out." She straightened and, trembling, said to Majnu, "The two of you take the balrog suits and go out the gut. I will stay behind."

"You w'stay huh?" Bhulna asked.

"I have nothing out there, no family, no fortune. What would I leave for?"

Peshi was not easily convinced. "You w'try to kill me as soon as I come out," he said.

"Peshi-brother," Bhulna said. "You of all people know we d'not kill."

There was silence. Then came the crackling, squealing response. "But that woman, that liar, she d'not eat of this devoured god."

Nawiz spoke. "I shared a meal of the devoured god. I will not—I w'not kill you. If you go."

There was a long silence. And then the submersible broke the surface of the water, and the hatch clanged open. Peshi's bald head poked out. "I w'go," he said.

A small crowd of Bitters gathered around the pool of oxygenated fluid, where Peshi and Majnu were preparing to put on the balrog suits and swim the rest of the way through the arcthant's digestive tract. Peshi leered at Unina, Egg's mama, who had come bearing good news: Egg was now awake and had opened her eyes. Nawiz shifted her body so that she stood between Peshi and Unina.

"So you follow this cannibal religion now huh?" Peshi asked Nawiz.

Nawiz shook her head. "I shared some meal, and promised I w'not kill you. I said nothing about any of those others."

Bhulna, looking horrified, put a hand on Nawiz's arm. "It i'some terrible sin to kill."

Nawiz laughed. "Oh, I a'some great and terrible sinner. And I promise you, those Salties w'know how terrible I am!"

Peshi shrugged, took a deep breath, and sank below the surface.

Majnu lowered himself until his chin just touched the liquid. "So," he said.

"So," Nawiz said.

"I'll alert the authorities, have them send a rescue party."

"For a bunch of fishers stuck in the belly of an arcthant for years? I'll believe it when it happens." She shook her head.

But Majnu had more to say. "It occurs to me," he said, "it was never me you really wanted. You hadn't even met me."

"No," she admitted.

"Bhulna told me what you said. You wanted to have a world to rule over." Nawiz felt a warmth to her face. "And now," he said, raising a dripping arm to gesture at the vault of Wakangshi's stomach, "now you have one."

Then Majnu slipped beneath the surface, leaving behind Nawiz and her rising astonishment.

RedKing

Craig DeLancey

TAIN HELD A pistol toward me. The black gel of the handle pulsed, waiting to be gripped.

"Better take this," she said.

I shook my head. "I never use them."

We sat in an unmarked police cruiser, the steering wheel packed away in the dashboard. Tain's face was a pale shimmer in the cool blue light of the car's entertainment system. "Your file says you are weapons trained."

"Yeah," I said, "I got one of those cannons at home, locked in my kitchen drawer."

Tain turned slightly toward me. She still held the gun out, her fingers wrapped around the barrel. "You gonna get me killed, code monkey?"

I considered telling her it was quaint to think that protection could be secured with a gun. But instead I told her, "I start waving that around, I'm more likely to shoot you than the perp. Just get me to the machines. That's how I'm going to help you."

She thought for a moment, then nodded. "Well, at least you're a man who knows his limitations." She turned the pistol around, held it a second so that the gun locked to her hand print, and then she tucked it under her belt at the small of her back.

She dimmed the dash lights. I was running a naked brain—standard procedure for a raid—and so the building, the sidewalk, and the road reduced down to the hard objects that our paltry senses could latch onto: a world without explanations, ominously obscure.

We both leaned forward and looked up at the building before us, eighteen stories of concrete. The once-bright walls had faded to the color of mold. A half-hearted rain began, streaking the grime on its narrow windows.

The clock on the dash read 2:30 A.M. No one in sight. Most of the lights in the building were out now.

"You know the drill?" Tain asked me.

"I know this kid we're arresting probably wrote RedKing," I told her. "That's all I need to know."

Unsatisfied with this answer, she repeated the rap. "Twenty-seven-year-old male. Got his name legally changed to his code handle: Legion. Five prior convictions for 909." Design, manufacture, and distribution of cognition-aversive and intentionally addictive software. "No record of violence. But he's still a killer, so consider him dangerous. We go in fast, my people take him down, and you save what you can from his machines."

"I know my job."

"Right." She pushed open her door. I followed her into the rain, heaving my backpack on. I tightened its straps and then snapped them across my chest.

A Korean food truck, covered with twisting dim snakes of active graffiti, idled across the street. Its back door swung open, and cops in black, holding rifles, poured out.

We ran as a group for the entrance to the tower.

A few kids stood in the lobby, smoking, and they turned pale and ran for the stairs when we parted the front doors. Their untied sneakers slapped at the concrete floor. We ignored them, but two cops took position in the lobby to ensure no one left. Tain had a set of elevator keys and she took command of both lifts. We squeezed into the elevator on the left, shoulder to shoulder with four other cops in full gear, their rifles aimed at the ceiling. The smell of leather and gun oil overwhelmed everything else while the LED counter flicked off sixteen flights.

A chime announced our arrival. We made a short run down a dim hall and stopped before a door with an ancient patina of scratched and flaking green paint. The cops hit it with a ram and we filed in quick and smooth. I broke to the left, following half the cops through a dingy common room with a TV left on mute, the flickering images casting a meager glow over an open pizza box on an empty couch.

A door by the TV led to a dark room. Two cops rousted the suspect out of bed and zip tied him in seconds. Legion was a pale, thin kid with trembling, sticklike arms. He gazed around in shock. A woman leapt out of the bed and stood in the corner, shouting, clutching the sheets over her naked body. Somewhere a baby started screaming.

Tain's cops were good: They moved quietly, not all hyped on adrenaline, and they stayed out of my way as I ran through the apartment, checking each room for machines. But the only computers were in the bedroom: a stack of gleaming liquid-cooled Unix engines atop a cheap, particle board desk. Not heavy iron, but good machines: The kind rich kids bought if they played deep in the game economies.

Legion began to yell, calling for the woman to bring him clothes while two cops dragged him out. The woman screamed also, demanded a lawyer, demanded her baby. I did my best to tune out all that noise, pulled a cable from the side of my backpack, and jacked my field computer straight into the top deck. Data streamed through my eyeplants—the only augmentation I was allowed to run here—and I tapped at a virtual keyboard. In a few seconds I dug under the main shell and started a series of static disk copies. While in there, I ran a top check to show the processes that threaded across the machines: nothing but low level maintenance. Tain's crew had got Legion before the kid could trigger a wipe.

I turned, found Tain's eye, and nodded.

"Okay," she shouted. "Wrap it up."

☼　　☼　　☼

It started with the gamers. It wasn't enough to stare at screens any longer. They wanted to be there, in the scene. They wanted to smell and hear the alien planet where they battled evil robots, to feel the steely resolve of their avatar and enjoy her victories and mourn her losses. They wanted it all.

That meant moving hardware into the skull, bypassing the slow crawl of the senses. Once we'd wired our occipital lobes, you could predict the natural progression of commerce: Not just visuals, but smell, and sound, and feel, and taste had to come next. So the wires spread through our neocortexes, like the roots of some cognitive weed. Autonomic functions came after, the wires reaching down into the subcortical regions of pleasure and pain, fear and joy. We gave up all the secrets of our brains, and sank the wires ever deeper.

Then people started to wonder, what other kinds of software could you run on this interface?

Pornography, sure. The first and biggest business: orgies raging through the skulls of overweight teenage boys lying alone in their unmade beds.

But after that, people began to demand more extreme experiences. A black market formed. For the buyer, the problem is one of imagination: What would you want to feel and believe, if you could feel and believe anything? For the coders, the problem is one of demand: How can you make the consumer come back again? The solution was as old as software: Write code that erases itself after a use or two, but leaves you desperate to spend money on another copy.

That code was dangerous, but it wasn't the worst. The worst was written by the coders who did not want money. They were users themselves, or zealots, and their code might just stick around. It might not want to go.

RedKing was a program like that. RedKing was as permanent as polio. And RedKing made people kill.

When we got outside, a dozen press drones hovered over the street.

"Damn," Tain said. "How do they find us so fast?"

"Hey, code monkey!" a voice called. We turned and saw a short, thin woman, with very short dark hair. Drones buzzed above her, filming her every move as she hurried toward us.

"Ellison," I said, "what brings you to this side of town?"

She had a big mouth that probably could produce a beautiful smile, but she never smiled. Instead, her voice was sharp and quick. "You got a statement? A statement for *Dark Fiber*? This have anything to do with RedKing?"

"No statement," Tain said.

"Come on, code monkey," Ellison said, ignoring Tain. "You gotta give me something."

"I'll catch you later," I said.

"He will not catch you later," Tain said. She took my elbow. "No press," she hissed at me. She slapped a small news drone that flew too close. It smacked into the pavement and shuddered, struggling to lift off again. We stepped over it.

"Ellison has helped me out a few times," I told Tain as we walked away. "And sometimes I help her out."

"While you're working for me, you only help me out. And the only person that helps you out is me."

We got in the car.

At the station, they gave me a desk pressed into a windowless corner by the fire exit, under a noisy vent blowing cold air. The aluminum desk's surface was scarred as if the prior owner stabbed it whenever police business slowed. I was filling in for their usual code monkey, and I got the impression they didn't aspire to see me again after this job. I didn't care. The desk had room for my machine and Legion's stack of machines, the cold air was good for the processors, and I wouldn't have time to look out a window anyway.

Within an hour I had scanned Legion's machines twice over, mapped out every bit and byte, dug through all the personal hopes and dreams of the scrawny guy now shivering in the interrogation room.

I sighed and went looking for Tain. I wandered the halls until I found the observation room with a two-way mirror looking in on the suspect. Tain stood over him.

"She's been in there a while," one of the cops standing before the window told me between sips of coffee.

"I want my lawyer," the kid said. His voice sounded hollow and distant through the speaker. He sat in a metal chair, and I wondered if he knew it measured his autonomic functions while he talked. Some people refused to sit when they got in an interrogation room.

"You made your call. Your lawyer's on her way." Tain bent forward. Her strong arms strained at the narrow sleeves of her coat as she laid a tablet on the table. Even from a distance, we could see the tablet displayed the picture the news had been running all week: a teenage kid with brown disheveled hair, smiling with perfect teeth. He looked innocent, and maybe rich.

Legion glanced down. "I'm not saying anything till I get my lawyer."

Tain pointed at the picture. "Phil Jackson."

"I had nothing to do with that."

"With what?" Tain asked, with exaggerated innocence.

"I watch the news."

"I didn't take you for someone who watches the news, Legion." Tain tapped the tablet decisively. "Seventeen. Doing fine in school. Lonely, but what high school kid doesn't think he's lonely, right? So little Phil Jackson loads a copy of RedKing into his head. Spends a week delirious, happy maybe, thinking he's king of the world—who knows what it makes him think? Then he cuts his mother's throat, hits his father with the claw of a hammer, and jumps off the roof."

Legion looked up at Tain and smirked. Tain became as taut as a spring. She wanted to hit him. And Legion wanted her to hit him. It would provide great fodder for his lawyer.

But she held her fists. Legion waited, then said softly, as if he could barely manage to stay awake, "I told you, I watch the news."

"What they didn't tell you on the news, Legion, is that we got the code out of that kid's implants, and our code monkeys decompiled it, and you know what they found? Big chunks of stuff written by you. Unmistakable provenience. Big heaps of Legion code." Tain let her voice grow soft and reasonable. "We've got fifty-four confirmed casualties for this virus. It's only going to get worse. And the worse it gets—the more people that commit crimes or hurt themselves—the worse it's going to be for you, Legion."

He clamped his jaw and mumbled, "My lawyer."

"I'll go get her for you. You sit here and look at the kid that your code killed."

Tain kicked the door. The cop outside opened it. In a second she was around the corner and when she saw me she walked up close.

"Tell me what you got, code monkey."

"Nothing," I told her.

Her heavy black brows drew together over her pale, inset eyes. I held up my hands defensively.

"Hey, no one wants to find the raw code for RedKing more than I do. But I've scanned every bit of his machines, and I got next to nothing."

Tain dragged me to her office, her grip tight on my elbow, and closed the door.

"You're saying your division made a mistake when they linked this guy to the code?"

I sat down on a hard metal chair by the door. Tain followed my example and flopped back into the chair behind her desk. It squeaked and rolled back.

"No. There's code on Legion's machines that is unique and that matches identically big chunks of the RedKing program. But there isn't a lot there. And it's ... general."

"What do you mean? What kind of code?"

I hesitated. "A toolkit. For running genetic algorithms."

"What's that doing in there?"

I frowned. "I'm not sure yet. I have a hunch, and it's not good news. I'd rather follow up a little, study the code, before I say more."

"Don't take too long. So why isn't this toolkit enough to convict?"

"Hackers tend to give toolkits away, on some user board or other. You can bet he'll claim he did, first time we ask about the details."

Tain frowned in disgust. "You see the autonomics on that kid while I was interrogating him? He flatlined everything. Skin response. Heart rate. Temperature and breathing. All unchanging. He fears nothing, he cares about nothing."

"Oh," I said, "he cares about one thing. His credibility. That's what's driving him."

"Okay, fair enough. You code types have your whole thing with cred. But what I'm trying to say is, the guy is a classic psychopath."

I nodded. "He's a bad guy. But can we prove he's our bad guy?"

She stared at the image on her active wall: mountains at the edge of a long green prairie. It was surprisingly serene for this nervously energetic woman.

"I got nothing," she mused. "He's not gonna talk; psychopaths don't break under threat. My code monkey can't link him to RedKing. And we don't know what RedKing does or why it made a kid kill his own mother. We've identified dozens of infected people, and they all acted differently."

I let that hang a long time before I stated the obvious. "Only one thing to try now. I load it up and see what I can tell from running the copy we got in quarantine."

Tain leaned her head forward and looked at me through her dark eyebrows. "You know why we called you in? Why you're here? Our usual code monkey is on extended leave. She fried her head trying just that."

"Occupational hazard," I said.

"Don't tough guy me. My father was a cop, and my grandfather. When they busted a heroin ring, they didn't go home and shoot smack to try to understand addiction from the inside."

"It's not the same," I said.

"Looks the same to me."

"All right, maybe it is. But what if, what if there was a new drug every week, all the time, and you couldn't know what it would do to people—what it would make people do—if you didn't just try it. Then I bet your grandfather, or your father, would have shot up. Because they wanted to fight it, right? And they needed to know how to fight."

"Bullshit," she said. But she didn't say anything more. She didn't say no.

They put me in a conference room, bare white walls, a table that tipped back and forth if you leaned on it. Tain stared at me, her jaw working, while the tech brought me a memory stick. I slotted it into my field deck immediately, not wanting to give Tain time to change her mind. I'd set up a buffer and then a process echo, so my deck could record everything that was happening.

I plugged straight into my skulljack and in a few seconds I copied the code over into my implants.

"I got an interface," I said. "Pretty simple."

A single sentence appeared in my visual field. *Do you want to be King?* it asked. I looked at the word *yes* and willed it to click, giving it permission to run on my brain OS.

A rush of colors washed over me. I felt cold, exhilarated, as if I fell down a bright well of light. I think I shouted in something like joy.

Then it was over. There stood Tain, her eyebrows up in an expression of alarm mixed with disapproval.

"How long?" I asked.

"Long? You just plugged in."

I frowned.

"Well?" Tain asked.

"It's…." I thought about it. "After the initial rush it's nothing. Nothing yet, anyways. I don't know."

I looked around, meeting Tain's eyes, then the eyes of the cop waiting bored by the door. I did have a slight sense that maybe I felt a little … tenuous. But it was nothing definite. It's hard when you are waiting to hallucinate. You tend to start to work yourself into a psychedelic state if you try too hard to expect one.

"Let me clear the buffer and start it up again."

I took a deep breath and did it. We waited a while. "Nothing," I said.

Tain sighed. "Bad batch of code? Maybe they sent you the neutralized compile."

I shrugged.

"All right," she said. "Shut it down. Look over your sample again, see if something is wrong with it. I'll call Code Isolation and see if they sent you the wrong sample."

We pulled the plugs. Someone knocked at the door. "Stay here," Tain said. She went out into the hall and the other cop followed her.

I lifted my deck off the table. That's when I realized my deck's wireless had been left on.

I slipped out of the conference room and walked quickly back to my desk, trying to stay calm. Or at least trying to appear calm. When I set my deck down I looked back. The door to my office was open, showing the long hall that stretched all the way to the center of the building, a corridor that diminished into infinity. And, along the sides of the hall, it seemed every cop in the building stood, hand on holster, looking at me. And down the center of the hall came Tain.

I turned and hit the crash bar to the emergency exit next to my desk. As I passed through, I cracked the red fire alarm crystal by the door. An alarm began to shriek.

"Stop!" Tain shouted. I didn't look back to see if she aimed a gun at me. I threw the door shut and ran down the steps.

I was on the street before they could get word out to stop me. The fire alarm was painfully loud, causing a lot of confusion. A few cops milled by the station's front steps, wondering if the alarm was a drill or mistake. I walked past them and to the block's corner. When I turned out of sight, I ran.

By the time I reached the subway steps my chest hurt and a sharp stitch slowed me to a hobble. I'm a code monkey, not a runner. But I made it down inside, hair lifted by the stink of hot air that a coming train pushed out of the dark. I turned all my implants on, wanting to get the full input now. I mustered a last burst of energy and slipped down the next set of steps and onto the train just as its doors shuddered closed.

Only a handful of people sat in the car. No one met my gaze. Still. Someone here could be undercover. Hard to know. I stared around, wondering what I should do next. If the whole department was infected, what would be the right course of action? Report to Code Isolation? That would be procedure. Only, I thought, I should get myself secure first. I needed a place to hide. I needed my gun.

It was easy to outsmart them. It would be foolish for me to go home, but then they'd know it was foolish for me to go home, and so they wouldn't look for me at home.

So I went home. I took the back door, the one that opened onto the parking lot for the few of us with cars. A short elevator ride, a few steps down an empty hall, and I pushed my way into my apartment.

In the kitchen, under the pale LEDs of my undercounter light, I keyed open my safety drawer. My gun sat with my passport and some spare cash. I picked it up and held it. The grip vibrated once to tell me it recognized me. I stuck it into my coat pocket.

Time to go. No sense in pushing my luck. I was smarter than all of them, sure, but even idiots could fall into fortune. So: I reconsidered. Should I report to Code Isolation? As I thought about it, the idea paled. Code Isolation had sent me the program I'd run on my deck. They had to have known my deck would transmit it. They were likely infected already.

I'd have to solve this on my own. And I could. It was just a matter of recognizing that anyone, everyone could be my enemy—and then outsmarting them all. I felt a thrill of excitement, a soaring determination. Because I realized I could do it. I could trick them all.

First step would be to lose myself in a crowd.

The Randomist was a noisy bar half a block from my apartment building. I'd walked by it hundreds of times but had never gone in. The boisterous cheerfulness of the crowd, the painful sense that one had to be very hip to fit in, had alienated me immediately the few times I'd considered stopping for a quick drink. But now I went directly in under the electric blue archway.

I got a beer at the bar, something local and artisanal with a silly name. The bartender slid it to me but smiled insincerely. "Hey, buddy, how about turning it down a little?"

"What the hell you talking about?" I asked.

"You've got your implants turned all the way out. It's hard to walk past you, you're broadcasting so much. And what is it you're blasting? Some kind of program? That's not cool."

"Drop dead," I told him. I took my drink and turned away, all the hairs on my neck raised. He might work for the cops, I realized. An informant for the infected precinct. I might have to shoot him.

But the crowd swallowed me instantly, and I relaxed. Forget the bartender. He couldn't see me or get me in this dense mass of people.

Bumping shoulder to shoulder as I pushed through, I felt a great worry lift. The cops would never find me in here. And I loved this crowd, with their implants humming all around me invitingly.

There was a beautiful girl in the back, standing alone, waiting for someone. I decided she was waiting for me.

"You're a loud one," she said, as I walked up.

"I like to speak my mind," I said.

"More like shout it."

But she didn't leave. I leaned in close.

"What's your name?" I asked.

"Sparrow. What's that you're broadcasting, anyway? You an ad? One of those walking ads? Come on, turn down your broadcast. I'm serious. It's too much."

I shook my head. "Let me tell you what I do, Sparrow. I'm a cop. But a special kind of cop. I protect people from the only real threat, the threat of their computers and their implants going bad. I'm fantastic at it. I'm the smartest person in the world."

"Yeah? You don't look like a cop."

"I could show you my gun." I put my hand in my pocket and felt the handle thrum against my palm.

She frowned, not sure if I had intended some dirty joke. She pointed over my shoulder. "Now she, she looks like a cop."

I turned. Tain stood there, a few steps away, under a red light. She was all shadows and angles in the dim focused glare. Her hand was at her hip.

I scanned the room. People were starting to freeze in place and fall quiet as seven uniforms filed in. I counted them slowly. Then an eighth. Then a ninth, slipping behind the bar.

There were seventeen rounds in my gun. I could shoot all these cops and still have seven rounds left. I pulled my gun from my jacket pocket.

Tain's hand didn't move, but Sparrow screamed as a blur shot forward and two darts stuck into my chest. My body went rigid as a current slammed my nerves into overdrive.

I heard my gun clatter on the hard floor. I blacked out.

When I came to, someone was sitting on me.

No, that wasn't it. My hands. My hands were strapped down. And something gripped my head. A hat or helmet. I opened my eyes.

A white room. A hospital room. The sharp stink of disinfectant wafted over me. Every muscle in my body ached. Tain stood nearby, talking to a doc in a white coat. Behind her a big window was black with night, mirroring the white room back at us. A code monkey stood behind Tain, field deck strapped on her back. Stepin, a field agent specializing in brain system wipes. She was short and broad shouldered, with a calm but distracted look that made it seem she was always thinking hard about something distant and slightly sad.

"They got you, too," I said.

Stepin looked over at me.

"Who got me?" she asked.

I looked at Tain. "Her. The others in the precinct. They're contaminated with RedKing. You can't trust them. If you're not infected, step away from her, Stepin. Get me out of this. I'm the only person who can stop this. I can fix everything."

Tain took a step forward. "How do you think we got contaminated? You're the one who loaded up the RedKing."

"My computer's transmitter was on," I said, looking at Stepin because it was useless to appeal to Tain. Tain would be gone now, inhuman. "I thought I was loading the virus but instead I was transmitting it."

"Put him under," Stepin said. "I've got to do a complete OS replacement. It'll take me a few hours."

The doctor stepped forward and adjusted my IV. A huge weight closed down on my eyes. As the darkness fell, I heard Stepin say to me softly, "Field computers don't have transmitters. You know that."

When I woke, I was alone in the room. The straps lay open, my wrists and legs freed. Sunlight streamed through the window at a nearly vertical angle. I'd been here a long while, asleep on tranqs. I had a bad headache but otherwise felt normal. I opened my brain menus, and found they worked fine, although the arrangement was all factory normal. I logged into my work desktop and began to review my notes.

Some program had detected my waking, because in a few minutes a nurse brought me food, and then an hour after that Tain arrived, wearing new clothes.

We looked at each other. I chewed air, trying to get started on an apology. Tain let me struggle a while, before she nodded once. She pulled up a chair.

"All right, code monkey, just tell me what happened. We knew something was wrong when you left the test room."

"RedKing is subtle," I told her, relieved to be talking about code. "First, it convinces you that nothing has changed. And that remains throughout: I literally could not even imagine that I was running the virus in my head. I don't know how it inhibits such a basic belief, but it does it very well. That's a breakthrough of some kind. We'll have to study it very carefully and—"

"Don't tell me your research plans," Tain interrupted. "Tell me what it does."

"Right. It made me paranoid of anyone who might be a threat to the virus. I think my brain tried to make sense of my irrational fear of you and the others, and so I concluded you had the virus. I probably invented the idea that my computer had transmitted it in order to explain my fear to myself. Also, I began to feel … smart. Super intelligent. I became convinced that I could solve any problem. That I was smarter than anyone."

"You were reaching for your pistol when I tazed you."

I nodded. "I meant to shoot you all. It was … bizarre. I didn't see you as people. I saw you as puzzles. Puzzles to be solved by my brilliant mind."

Tain leaned back. Her jaw worked a while as she thought it through. Finally, she said, "So, what we have is code that convinces you that you are a genius, and makes you paranoid, and makes you see other human beings as worthless."

I sighed. "It's worse than that."

"How?"

"Two things. First, I think I tried to spread it last night. To transmit it."

"It's too much code to transmit implant to implant."

"I'm not sure. I think there might be a workaround, to make people call it up off of some servers. You have to test everyone in that bar."

She stood, shoving her chair back. "Damn. We'll have to act fast."

"Get me out of here and I can help. We can get a court order to trace the bar charges and track everyone down."

"Damn," Tain repeated. She got a faraway look as she started transmitting orders from her implants. "What a mess. We're back where we started, and things are even worse."

"Maybe not," I said. "If I'm right, and the program loads from another server, then that's a weakness. If we can find someone infected, and can find the address that they downloaded RedKing from, we can find Legion's hidden servers."

"All right. That's something. So what's your second bit of bad news?"

"I've been reviewing the decompile, and I've confirmed my hunch. But before I explain that, I want to see Legion. We need to set up a meeting with him."

"Why?"

Before I could answer, the door to the room banged open. Ellison strode in. "Hey, code monkey, you sick or something?" She looked at Tain, made it clear that she was not impressed by the lieutenant, and looked back at me. "Or you get shot? That'd be newsworthy, if you got shot."

"You will get out of here right now," Tain said.

"Hey, is that any way to treat a guest? I was invited."

Tain glared at me. I held up a hand to urge her to wait a minute.

To Ellison I said, "I got something for that crappy blog of yours."

"Blog. Yeah, really funny, code monkey. I never heard that one before. But *Dark Fiber magazine* gets more hits in an hour than there are cops in America. So don't misunderstand who has the clout in this relationship."

"I got something about RedKing."

Ellison immediately looked cagey. She gave Tain a sidelong glance. "Okay. I'm interested."

"Of course you are. Only: We don't have the whole story yet. But I can tell some of it. An important part of our investigation, let's say."

"You're asking me to help you get a piece of the story out. All right: Can you promise that I'll be first to get the whole story when you put it together?"

"Tain," I said, "set up that meeting we were talking about. Because you and I will be ready in a few hours."

There were four of us now in the small interrogation room. I sat across from Legion, in one of the metal chairs. Both Tain and Legion's lawyer stood. Everyone eyed me suspiciously.

"My client has already made a statement," Legion's lawyer said.

"To me," Tain said. "But our code security agent would like to ask a few questions."

"My client does not have to answer any more questions."

"No. But he can listen to them, can't he?"

Silence. Legion looked around the room, feigning boredom. Finally his eyes settled on me. I met his gaze and held it.

"RedKing is brilliant code," I said. "A small packet can be transmitted head to head and make a network call for the rest of the code."

"That's been done before," Legion said.

The lawyer stepped closer. "Mr. Legion, I strongly advise you to say nothing."

I nodded. "But the way it tricks implants into seeing RedKing as an operating system upgrade—that's very good. I didn't know such a thing could be done. But that's not the special thing." I glanced at Tain to let her know that this was my second bit of bad news. "The special thing is that it mutates. That code we found on your machines? A genetic algorithm toolkit. You wrote RedKing to mutate. As it spreads itself, it changes a little bit each time it's copied. That's why its operational profile is so variable. Eventually, there'll be a version that probably won't kill people—after all, dead users can't transmit the code—but it will just spread and spread. If your program works, it'll be the most influential, the most important virus ever written. It's historic."

Legion smiled. "Why tell me about this?"

"You read *Dark Fiber*?"

"I read lots of things."

I set a tablet on the table and turned it around. The cover of *Dark Fiber* blared a headline in big letters: REDKING CULPRITS FOUND?: POLICE SUSPECT CRIMEAN HACKER GROUP VEE.

Legion flinched. For the first time, his mocking smile faded as he read a few lines of the news story.

I leaned forward. "Here's what's before you." I held up a finger. "Option one. Admit you wrote RedKing. You can plead that you never knew it would be dangerous. The fact that you confessed will count in your favor. You'll get a few years, and you'll keep some net privileges. But—here's the important point—you'll be immortalized as the creator of the greatest brain hack ever."

I held up a second finger. "Or, option two. Deny you wrote RedKing. Maybe we can't convict you, maybe we can—let's call it fifty-fifty odds. But if you walk free or you go to prison, either way, you lose your chance for the world's biggest cred upgrade. You'll have given up immortality for a fifty percent chance of escaping a few years Upstate."

"I think my client has heard enough," the lawyer said. She pulled at Legion's sleeve, but the kid did not move. Tain held her breath.

"Vee can't hack," Legion said.

"You and I know they're just some teenage thugs whose only skill is to steal credit info off old ladies. But this story has been picked up by a dozen other news companies. Reporters can't tell a real hacker from a kid wearing a mask. And Vee was delighted to claim credit. They've already released a confession video."

"Only I could have written RedKing."

I nodded.

"Mr. Legion," the lawyer growled, "I have to advise you that—"

"Only me," Legion said.

Tain exhaled.

"You get everyone from the bar?" I asked Tain. We sat in her office, looking at her wall screen image of mountains.

She nodded. "Only one has proven infected, a young woman. Stepin is working on tracing back the code."

"I'm sorry I caused so much trouble."

"Getting Legion to talk has made up for some of it. How did you know he would crack?"

"It's a coder thing. Once I'd experienced RedKing, I knew it was a once-in-a-lifetime hack. No one like Legion would be able to stand someone else taking credit for it."

"And how is your friend Ellison going to take it when she discovers your story about Vee was bogus?"

"Ellison will be fine as long as she gets to break the story that Legion confessed. She'll be better than fine: We gave her two good stories, and one of them was even true."

Tain cracked a smile that broke into a laugh. But it died quickly.

"What will it be like, if thousands of people get this virus? Maybe thousands already have it. It's the end of goddamn civilization."

"I don't know," I said. "It's just this week's threat. With any luck we can contain RedKing."

"And then the next brainvirus will come along."

I nodded. "It's a race."

Tain squinted. "You got kids, code monkey?"

"No."

"I got a kid. Four years old. A second on the way."

"Congratulations."

"Yeah. But I swear, you know what, as soon as I put in my time, earn my pension, I'm going to get the wife and move out to Montana." She gestured at the wall image. "And there, I'll never get the implants in my kids. I'll make sure they live in the real world."

"Sounds like a plan," I said. "Me, I'm not much use at anything but coding."

She grunted. "You wanna stick around awhile? Our old code monkey, she's moving to a desk job at Code Isolation."

"All right."

She reached into a drawer and pulled out a big pistol. It fell on her desk with a heavy thud.

"Only, put your damn gun back in your kitchen drawer and lock it up before you hurt somebody."

Vortex

Gregory Benford

"What we observe is not nature itself but nature exposed to our method of questioning."

—Werner Heisenberg

INTERPLANETARY DIPLOMACY

MARS SOMETIMES FELT like a graduate seminar for which she lacked the prerequisites.

"Before we go in," Julia said to Viktor, "let's have a strategy."

International diplomacy, not my department, Julia thought. They were joining Liang, leader of the Chinese astrobio team, in the spiffy new Chinese rover. They huffed across the messy corral of vehicles and gear between their habitat and the waiting rover, talking on suit-comm.

Viktor said, "Tell him truth. Often disarms people."

"Honesty as a startling approach, then?" She chuckled. "We've been married decades and you still surprise me."

They climbed into the shiny blue Chinese rover, fresh down from orbit, and purred through the lock. They rinsed their suits before entering the surprisingly lush passenger compartment. Liang was a lean, handsome man with graying hair, smiling as they sat. The murmuring rover started the trip to the Chinese cave emplacement.

"I am happy to greet you in better transport," he said with a thin and somehow sure smile.

"Looking forward, much, to seeing your discovery," Viktor said, patting the upholstered bucket seats with appreciation. Their own old rover had hard bench seats that made long trips wearing.

"I hope you are not disturbed by Earthside news," Liang said.

"Had not heard," Viktor said.

"More disputes between our countries."

"Since I'm Australian, Viktor's Russian and you're Chinese, it's hard to believe we can be antagonists all at once," Julia said wryly.

"Well, we see the Americans as like you Australians," Liang said with a fixed face. "Russians are not our friends, either."

We drag our past around with us, Julia thought behind her steady smile, *and so does Mars.*

"But we are scientists here, not nationalists," Viktor said.

They all three nodded. "I trust the limited fighting in Korea will not spread," Liang said. Calm words, but his eyes were intense, narrow.

As they lumbered across the red-brown sands she looked out the broad side windows, watching the human imprint slide by. Humans on Mars had carried the emerging symbiosis of human and machines to new heights. Within a few years of the First Expedition—of which only she and Viktor still lived on Mars—wireless sensors lay scattered, to collect better local data on the Marsmat's methane releases from subsurface. Robots came next—not clanking metal humanoids, but rovers and workers of lightweight, strong carbon fiber, none looking remotely like people. Most were either stationary, doing routine tasks, or many-legged rovers. The First Expedition was a private enterprise and grabbed headlines for years, so follow-up national expeditions were inevitable. The Chinese chose to send their own, building on their disastrous Second Expedition. Viktor and Julia had suffered their minor falls and sprained ankles, so now only in exploration did humans risk climbing around on steep slopes. Much of their work was within safe habitats, tele-operation for exploring and labor. But no machine could deal with the Mat.

"We welcome you to see the unusual activity we have found," Liang said, his eyes studying Julia carefully.

Okay, try the truth.

"We haven't seen anything odd," Julia said.

"You see what?—big rushes of liquids, vapor?" Viktor leaned forward intently against the rover's sway. "Do those big elephant-ear flaps close behind you, blocking way out?"

"The reverse," Liang said mildly, eyes still wary. "They close us out."

"So you can't get in?"

Liang nodded ruefully. *So they wonder if we can help them knock on the door ...* Julia pondered this and Liang took the moment to unwrap a surprise, some dumplings whose aroma filled the air.

"To give us energy," he said. They all dug in. Liang had fragrant tea in a thermos, too. Years on Mars had taught a central lesson: People crave the flavors and textures of the planet they left behind, the connection to something like home in an alien land.

ENTRANCE IRIS

They did a lock and wash at the Chinese base. Thrifty, the Chinese had built a big habitat at the cave entrance in the steep wall of Gusev crater. Julia and Viktor had found the yawning opening, concealed by a landslide, with some seismic studies. They discovered it in the fifth year of the continuing First Expedition, known Earthside as the Julia & Viktor Perpetual Show. Their contract specified regular broadcasts for the entire mission, so when they elected to stay, they had to keep making up staged events to transmit. *Thank God we can finesse this descent,* Julia thought as they walked through the lavish Chinese habitat, *by just not telling them we're doing it. If nothing much happens, no report.*

There was a bit of tea-sipping ceremony in the social room, meeting the descent team members, coordinating com links and smiling a lot.

"You have experience in opening the elephant flaps?" Liang asked, apparently expecting a firm *yes.*

Viktor said, "Done in early days, yes. Julia more than me."

"Once we learned not to irritate it, no problem," Julia added softly. Too late, she saw this implied the Chinese had screwed up. But Liang kept his face blank. *Better diplomat than I am.*

The roomy habitat's rear exit fed directly onto the cave entrance, where the anchored robots who assisted descents stood at the hoist apparatus. Somebody in the habitat made the bots all turn and awkwardly bow as the humans approached. Julia laughed with the others. She had not been here since the new Chinese expedition landed and noted that their new cable rig was first class. It worked from a single heavy-duty winch, with a differential gear transferring power from one cable to the other depending on which sent a command to the tending robots. It was the same idea as the rear axle in a car and saved mass.

Methods had marched on. Sitting warm and snug in the habs, she and Viktor and rotations of crews from China and Europe had robotically tried out dozens of candidate vents. Increasingly, robots did the three Ds—dull, dirty, dangerous.

In a decade they found that most fissures, especially toward the poles, were duds. No life within the upper two or three kilometers, though in some there were fossils testifying to ancient Mats' attempted forays. Natural selection—a polite term for Mars drying out and turning cold—had pruned away these ventures. The planet's axial tilt had wandered, bringing warmer eras to the polar zones, then wandered away again. Life had adapted in some vents, but mostly it had died. Or withdrawn inward.

Not this vent, though. It was forty kilometers from the first vent discovered, with a convenient cave entrance, and the Chinese had made it their major exploration target. They got shelter and access.

The team lowered down twenty meters into it and came to the flat staging area. Unlike the First Expedition, everybody wore white suits—surprisingly spotless, still. Here they picked up the recording and safety gear already delivered by the robots. Bare rock; the robots had cleared away talcum powder-like Mars dust.

Julia knew she would have to report on this so she got Viktor to stand and deliver an opening line: "Now we go down a deep hole to cross examine life form that looks like carpet."

She laughed despite herself. "Never pass up a chance, do you, weird husband?" He shrugged, a gesture that in their new slimsuits was visible on camera. These days her pressure suit was supple, moving fluidly over her body as she walked and stooped. The First Expedition suits had been the best of their era, but they'd made you as flexible as a barely oiled Tin Man, as dexterous as a bear in mittens. These comfy suits had self-cleaning liners and 'freshers and solved the basic problem—most of the older suits' weight hung on the shoulders.

Another descent. She could barely remember the days, decades before, when she had broadcast several times a day, sometimes from this same spot. But back then, they had been breaking new ground nearly every day. And betting pools on Earth gave new odds every time they went out in the rover, for whether they'd come back alive. The good ol' days.

"Suit lights off," Viktor sent on com.

They advanced toward the first big iris. A double pressure lock, the microbial mat version of the locks humans used to retain air. As their eyes adjusted, all around them a pale ivory radiance seeped through the dark. Julia knew the enzyme, something like Earth's luciferase, an energy-requiring reaction she had observed in a test tube during molecular bio lab, a few thousand years ago. She recalled as a girl watching in awe "glow worms"—fly larvae, really—hanging in long strands in New Zealand caves, luring insect prey. The Marsmat version was similar, though DNA studies had shown that the Mars subsurface ecosphere had parted company with Earthside evolution over three billion years before. These hardy tapestries of dim gray luminosity, able to survive in near vacuum, were fed from below— from beyond the entrance iris.

They stopped at the three meter wide gray iris, resembling a crusty elephant ear, and stood in silence. Julia and Viktor knew this moment well, this respectful pause experienced in the company of many other crews.

"It closed up yesterday," Liang said. "Nothing we do helps open it."

"Time to use trick," Viktor said.

He reached around to his hip pack and fished out a square box, two wire leads with alligator clips already attached. He fastened one to the outer edge of the iris and another near the center, where the folds overlapped to seal it. He pressed the discharge button at the box's center. The iris stirred, jerked—and slipped slowly open, driven by the current from the battery.

Liang said, "You never mentioned this method."

"Earthside would accuse us of torturing Mat," Viktor said. "Committees, reports, lectures—all from people never been here."

"So the Mat responds to—"

"High current," Julia said. "I got trapped once, Viktor got me free. Turned out I'd done some damage; the Mat answered. Viktor trumped it, though. The Mat uses electrical potentials to muscle its own mass around."

"You did not report this method—"

"Come on through!" Viktor urged, leading the way. Warm wreaths of moist gases wrapped around them, frayed away. The Mat kept itself secured from the near-vacuum above with folded sticky layers. This cave iris was classic, grown at the narrow turn. Viktor held the iris open with more e-jolts as the crew quickly moved through it. Their head beams stabbing into the murky fog as they entered.

"Think is safe?" Liang asked.

Julia came through last, eyes darting. She would put very little past the strange intelligence that surrounded them now, as they threaded their way through the bowels of a life form that was in many ways still beyond their comprehension. The Mat pulsed suddenly, a blue and ivory glow. It knew they were there.

Again Julia felt the churn of somber, slow luminosities stretching into the foggy darkness beyond their lamps' ability to penetrate. There was a sense of silent vitality in the ponderous ferment of vapor and light, a language beyond knowing. As a field biologist she had learned to trust her feel for a place. This hollow of gauzy light far beneath a dry world had an essence she tried to grasp, not with human ideas but by opening herself to the experience itself. To Mars, singing through her bones.

The iris quickly closed behind them as they reached a murky vault that stretched beyond view. Its petals made a tight seal around their cables, decades-old evidence that the Mat learned how to meet challenges. It had done that at the first discovery site, and apparently the knowledge spread—a first sign that the Mat was a global intelligence. Or else had evolved this defense mechanism long ago— against what? Despite decades of wondering which explanation was right, she still did not know.

Snottites gleamed in their handlamps, dangling in moist lances from the ceiling. She steered well clear of the shiny colonies of single-celled extremophilic bacteria—like small stalactites, but with the consistency of mucus. She waved the team back. "Those mean the Mat is moving a lot of fluid around."

Snottites got their name from how they looked, and their energy from digesting the volcanic sulfur in the warm water dripping down from above. Brush one of those highly acidic rods and their battery acid would cut through a suit in moments. A sharp, short *ouch*, quite fatal. The Chinese nodded, backing away. *Good; they've learned some of the many dangers here.*

Meters above in the dim pearly glow she saw Mat sheets hanging in a vast cavern. Under their beams this grotto came alive with shimmering luminescence: burnt oranges, dapplings of vermilion, splashes of delicate turquoise. Another silence. *Inside the beast.*

All around, a complex seethe of radiance. On Earth, mats of bacteria luminesced when they grew thick enough—quorum sensing, a technical term. A lot of Earthside biologists thought that explained this phenomenon, too. But they had never stood in shadowy vaults like this—the thirteenth such large cavern found in over twenty years of exploration. To see the rich, textured ripples of luminosity that slowly worked across the ceiling and down the walls was to dwell in the presence of mystery. Just ahead, thin sheets of mat hung like drapes. Wisps of mist stirred when they passed by. Unlike scuba gear, their suits did not vent exhaled gases, so they would not poison this colony of oxygen-haters. During the first explorations she had done just that.

They reached a branching point and elected to go horizontally into the widest opening. Their beams cast moving shadows, deepening the sense of mystery. Within minutes they found orange spires, moist and slick. Beyond were corkscrew formations of pale white that stuck out into the upwelling gases and captured the richness. More pale, thin membranes, flapping like slow-motion flags. The bigger ones were hinged to spread before the billowing vapor gale. Traceries of vapor showed the flow direction, probably still driven by their opening the iris diaphragm. One spindly, fleshy growth looked like the fingers of a drowned corpse, drifting lazily in the current. It reminded her that so far, thirteen people had died exploring the Mat, all around the planet. There would be more deaths. She always reminded new crews that Mars was constantly trying to kill them.

But something was wrong. She had been here when the Chinese first arrived, waiting for their major gear to set up the plumy habitat they now used—and the Mat then was vibrant, alive. Now big swaths of it were dull, gray.

"Was it like this last time you were here?" she asked.

"Yes, we were studying the change when the iris lock began closing. We barely escaped."

Julia studied the postures of the Chinese team. Did they look embarrassed? "Smart. It can respond quickly. Earthside says the samples we sent back in 2025 imply the Mat was here about 3.5 billion years ago, and we share DNA—so it's been evolving as a single entity since then. It can be quick, but prefers slow. I think it sees us as mayflies."

They looked puzzled. Liang kept his face blank.

"Look—here, pressure is precious. The Mat evolved to seal off passages, build up local vapor density. Then it could hoard the water and gases it got from below. But it has to seal breaches fast. It's killed people before; be careful."

The closest comparison Julia and other biologists had been able to make was to Earthly stomates, the plant cells that guard openings in leaves. The iris opened or closed the holes by pumping fluid into the stomate cells, changing their shape. But analogies were tricky because the Marsmat was neither a plant nor an animal—both Earthly categories—but rather another form of evolved life entirely, another kingdom altogether. Some thought it should be classed with the Earthly biofilms, because some Marsmat DNA closely matched—but the Mat was hugely more advanced.

Yes, the Chinese were both embarrassed and puzzled, judging by their faces. "Get samples of damage," Viktor told them. That unfroze them and they spread out, taking small snips.

Liang eyed the entire chamber. "The damage looks worse. It is spreading."

"Glad we could help," Julia said, though not really glad at all. She knew this sickly gray plague was different. Her alarm bells were ringing. "Let's stop pestering it—out!"

MICROBIAL WISDOM

Julia studied their distant Marsmat sites by reviewing past observations, looking for any signs of the gray swaths they had seen. Every time she looked, the intricate Byzantium of the Mars underworld captivated her.

Earthside subterranean life—microbes, mostly—ran many kilometers deep. In total mass it just about equaled the oxygen-loving life above. Underground Mars life had natural advantages over Earthside. Lower gravity meant that cracks and caverns could be larger. The early plate tectonics of Mars had shut down, so the whole planet froze up. Olympus Mons was the largest volcano in the solar system because the lava that built it came up the same chimney, and nothing moved, ever—so the chimney erected a vast shield mountain. On Earth, the same sort of persistent eruption built the Hawaiian island chain, where tectonics kept steadily moving the upper surface, dotting the ocean with new volcanic piles that made the islands.

The static Martian crust meant that, once formed, caves and cracks were never closed up again by the ceaseless movement of rock layers, as they were on Earth. Mars was also cooler, right down to its core. So milder temperatures prevailed further beneath the surface, and the working volume of rock available for life to thrive in was bigger than the inhabitable surface area of Earth. Even the pores were larger, due to the lesser gravity and rock pressure. *Plenty of room to try out fresh* patterns, she thought. *Over four billion years. Over the whole planet. All one big ... mind?*

They still didn't know how all-embracing was the network of habitable zones available to the Marsmat. Seismic data alone could not tell them what all those open volumes held. To learn that they had to make laborious descents, their reach prolonged by oxygen bottles and supplies stashed earlier—hard, grueling work. Living in a suit for days was not just tiring—it ground down the spirit. The gloom of those chambers, the pervasive atmosphere of strangeness, the creeping claustrophobia—all took their toll through the years. Everywhere they had gone, there was the Marsmat, linked by intricate chemical cues, vapors, fluids.

Julia sat in their very own, original First Expedition habitat—upscaled a lot, but homey—and pondered the 3-D cavern maps of the entire nearby area—a Byzantine spaghetti of life zones.

Viktor said from his work desk, "Time for dinner."

She said, "In a minute. Vulet over in the main hab is looking through all our old videos for me."

"For great discoverer, *da.*" Julia's Earthside fame was a running joke between them now for two decades. "Vulet says—here, quote: 'The Mat's reaction to repeated violations of its integrity by humans—oxygen exposure from leaks and exhalations from their early suits—never presented the gray swaths seen now in China Cave.' So it's new."

"Chinese at fault?"

"I don't want to provoke them."

"Must poke to know."

Amazing, Julia thought, *how large a month of the hab's shit was!*

The next morning she had showed up for her Task Assignment. The Mars Code: Everybody works. No exceptions. Especially for Earthers fresh in—no tourism!

As she passed through the main hab mess hall, some of the new Earthside socko music was playing and people were dancing to it. To her it sounded like a rover flange coupling had gotten loose, flapping against the hull, and so the hell with it.

Mars Operations minimized manual labor, but robots couldn't handle everything. Like this. First their team pulled the plastic bag from the hab underskirting and onto the hauling deck of a truck that growled like a caged animal, which in a way it was. It doubled as a mobile power source, one hundred kilowatts electrical, able to crawl anywhere on hard, carbon fiber treads. She boarded the hauler and checked the long-term weather while she waited for interior systems to self-check: A category four storm was coming, with winds gusting to eighty kilometers per hour.

She noted that the air lock seal was hissing, so either it had snakes in it or needed a smart patch. She told her helmet to send an alert to Main Hab. To Earthside, equipment failure was alarming; for Julia, it was just "Thursday." Holes? Duct tape. Electro: Re-rig it in the shop. Computer? Pull a board, usually, and let the smart 3-D printer figure out what needed doing. Mars liked improvisation.

While she worked, the team lugged the goodie bag of brown across the landscape—a big, rich gift to Mars inside a mercifully opaque plastic sack, compacted and frozen solid. The Planetary Protocols demanded that human waste be taken several kilometers from habitats, then buried in perchlorate-rich sands. But not too deep—the site had to be water-poor, unable to let waste trickle down into the volumes where the Mat lived.

Ecology wasn't just some science here, it was life itself. The hab used toilets that neatly separated solid and liquid waste—nature gave them separate exits, after all—and the urine got recycled, since it held eighty percent of the useful nutrients in their wastes. Kitchen scraps, of course, went back into the greenhouses. In the early days building the greenhouse, they had used "humdung," the Earthside euphemism, for building the topsoil. Soon enough Earthside had reduced the term to TOTS, Take Out The Shit, an acronym that quickly became a hip shorthand Earthside for doing drudge work.

The one trick the bioengineers had not yet managed was converting most of the solid wastes to anything useful or even non-sickening. Let somebody else "realize existing *in situ* resources," as the manuals had put it, by composting. Frozen, it would keep.

Yesterday's ground crew had already dug the pit for it, a few klicks away across rocky terrain, using a Rover Boy backhoe. The perchlorate dust was the bizarre surface chemistry's sole advantage— it plus the constant UV made the risk of contaminating the biosphere below tiny. Perchlorates ate up fragile biological cells in seconds. This surface was the most virulent clean room in the solar system, down to five meters. Any mess that escaped, Mars would kill every single cell within an hour.

As she worked she thought. The Chinese kept their methods secret—that had been only the second time she had been invited into their main hab. So she knew nothing about how thorough they were. Humans were walking litterbugs. They shed human dander, duly vacuumed up and used in the greenhouse for valuable proteins and microorganisms. Early on, she had set out a sample—"a dish of dander," she had called it in a published Letter to *Nature*—and Mars had killed every single cell. That kept the Marsmat isolated from both the searing surface and the alien, invading humans.

It took two hours for them to deploy the big waste bag, more to get the awkward plastic liner pinned up and protocols followed. Mars taught hard lessons. How much Mother Earth did for humans without their noticing, for one.

Here, recycling air, water and food was an intricate dance of chemistry and physics, so they had to tinker with their systems constantly. The greenhouse helped, but the dance of myriad details never ended. Watch the moisture content of the hab's air or they would all get "suit throat"—drying out of the mucous membrane until voices rasped. Even then it was hard work in a suit that couldn't get its heating right—cold feet, hot head. She felt drained on the backhoe ride back.

THINK GLOBALLY

She and Viktor sat in the Global Mat Monitoring room, surrounded by screens. There were views from mats in vents and caves all over Mars, concentrated toward the equator, where the mat density was highest.

Most of her colleagues here were exobiologists, mingled with hardcore mathist types. The mathists tried to invent ways to communicate with the Marsmat, using screens for signaling and occasionally physical models. The Mat sometimes responded with figures it slowly shaped from itself. Julia had prompted the first, during the First Expedition's foray into Vent A. The Mat had echoed Julia's body shape as a hail.

Now big digital screens stood in dozens of Mat sites, trying to build a discourse with the Marsmat. The work went painfully slowly. Drawings of simple rectangles and triangles sometimes got a reply, usually not. The mathists had to visualize four-dimensional surfaces in a non-Euclidean geometry, just to make sense of some Mat shapes which might be messages. They used terms like "finite state grammars" and talked fast. Apparently, this work took inordinate quantities of caffeine. Mathists further proved that high intelligence did not necessarily guarantee fine table manners. She was happy to leave them to it.

Masoul, a slim Indian woman sitting with them, ran the Monitoring room and kept treating Julia and Viktor like minor gods. *If she only knew what job I was doing a few hours ago....* Masoul said, "We have seen no major changes far away, but in the Gusev region, two hundred kilometers diameter, we see fluid buildup and movement."

"When?" Viktor asked.

"For several months now."

"Any progress on talking to the Mat?"

Masoul gave them a weary smile. "It is very slow work. We have a vocabulary of shapes and geometries, which the Mat echoes. Then it shapes a series of other forms, but we do not know what they mean."

Julia asked, "It shows numerical continuity?—counting in order?"

Masoul said, "Yes, but some of us feel that may involve mimicry. Like dolphins, which are unsurpassed in imitative abilities among animals, the Mat may just echo. Of course, both can also invent signals."

"What could select for echoing?" Viktor wasn't a biologist but knew this was always the fallback question: How could the Mat be under selective pressure when it was alone on the planet?

"We think the Mat, so dispersed, may need to talk to parts of itself. We compared data shape formations and pigmentation changes in distant sites. They differ."

"How many species you now figure in Marsmat?" Viktor pressed her.

She gave a small chuckle. "The biologists' mud fight. We think about three thousand different ones, but it's probably more."

"Microbial mats use all of the metabolism types and feeding strategy that have evolved on Earth, plus some," Julia said. "Our cute Marsmat has gone far beyond that. But we can't talk to it!"

Masoul blinked, startled by Julia's irked head-jerk. "It shows—here, see, this is new."

She ran a video of a Mat responding to a screen displaying another Mat, from a different site. Fast forward: incremental changes. Within a day it had reshaped itself to resemble the distant Mat.

"Um," Julia said. "The same mirror test we use on animals like chimps and dolphins. Good!" The method was simple: Put a bit of blood on a chimp's forehead. If it then touched its own forehead in the same place, the chimp realized the reflection is actually him, not another chimp: a crude test of self-awareness.

Masoul brightened at this approval. "It loves mirrors. At several sites, it reacts with fluid movements when we place a large mirror in a cavern."

"Which means ... what?" Viktor asked.

"Earthside has jumped on the study of Mats, so we have a lot of info. In Africa there are big mold-like organisms that can partition its chemical processes, separating out chemicals. It's almost as if the mold were emulating a larger brain piece by piece, saving the results of one module to feed into the next."

Viktor frowned. "So dumb Earthside media are sort of right? I guess we have intelligent slime mold from outer space."

"When you have a Ph.D., you call them hypotheses, not guesses," Masoul said.

Indeed, Julia and Viktor both had doctorates, based on their papers reporting the First Expedition discoveries. Plus many honorary degrees, some apparently bestowed in hopes they would show up for the ceremony. But the Marsmat was a lot harder to fathom than listening to the whistles and clicks of dolphins.

TEA FOR TWO

Julia met Liang just beside the sign, made from a crate:

The Garden of ETON (EXTRA-TERRESTRIAL ORGANIC NUTRITION)

"You don't need those," she said, gesturing at Liang's huge insectile sunglasses. "Not much UV here."

"I see—you have water screen." This was his first visit; the Chinese kept to themselves, worked round the clock. He pointed at the dome where the transparent walls held a meter thick layer of water, warmed by the big nuke, absorbing UV and solar storms. The walls held nearly a full Earth atmosphere and subtracted the UV without editing away the middle spectrum needed for plant growth. All so he and Julia could stroll through aisles of luscious leafy crops. The "grass" was really a mixture of mosses, lichens and small tundra species, but it felt great to stroll on it. Only the toughest stuff from Earth made it here—including a baobab, a tall, fat, tubular tree from western Australia, with only a few thin spidery limbs sprouting from its crown, like a nearly bald man.

Distraction psychology was everything here, from the new habitat for most of Expeditions Two through Seven, and especially in the ten square kilometer greenhouse. That meant heating every habitat's water jacket with their nuclear reactor waste therms, so everything was pleasantly warm to the touch. The walls radiated a comfortable reassurance that the stinging, hostile world outside could have no effect here. Still, indoors on Mars was like being in a luxury gulag. The Siberia outside was never far from mind.

She circled them around the constant-cam that fed a view to Earthside, for the market that wanted to have the Martian day as a wall or window in their homes. She knew this view sold especially well in the cramped rooms of China and India. It was a solid but subtle advertisement.

Earthside could see most of the whole base with their snooper cameras—except in the greenhouse bar. They kept secret from Earthside this little robo-served outdoor restaurant and the distillery it ran. On the patio she liked to look at the eternal rusty sands through eucalyptus trees—surreal blue-green and brownish pink, the only such sight in the solar system.

The eucalyptus stand towering at the dome's center was her pet project. She had insisted on getting some blue gum trees from her Australian home, the forests north of Adelaide. Then she had to prepare the soil, in joyful days spent spading in the humus they had processed from their own wastes. The French called it *eau de fumier* or "spirit of manure" and chronicled every centimeter of blue gum growth—which was fast. But their trunks were spindly, with odd limbs sticking out like awkward elbows—yet more evidence that bringing life to Mars was not going to be easy.

They enjoyed drinks in glasses you could have stood umbrellas in—Liang a straight vodka slush, Julia a gin and tonic. Under 0.38 gee, there was plenty of time to catch a tipping glass. Not that you needed an umbrella on Mars, for, say, the next thousand years.

Liang was so tense, she deliberately kicked back in her chair, at an angle much easier in lesser gravity. "Took me years to get Earthside management to figure this out and send us the carbon struts." She pushed toward him a bowl of fried, salty mixed insects from the dispenser and they both dug in.

She ducked as a white shape hurtled by, narrowly missing her head. "Chicken alert!" It squawked and flapped, turning like a feathered blimp with wings. "Who would have thought chickens could have so much fun up here, in low grav? Plus we get fresh eggs."

He gave her a chilly smile. She marveled at its mechanical insincerity. "The damage. It still spreads."

"You've made no more descents?"

A nod. "We study it from cameras, just wait."

"The gray—"

"Worse. Older parts, black now."

"You've looked at causes?"

"Of course. Ours is a more advanced site than yours."

"This is a life-form we have no intuition about. All these Mears, we've never seen anything—"

"What 'mears' means?"

"A Martian year. Look, from our perspective, it's immortal. It's faced enormous threats as Mars dried out, meteors hammered it, God knows what else—then we made our stupid mistakes venting oxy in the Vent A descents decades back—"

"You were crude. We are not."

Liang was stiff about something, but what? Outside, the wind whistled softly around the dome walls. Another reason she enjoyed the big dome—the sighing winds. Sounds didn't carry well in Mars' thin atmosphere, and the habs were so insulated they were cut off from any outdoor noise.

"Um. Meaning?"

"You listen Earthside? The Americans, they used some new weapon to kill all the senior leadership—"

"Of the Peoples' Republic of Korea, yeah. Thermobaric bombs—air ignition of fuel, shock wave, big blast effect. Pretty effective in those Party enclaves all bunched up at the city centers."

A glare, eyes large. "This makes our collaboration impossible."

"We're not a USA expedition! Our stockholders—"

"We cannot work with you."

"Look, Australia isn't the USA. Not nearly! But our science here comes first, right? I think there's some new factor causing the Mat diebacks. I dunno what, but—"

He sat back, displaying all the personality of a paper cup.

"I came here to serve notice. Do not come to our site again."

She gave him a hard look. "So politics comes first?"

He gave her a hard look, said nothing.

"We find ourselves, the entire human presence on another world, carrying out the dictates of people on the other side of the solar system."

No response. She got up and walked away, pretty nearly the hardest thing she had ever done. *Time to calm down.* She decided to make use of the psychers' classic advice: Take a walk. Breathe deeply. Let the greenhouse calm her. Plus the G&T.

Masoul said, "I called you here because things are moving fast. The fluid flux is building. Seismic rumbles, even—between Vent A and the

Chinese cave. There are electrical signals in the Mat, too, highest level we've ever seen."

Viktor said, "What's it mean?"

Masoul frowned. "That gray damage? I tapped into the Chinese feed—they keep it sequestered for days before letting us look, but I hacked their blocks. The gray is growing. The older spots are going black, too."

"Forget about working on this problem with them," Julia said. "Latest news feed says this damned war has stalled—nobody wants to be first to use nukes. So they're knocking out each others' satellites."

Viktor stood up, agitated. "Go on longer, could cut off our Mars capability. We'll not get resupplied."

"Or go home," Masoul said. "I'm slated to go back next year. I gather North Korea's regime has lost its grip on the country, after the Americans decapitated its Party sites. Who's in the right here?"

Viktor grimaced. "Wars don't determine who's right, only who's left."

WINDS OF MARS

Glancing back at their original hab, she was struck by how clunky it looked. A giant tuna can, its lines were not improved by the sandbags they'd stacked on the top for radiation protection. Still, it had the familiarity of home, and they'd lived in it fairly comfortably for over two decades now, a hab for two.

Compared to Airbus's sleek nuke standing on its tail like a twencen space movie, their gear was now Old School. The Chinese had landed there, then deployed their elegant hab and gear into the cave beyond.

Their rover purred and lurched as Viktor took it at max speed toward where this had all started—Vent A. The seismic data showed building pressures all along this region of Gusev crater.

Three billion years ago, this had been a vast lake. Now only a desert remained where great breakers had once crashed on a muddy shore. As they passed by a bluff, she could see fossil rocks from the early surface life of the Marsmat. These had first been noticed far back in 2014, a powerful clue. Most of the ancient water that fed those eras still slumbered under the rusted pink-brown sands. Now some of it was building up below.

They received bulletins from Earthside's war as they lumbered out. More explosions in orbit, space capabilities used like pawns in a brutal global chess game. *Mars has a lot of past, and so do we.*

As they reached the vent, Phobos rose in the churning ruby sky. "Chinese!" Viktor called. There they were, white suits moving in the slow-motion skipping dubbed "Mars gait" by Earthside media.

"They must've felt it in the cave," Julia said. "Step on it!"

They got out and fought against the gathering storm now heading into Gusev, winds howling a hollow moan. She and Viktor had first met the Marsmat in a deep descent of Vent A, and now, decades later, it fumed with vapor as she had never seen it.

"Liang!" she called on suit com. "What's happening?"

The nearest figure turned. Julia could see from his tormented face that in Liang's mind the frontier between irritation and outright anger had grown thinly guarded, and as his irked mouth twisted she gathered that he had crossed the border without slowing down.

His voice rasped. "Felt quakes, came here. Iris opened, let out liquids, wind. We will deal with this! Go away!"

"We came offering *help*—hey, this is *our* vent!"

"Connected to the cave, same fluid surges." Liang's face now showed his jittery alarm. "I found why the gray damage. Our waste disposal, human dung—Mat got into it, despite our protocols. Was piping it down, must have—"

"Look out!" Viktor called.

She was used to dust devils on Mars, had seen hundreds—but not like this.

It came not from the storm but from Vent A. The furious vortex was a sulfur-rich yellow stream jetting out of the vent, corkscrewing up. Odd gray clots danced in it, whirling out and up. The blast of it knocked her down.

She scrambled to her feet and saw the Chinese run, chattering their panic on com. Winds howled with a strange shrill song.

The vortex rumbled now as it twisted high into a ruddy sky. "Blotches!" Viktor said. "See?—gray mass. It's ejecting bad stuff."

She saw dark masses of it whirring upward in the spreading helix. Something smacked into her helmet. More spattered on her suit and she saw it was the gray, mingled with living parts of the Mat itself.

"We did not know—I thought—" Liang was struggling with his confusion, his rage.

"You put your shit *where*?" she shouted over the hammering storm.

"Froze, dried, buried in cave—"

"Not far enough away." *Stupid,* she thought but did not say.

"I had not known—it can expel! Must know its body." Liang's reserve had shattered.

They hunkered down together against the gale. The vortex blow was easing, winds moaning, wet debris peppering the rusty sands. She watched it in wonder. "Could be, this is a way to transport its genetics, too. Spread it around the planet, looking for new wet spots to populate. Earthside slime molds develop a treelike fruiting structure, spores— toss them to the winds at the reproductive airborne stage. The Mat must've done that way back, when there was some real atmosphere. Helped build its global mind."

"I...." Liang clung to her, as if he could not stand. "I do not know, such strange place. New ideas...."

"Look, the Mat fixes itself. It's smart that way."

Viktor said, "Sharp, Mat is. Blows out its dead, spreads itself, both at once."

Liang peered up into the howling vortex that plowed into the sky. "I ... I should ... seen this, before."

Julia said, "Nobody has much foresight, especially here. Look at Earthside! We're a funny species—we fall forward, catch ourselves. Two-footed terrors." She could joke him through this, get him straight, maybe.

"And the Korean...." Too much was happening, too fast, for Liang.

"If Earthside loses its orbital capability, we'll have to hold out here on our own. That'll take cooperation. We'll be the new Martian race."

"The war, now this—" Liang gazed around at the whipping winds, as if grasping the strangeness of Mars for the first time.

"It's just life finding its way."

She could not understand why people feared new ideas. She was frightened by the old ones.

The Visitor from Taured

Ian R. MacLeod

1.

THERE WAS ALWAYS something otherworldly about Rob Holm. Not that he wasn't charming and clever and good-looking. Driven, as well. Even during that first week when we'd arrived at university and waved goodbye to our parents and our childhoods, and were busy doing all the usual fresher things, which still involved getting dangerously drunk and pretending not to be homesick and otherwise behaving like the prim, arrogant, cocky, and immature young assholes we undoubtedly were, Rob was chatting with research fellows and quietly getting to know the best virtuals to hang out in.

Even back then, us young undergrads were an endangered breed. Many universities had gone bankrupt, become commercial research utilities, or transformed themselves into the academic theme-parks of those so-called "Third Age Academies." But still, here we all were at the traditional redbrick campus of Leeds University, which still offered a broad-ish range of courses to those with families rich enough to support them, or at least tolerant enough not to warn them against such folly. My own choice of degree, just to show how incredibly supportive my parents were, being Analogue Literature.

As a subject, it already belonged with Alchemy and Marxism in the dustbin of history, but books—and I really do mean those peculiar, old, paper, physical objects—had always been my thing. Even when I was far too young to understand what they were and by rights should have been attracted by the bright, interactive, virtual gewgaws buzzing all around me, I'd managed to burrow into the bottom of an old box, down past the stickle bricks and My Little Ponies, to these broad, cardboardy things that fell open and had these flat, 2-D shapes and images that didn't move or respond in any normal way when I waved my podgy fingers in their direction. All you could do was simply look at them. That and chew their corners, and maybe scribble over their pages with some of the dried-up crayons that were also to be found amid those predigital layers.

My parents had always been loving and tolerant of their daughter. They even encouraged little Lita's interest in these ancient artefacts. I remember my mother's finger moving slow and patient across the creased and yellowed pages as she traced the pictures and her lips breathed the magical words that somehow arose from those flat lines. She wouldn't have assimilated data this way herself in years, if ever, so in a sense we were both learning.

The Hungry Caterpillar. The Mister Men series. *Where The Wild Things Are.* Frodo's adventures. Slowly, like some archaeologist discovering the world by deciphering the cartouches of the tombs in Ancient Egypt, I learned how to perceive and interact through this antique medium. It was, well, the *thingness* of books. The exact way they *didn't* leap about or start giving off sounds, smells, and textures. That, and how they didn't ask you which character you'd like to be, or what level you wanted to go to next, but simply took you by the hand and led you where they wanted you to go.

Of course, I became a confirmed bibliophile, but I do still wonder how my life would have progressed if my parents had seen odd behavior differently, and taken me to some pediatric specialist. Almost certainly, I wouldn't be the Lita Ortiz who's writing these words for whoever might still be able to comprehend them. Nor the one who was lucky enough to meet Rob Holm all those years ago in the teenage fug of those student halls back at Leeds University.

2.

So. Rob. First thing to say is the obvious fact that most of us fancied him. It wasn't just the grey eyes, or the courtly elegance, or that soft

Scottish accent, or even the way he somehow appeared mature and accomplished. It was, essentially, a kind of mystery. But he wasn't remotely standoffish. He went along with the fancy dress pub crawls. He drank. He fucked about. He took the odd tab.

One of my earliest memories of Rob was finding him at some club, cool as you like amid all the noise, flash, and flesh. And dragging him out onto the pulsing dance floor. One minute we were hovering above the skyscrapers of Beijing and the next a shipwreck storm was billowing about us. Rob, though, was simply there. Taking it all in, laughing, responding, but somehow detached. Then, helping me down and out, past clanging temple bells and through prismatic sandstorms to the entirely non-virtual hell of the toilets. His cool hands holding back my hair as I vomited.

I never ever actually thanked Rob for this—I was too embarrassed—but the incident somehow made us more aware of each other. That, and maybe we shared a sense of otherness. He, after all, was studying astrophysics, and none of the rest of us even knew what that was, and he had all that strange stuff going on across the walls of his room. Not flashing posters of the latest virtual boy band or porn empress, but slow-turning gas clouds, strange planets, distant stars and galaxies. That, and long runs of mek, whole arching rainbows of the stuff, endlessly twisting and turning. My room, on the other hand, was piled with the precious torn and foxed paperbacks I'd scoured from junksites during my teenage years. Not, of course, that they were actually needed. Even if you were studying something as arcane as narrative fiction, you were still expected to download and virtualize all your resources.

The Analogue Literature Faculty at Leeds University had once taken up a labyrinthine space in a redbrick terrace at the east edge of the campus. But now it had been invaded by dozens of more modern disciplines. Anything from speculative mek to non-concrete design to holo-pornography had taken bites out of it. I was already aware—how couldn't I be?—that no significant novel or short story had been written in decades, but I was shocked to discover that only five other students in my year had elected for An Lit as their main subject, and one of those still resided in Seoul and another was a post-centarian on clicking steel legs. Most of the other students who showed up were dipping into the subject in the hope that it might add something useful to their main discipline. Invariably, they were disappointed. It wasn't just the difficulty of ploughing through page after page of non-interactive text. It was linear fiction's sheer lack of options, settings, choices. Why the hell, I remember some kid shouting in a seminar, should I accept all the miserable shit that this Hardy guy rains down on his characters? Give me the base program for *Tess of the d'Urbervilles*, and I'll hack you fifteen better endings.

I pushed my weak mek to limit during that first term as I tried to formulate a tri-D excursus on *Tender Is The Night*, but the whole piece was reconfigured out of existence once the faculty AIs got hold of it. Meanwhile, Rob Holm was clearly doing far better. I could hear him singing in the showers along from my room, and admired the way he didn't get involved in all the usual peeves and arguments. The physical sciences had a huge, brand new facility at the west end of campus called the Clearbrite Building. Half church, half pagoda and maybe half spaceship in the fizzing, shifting, headachy way of modern architecture, there was no real way of telling how much of it was actually made of brick, concrete and glass, and how much consisted of virtual artefacts and energy fields. You could get seriously lost just staring at it.

My first year went by, and I fought hard against crawling home, and had a few unromantic flings, and made vegetable bolognaise my signature dish, and somehow managed to get version 4.04 of my second term excursus on *Howard's End* accepted. Rob and I didn't became close, but I liked his singing and the cinnamon scent he left hanging behind in the steam of the showers, and it was good to know that someone else was making a better hash of this whole undergraduate business than I was.

"Hey, Lita?"

We were deep into the summer term and exams were looming. Half the undergrads were back at home, and the other half were jacked up on learning streams, or busy having breakdowns.

I leaned in on Rob's doorway. "Yeah?"

"Fancy sharing a house next year?"

"Next year?" Almost effortlessly casual, I pretended to consider this. "I really hadn't thought. It all depends—"

"Not a problem." He shrugged. "I'm sure I'll find someone else."

"No, no. That's fine. I mean, yeah, I'm in. I'm interested."

"Great. I'll show you what I've got from the letting agencies." He smiled a warm smile, then returned to whatever wondrous creations were spinning above his desk.

3.

We settled on a narrow house with bad drains just off the Otley Road in Headingley, and I'm not sure whether I was relieved or disappointed when I discovered that his plan was that we share the place with some others. I roped in a couple of girls, Rob found a couple of guys, and we all got on pretty well. I had a proper boyfriend by then, a self-regarding jock called Torsten, and every now and then a different woman would emerge from Rob's room. Nothing serious ever seemed to come of this, but they were equally gorgeous, clever, and out of my league.

A bunch of us used to head out to the moors for midnight bonfires during that second winter. I remember the smoke and the sparks spinning into the deep black as we sang and drank and arsed around. Once, and with the help of a few tabs and cans, I asked Rob to name some constellations for me, and he put an arm around my waist and led me further into the dark.

Over there, Lita, up to the left and far away from the light of this city, is Ursa Major, the Great Bear, which is always a good place to start when you're stargazing. And there, see close as twins at the central bend of the Plough's handle, are Mizar and Alcor. They're not a true binary, but if we had decent binoculars, we could see that Mizar really does have a close companion. And there, that way, up and left—his breath on my face, his hands on my arms—maybe you can just see there's this fuzzy speck at the Bear's shoulder? Now, that's an entire, separate galaxy from our own filled with billions of stars, and its light has taken about twelve million years to reach the two of us here, tonight. Then Andromeda and Cassiopeia and Canis Major and Minor.... Distant, storybook names for distant worlds. I even wondered aloud about the possibility of other lives, existences, hardly expecting Rob to agree with me. But he did. And then he said something that struck me as strange.

"Not just out there, either, Lita. There are other worlds all around us. It's just that we can't see them."

"You're talking in some metaphorical sense, right?"

"Not at all. It's part of what I'm trying to understand in my studies."

"To be honest, I've got no real idea what astrophysics even means. Maybe you could tell me."

"I'd love to. And you know, Lita, I'm a complete dunce when it comes to, what *do* you call it—2-D fiction, flat narrative? So I want you to tell me about that as well. Deal?"

We wandered back toward the fire, and I didn't expect anything else to come of our promise until Rob called to me when I was wandering past his room one wet, grey afternoon a week or so later. It was deadline day, my hair was a greasy mess, I was heading for the shower, and had an excursus on John Updike to finish.

"You *did* say you wanted to know more about what I study?"

"I was just...." I scratched my head. "Curious. All I do know is that astrophysics is about more than simply looking up at the night sky and giving names to things. That isn't even astronomy, is it?"

"You're not just being polite?" His soft, granite-grey eyes remained fixed on me.

"No. I'm not—absolutely."

"I could show you something here." He waved at the stars on his walls, the stuff spinning on his desk. "But maybe we could go out. To be honest, Lita, I could do with a break, and there's an experiment I could show you up at the Clearbrite that might help explain what I mean about other worlds ... but I understand if you're busy. I could get my avatar to talk to your avatar and—"

"No, no. You're right, Rob. I could do with a break as well. Let's go out. Seize the day. Or at least, what's left of it. Just give me..." I waved a finger toward the bathroom. "...five minutes."

Then we were outside in the sideways-blowing drizzle, and it was freezing cold, and I was still wet from my hurried shower, as Rob slipped a companionable arm around mine as we climbed the hill toward the Otley Road tram stop.

Kids and commuters got on and off as we jolted toward the strung lights of the city, their lips moving and their hands stirring to things only they could feel and see. The Clearbrite looked more than even like some recently arrived spaceship as it glowed out through the gloom, but inside the place was just like any other campus building, with clamoring posters offering to restructure your loan, find you temporary work, or get you laid and hammered. Constant reminders, too, that Clearbrite was the only smartjuice to communicate in realtime to your fingerjewel, toejamb or wristbracelet. This souk-like aspect of modern unis not being something that Sebastian Flyte, or even Harry Potter in those disappointing sequels, ever had to contend with.

We got a fair few hellos, a couple of tenured types stopped to talk to Rob in a corridor, and I saw how people paused to listen to what he was saying. More than ever, I had him down as someone who was bound to succeed. Still, I was expecting to be shown moon rocks, lightning bolts, or at least some clever virtual planetarium. But instead he took me into what looked like the kind of laboratory I'd been forced to waste many hours in at school, even if the equipment did seem a little fancier.

"This is the physics part of the astro," Rob explained, perhaps sensing my disappointment. "But you did ask about other worlds, right, and this is pretty much the only way I can show them to you."

I won't go too far into the details, because I'd probably get them wrong, but what Rob proceeded to demonstrate was a version of what I now know to be the famous, or infamous, Double Slit Experiment. There was a long black tube on a workbench. At one end of it was a laser, and at the other was a display screen attached to a device called a photo multiplier—a kind of sensor. In the middle he placed a barrier with two narrow slits. It wasn't a great surprise even to me that the pulses of light caused a pretty dark-light pattern of stripes to appear on the display at the far end. These, Rob said, were ripples of the interference pattern caused by the waves of light passing through the two slits, much as you'd get if you were pouring water. But light, Lita, is made up individual packets of energy called photons. So what would happen if, instead of sending tens of thousands of them down the tube at once, we turned the laser down so far that it only emitted one photon at a time? Then, surely, each individual photon could only go through one or the other of the slits, there would be no ripples, and two simple stripes would emerge at the far end. But, hey, as he slowed the beep of the signal counter until it was registering single digits, the dark-light bars, like a shimmering neon forest, remained. As if, although each photon was a single particle, it somehow became a blur of all its possibilities as it passed through both slits at once. Which, as far as anyone knew, was pretty much what happened.

"I'm sorry," Rob said afterward when we were chatting over a second or third pint of beer in the fug of an old student bar called the Eldon that lay down the road from the university, "I should have shown you something less boring."

"It wasn't boring. The implications are pretty strange, aren't they?"

"More than strange. It goes against almost everything else we know about physics and the world around us—us sitting here in this pub, for instance. Things exist, right? They're either here or not. They don't flicker in and out of existence like ghosts. This whole particles-blurring-into- waves business was one of the things that bugged me most when I was a kid finding out about science. It was partly why I chose to study astrophysics—I thought there'd be answers I'd understand when someone finally explained them to me. But there aren't." He sipped his beer. "All you get is something called the Copenhagen Interpretation, which is basically a shoulder shrug that says, hey, this stuff happens at the sub-atomic level, but it doesn't really have to bother us or make sense in the world we know about and live in. That, and then there's something else called the many worlds theory...." He trailed off. Stifled a burp. Seemed almost embarrassed.

"Which is what you believe in?"

"Believe isn't the right word. Things either are or they aren't in science. But, yeah, I do. And the maths supports it. Simply put, Lita, it says that all the possible states and positions that every particle could exist in are real—that they're endlessly spinning off into other universes."

"You mean, as if every choice you could make in a virtual was instantly mapped out in its entirety?"

"Exactly. But this is real. The worlds are all around us—right here."

The drink and the conversation moved on, and now it was my turn to apologize to Rob, and his to say no, I wasn't boring him. Because books, novels, stories, they were *my* other worlds, the thing I believed in even if no one else cared about them. That single, magical word, *Fog*, which Dickens uses as he begins to conjure London. And Frederic Henry walking away from the hospital in the rain. And Rose of Sharon offering the starving man her breast after the Joab's long journey across dustbowl America, and Candide eating fruit, and Bertie Wooster bumbling back across Mayfair....

Rob listened and seemed genuinely interested, even though he confessed he'd never read a single non-interactive story or novel. But, unlike most people, he said this as if he realized he was actually missing out on something. So we agreed I'd lend him some of my old paperbacks, and this, and what he'd shown me at the Clearbrite, signaled a new phase in our relationship.

4.

It seems to me now that some of the best hours or my life were spent not in reading books, but in sitting with Rob Holm in my cramped room in that house we shared back in Leeds, and talking about them.

What to read and admire, but also—and this was just as important—what not to. *The Catcher in the Rye* being overrated, and James Joyce a literary show-off, and *Moby Dick* really wasn't about much more than whales. Alarmingly, Rob was often ahead of me. He discovered a copy of *Labyrinths* by Jorge Luis Borges in a garage sale, which he gave to me as a gift, and then kept borrowing back. But he was Rob Holm. He could solve the riddles of the cosmos and meanwhile explore literature as nothing but a hobby, and also help me out with my mek, so that I was finally able to produce the kind of arguments, links, and algorithms for my piece on *Madame Bovary* that the AIs at An Eng actually wanted.

Meanwhile, I also found out about the kind of life Rob had come from. Both his parents were engineers, and he'd spent his early years in Aberdeen, but they'd moved to the Isle of Harris after his mother was diagnosed with a brain-damaging prion infection, probably been caused by her liking for fresh salmon. Most of the fish were then factory-farmed in crowded pens in the Scottish lochs, where the creatures were dosed with antibiotics and fed on pellets of processed meat, often recycled from the remains of their own breed. Just as with cattle and Creutzfeldt-Jakob Disease a century earlier, this process had resulted in a small but significant species leap of cross-infection. Rob's parents wanted to make the best of the years Alice Holm had left, and set up an ethical marine farm—although they preferred to call it a ranch—harvesting scallops on the Isle of Harris.

Rob's father was still there at Creagach, and the business, which not only produced some of the best scallops in the Hebrides, but also benefited other marine life along the costal shelf, was still going. Rob portrayed his childhood there as a happy time, with his mother still doing well, despite the warnings of the scans, and regaling him with bedtime tales of Celtic myths, that were probably his only experience before meeting me of linear fictional narrative.

There were the kelpies, who lived in lochs and were like fine horses, and then there were the Blue Men of the Minch who dwelt between Harris and the mainland and sung up storms and summoned the waves with their voices. Then, one night when Rob was eleven, his mother waited until he and his father were asleep, walked out across the shore and into the sea, and swam, and kept on swimming. No one could last long out there, the sea being so cold, and the strong currents, or perhaps the Blue Men of the Minch, bore her body back to a stretch of shore around the headland from Creagach, where she was found next morning.

Rob told his story of without any obvious angst. But it certainly helped explain the sense of difference and distance he seemed to carry with him. That, and why he didn't fit. Not here in Leeds, amid the fun, mess, and heartbreak of student life, nor even, as I slowly came to realize, in the subject he was studying.

He showed me the virtual planetarium at the Clearbrite, and the signals from a probe passing through the Oort Cloud, and even took me down to the tunnels of a mine where a huge tank of cryogenically cooled fluid had been set up in the hope of detecting the dark matter of which it had once been believed most of our universe was made. It was an old thing now, creaking and leaking, and Rob was part of the small team of volunteers who kept it going. We stood close together in the dripping near-dark, clicking hardhats and sharing each other's breath, and of course I was thinking of other possibilities—those fractional moments when things could go one of many ways. Our lips pressing. Our bodies joining. But something, maybe a fear of losing him entirely, held me back.

"It's another thing that science has given up on," he said later when we were sitting at our table in the Eldon. "Just like that ridiculous Copenhagen shoulder-shrug. Without dark matter, and dark energy, the way the galaxies rotate and recede from each other simply doesn't make mathematical sense. You know what the so-called smart money is on these days? Something called topographical deformity, which means that the basic laws of physics don't apply in the same way across this entire universe. That it's pock-marked with flaws."

"But you don't believe that?"

"Of course I don't! It's fundamentally unscientific."

"But you get glitches in even the most cleverly conceived virtuals, don't you? Even in novels, sometimes things don't always entirely add up."

"Yeah. Like who killed the gardener in *The Big Sleep*, or the season suddenly changing from autumn to spring in that Sherlock Holmes story. But this isn't like that, Lita. This isn't..." For once, he was in danger of sounding bitter and contemptuous. But he held himself back.

"And you're not going to give up?"

He smiled. Swirled his beer. "No, Lita. I'm definitely not."

5.

Perhaps inevitably, Rob's and my taste in books had started to drift apart. He'd discovered an antique genre called Science Fiction, something which the AIs at An Lit were particularly sniffy about. And, even as he tried to lead me with him, I could see their point. Much of the prose was less than luminous, the characterization was sketchy, and, although a great deal of it was supposedly about the future, the predictions were laughably wrong.

But Rob insisted that that wasn't the point, that SF was essentially a literature of ideas. That, and a sense of wonder. To him, wonder was particularly important. I could sometimes—maybe as that lonely astronaut passed through the stargate, or with those huge worms in that book about a desert world—see his point. But most of it simply left me cold.

Rob went off on secondment the following year to something called the Large Millimeter Array on the Atacama Plateau in Chile, and I, for want of anything better, kept the lease on our house in Headingley and got some new people in, and did a masters on gender roles in George Eliot's *Middlemarch*. Of course, I paid him virtual visits, and we talked of the problems of altitude sickness and the changed asshole our old uni friends were becoming as he put me on a camera on a Jeep, and bounced me across the dark-skied desert.

Another year went—they were already picking up speed—and Rob found the time for a drink before he headed off to some untenured post, part research, part teaching, in Heidelberg that he didn't seem particularly satisfied with. He was still reading—apparently there hadn't been much else to do in Chile—but I realized our days of talking about Proust or Henry James had gone.

He'd settled into, you might almost say retreated to, a sub-genre of SF known as alternate history, where all the stuff he'd been telling me about our world continually branching off into all its possibilities was dramatized on a big scale. Hitler had won World War Two—a great many times, it seemed—and the South was triumphant in the American Civil War. That, and the Spanish Armada had succeeded, and Europe remained under the thrall of medieval Roman Catholicism, and Lee Harvey Oswald's bullet had grazed past President Kennedy's head. I didn't take this odd obsession as a particularly good sign as we exchanged chaste hugs and kisses in the street outside the Eldon and went our separate ways.

I had a job of sorts—thanks to Sun-Mi, my fellow An Lit student from Korea—teaching English to the kids of rich families in Seoul, and for a while it was fun, and the people were incredibly friendly, but then I grew bored and managed to wrangle an interview with one of the media conglomerates that had switched its physical base to Korea in the wake of the California Earthquake. I was hired for considerably less than I was getting paid teaching English and took the crowded commute every morning to a vast half-real, semi-ziggurat high-rise mistily floating above the Mapo District, where I studied high res worlds filled with headache-inducing marvels, and was invited to come up with ideas in equally headache-inducing meeting.

I, an Alice in these many virtual wonderlands, brought a kind of puzzled innocence to my role. Two, maybe three, decades earlier, the other developers might still have known enough to recognize my plagiarisms, if only from old movies their parents had once talked about, but now what I was saying seemed new, fresh, and quirky. I was a thieving literary magpie, and became the go-to girl for unexpected turns and twists. The real murderer of Roger Ackroyd, and the dog collar in *The Great Gatsby*. Not to mention what Little Father Time does in *Jude the Obscure*, and the horror of Sophie's choice. I pillaged them all, and many others. Even the strange idea that the Victorians had developed steam-powered computers, thanks to my continued conversations with Rob.

Wherever we actually were, we got into the habit of meeting up at a virtual recreation of the bar of Eldon that, either as some show-off feat of virtual engineering, or a post-post-modern art project, some student had created. The pub had been mapped in realtime down to the atom and the pixel, and the ghosts of our avatars often got strange looks from real undergrads bunking off from afternoon seminars. We could actually order a drink, and even taste the beer, although of course we couldn't ingest it. Probably no bad thing, in view of the state of Eldon's toilets. But somehow, that five-pints-and-still-clear-headed feeling only added to the slightly illicit pleasure of our meetings. At least, at first.

It was becoming apparent that, as he switched from city to city, campus to campus, project to project, Rob was be in danger of turning one of those aging, permanent students, clinging to short-term contracts, temporary relationships and get-me-by loans, and the worst thing was that, with typical unflinching clarity, he knew it.

"I reckon I was either born too early, or too late, Lita," he said as he sipped his virtual beer. "Even one of the assessors actually said that to me a year or so ago when I tried to persuade her to back my project."

"So you scientists have to pitch ideas as well?"

He laughed, but that warm, Hebridean sound was turning bitter. "How else does this world work? But maths doesn't change even if fashions do. The many worlds theory is the only way that the behavior of subatomic particles can be reconciled with everything else we know. Just because something's hard to prove doesn't mean it should be ignored."

By this time I was busier than ever. Instead of providing ideas other people could profit from, I'd set up my own consultancy, which had thrived and made me a great deal of money. By now, in fact, I had more of the stuff than most people would have known what to do with. But *I* did. I'd reserved a new apartment in swish high-res, high-rise development going up overlooking the Han River and was struggling to get the builders to understand that I wanted the main interior space to be turned into something called a *library*. I showed them old walk-throughs of the Bodleian in Oxford, and the reading room of the British Museum, and the Brotherton in Leeds, and many other lost places of learning. Of course I already had a substantial collection of books in a secure, fireproofed, climate-controlled warehouse, but now I began to acquire more.

The once-great public collections were either in storage or scattered to the winds. But there were still enough people as rich and crazy as I was to ensure that the really rare stuff—first folios, early editions, hand-typed versions of great works—remained expensive and sought-after, and I surprised even myself with the determination and ruthlessness of my pursuits. After all, what else was I going to spend my time and money on?

There was no grand opening of my library. In fact, I was anxious to get all the builders and conservators, both human and otherwise, out of the way so I could have the place entirely to myself. Then I just stood there. Breathing in the air, with its savor of lost forests and dreams.

There were first editions of great novels by Nabokov, Dos Passos, Stendhal, Calvino, and Wells, and an early translation of Cervantes, and a fine collection of Swift's works. Even, in a small nod to Rob, a long shelf of pulp magazines with titles like *Amazing Stories* and *Weird Tales*, although their lurid covers of busty maidens being engulfed by intergalactic centipedes were generally faded and torn. Not that I cared about the pristine state of my whispering pages. Author's signatures, yes—the sense of knowing Hemingway's hands had once briefly grasped this edition—but the rest didn't matter. At least, apart from the thrill of beating others in my quest. Books, after all, were old by definition. Squashed moths and bus tickets stuffed between the pages. Coffee cup circles. Exclamations in the margin. I treasured the evidence of their long lives.

After an hour or two of shameless gloating and browsing, I decided to call Rob. My avatar had been as busy as me with the finishing touches to my library, and now it struggled to find him. What it did eventually unearth was a short report stating that Callum Holm, a fish-farmer on the Isle of Harris, had been drowned in a boating accident a week earlier.

Of course, Rob would be there now. Should I contact him? Should I leave him to mourn undisturbed? What kind of friend was I, anyway, not to have even picked up on this news until now? I turned around the vast, domed space I'd created in confusion and distress.

"Hey."

I span back. The Rob Holm who stood before me looked tired but composed. He'd grown a beard, and there were a few flecks of silver now in it and his hair. I could taste the sea air around him. Hear the cry of gulls.

"Rob!" I'd have hugged him, if the energy field permissions I'd set up in this library had allowed. "I'm so, so sorry. I should have found out, I should have—"

"You shouldn't have done anything, Lita. Why do you think I kept this quiet? I wanted to be alone up here in Harris to sort things out. But...." He looked up, around. "What a fabulous place you've created!"

As I showed him around my shelves and acquisitions, and his ghost fingers briefly passed through the pages of my first edition *Gatsby,* and the adverts for X-Ray specs in an edition of *Science Wonder Stories,* he told me how his father had gone out in his launch to deal with some broken tethers on one of the kelp beds and been caught by a sudden squall. His body, of course, had been washed up, borne by to the same stretch of shore where Rob's mother had been found.

"It wasn't intentional," Rob said. "I'm absolutely sure of that. Dad was still in his prime, and proud of what he was doing, and there was no way he was ever going to give up. He just misjudged a coming storm. I'm the same, of course. You know that, Lita, better than anyone."

"So what happens next? With a business, there must be a lot to tie up."

"I'm not tying up anything."

"You're going to stay there?" I tried to keep the incredulity out of my voice.

"Why not? To be honest, my so-called scientific career has been running on empty for years. What I'd like to prove is never going to get backing. I'm not like you. I mean...." He gestured at the tiered shelves. "You can make anything you want become real."

6.

Rob wasn't the sort to put on an act. If he said he was happy ditching research and filling his father's role as a marine farmer on some remote island, that was because he was. I never quite did find the time to physically visit him in Harris—it was, after all, on the other side of the globe—and he, with the daily commitments of the family business, didn't get to Seoul. But I came to appreciate my glimpses of the island's strange beauty. That, and the regular arrival of chilled, vacuum-packed boxes of fresh scallops. But was this really enough for Rob Helm? Somehow, despite his evident pride in what he was doing, and the funny stories he told of the island's other inhabitants, and even the occasional mention of some woman he'd met at a ceilidh, I didn't think it was. After all, Creagach was his mother and father's vision, not his.

Although he remained coy about the details, I knew he still longed to bring his many worlds experiment to life. That, and that it would be complicated, controversial, and costly. I'd have been more than happy to offer financial help, but I knew he'd refuse. So what else could I do? My media company had grown. I had mentors, advisors, and consultants, both human and AI, and Rob would have been a genuinely useful addition to the team, but he had too many issues with the lack of rigor and logic in this world to put up with all glitches, fudges, and contradictions of virtual ones. Then I had a better idea.

"You know why nothing ever changes here, don't you?" he asked me as our avatars sat together in the Eldon late one afternoon. "Not the smell from the toilets or the unfestive Christmas decorations or that dusty Pernod optic behind the bar. This isn't a feed from the real pub any longer. The old Eldon was demolished years ago. All we've been sitting in ever since is just a clever formation of what the place would be like if it still existed. Bar staff, students, us, and all."

"That's...." Although nothing changed, the whole place seemed to shimmer. "How things are these days. The real and the unreal get so blurry you can't tell which is which. But you know," I added, as if the thought had just occurred to me, "there's a project that's been going the rounds of the studios here in Seoul. It's a series about the wonders of science, one of those proper, realtime factual things, but we keep stumbling over finding the right presenter. Someone fresh, but with the background and the personality to carry the whole thing along."

"You don't mean me?"

"Why not? It'd only be part time. Might even help you promote what you're doing at Creagach."

"A scientific popularizer?"

"Yes. Like Carl Sagan, for example, or maybe Stephen Jay Gould."

I had him, and the series—which, of course, had been years in development purgatory—came about. I'd thought of it as little more than a way of getting Rob some decent money, but, from the first live-streamed episode, it was a success. After all, he was still charming and persuasive, and his salt-and-pepper beard gave him gravitas—and made him, if anything, even better looking. He used the Giant's Causeway to demonstrate the physics of fractures. He made this weird kind of pendulum to show why we could never predict the weather for more than a few days ahead. He swam with the whales off Tierra del Fuego. The only thing he didn't seem to want to explain was the odd way that photons behaved when you shot them down a double-slotted tube. That, and the inconsistencies between how galaxies revolved and Newton's and Einstein's laws.

In the matter of a very few years, Rob Holm was rich. And of course, and although he never actively courted it, he grew famous. He stood on podiums and looked fetchingly puzzled. He shook a dubious hand with girning politicians. He even turned down offers to appear at music festivals, and had to take regular legal steps to protect the pirating of his virtual identity. He even finally visited me in Seoul and experienced the wonders of my library at first hand.

At last, Rob had out-achieved me. Then, just when I and most of the rest of the world had him pigeon-holed as that handsome, softly accented guy who did those popular science things, his avatar returned the contract for his upcoming series unsigned. I might have forgotten that getting rich was supposed to be the means to an end. But he, of course, hadn't.

"So," I said as we sat together for what turned out to be the last time in our shared illusion of the Eldon. "You succeed with this project. You get a positive result and prove the many worlds theory is true. What happens after that?"

"I publish, of course. The data'll be public, peer-reviewed, and—"

"Since when has being right ever been enough?"

"That's..." He brushed a speck of virtual beer foam from his grey beard. "...how science works."

"And no one ever had to sell themselves to gain attention? Even Galileo had to do that stunt with the cannonballs."

"As I explained in my last series, that story of the Tower of Pisa was an invention of his early biographers."

"Come on, Rob. You know what I mean."

He looked uncomfortable. But, of course, he already had the fame. All he had to do was stop all this Greta Garbo shit and milk it.

So, effectively I became PR agent for Rob's long-planned experiment. There was, after all, a lot for the educated layman, let alone the general public, or us so-called media professionals, to absorb. What was needed was a handle, a simple selling point. And, after a little research, I found one.

A man in a business suit had arrived at Tokyo airport in the summer of 1954. He was Caucasian but spoke reasonable Japanese, and everything about him seemed normal apart from his passport. It looked genuine but was from somewhere called Taured, which the officials couldn't find in any of their directories. The visitor was as baffled as they were. When a map was produced, he pointed to Andorra, a tiny but ancient republic between France and Spain, which he insisted was Taured. The humane and sensible course was to find him somewhere to sleep while further enquiries were made. Guards were posted outside the door of a secure hotel room high in a tower block, but the mysterious man had vanished without trace in the morning, and the Visitor from Taured was never seen again.

Rob was dubious, then grew uncharacteristically cross when he learned that the publicity meme had already been released. To him, and despite the fact that I thought he'd been reading this kind of thing for years, the story was just another urban legend and would further alienate the scientific establishment when he desperately needed their help. In effect, what he had to obtain was time and bandwidth from every available gravitational observatory, both here on Earth and up in orbit, during a crucial observational window, and time was already short.

It was as the final hours ticked down in a fervid air of stop-go technical problems, last minute doubts, and sudden demands for more money, that I finally took the sub-orbital from Seoul to Frankfurt, then the skytrain on to Glasgow, and some thrumming, windy thing of string and carbon fiber along the Scottish west coast, and across the shining Minch. The craft landed in Stornoway harbor in Isle of Lewis—the northern part of the long landmass of which Harris forms the south—where I was rowed ashore, and eventually found a bubblebus to take me across purple moorland and past scattered white bungalows, then up amid ancient peaks.

Rob stood waiting on the far side of the road at the final stop, and we were both shivering as we hugged in the cold spring sunlight. But I was here, and so was he, and he'd done a great job at keeping back the rest of the world, and even I wouldn't have had it any other way. It seemed as if most of the niggles and issues had finally been sorted. Even if a few of his planned sources had pulled out, he'd still have all the data he needed. Come tomorrow, Rob Holm would either be a prophet or a pariah.

7.

He still slept in the same narrow bed he'd had as a child in the rusty-roofed cottage down by the shore at Creagach, while his parents' bedroom was now filled with expensive processing and monitoring equipment, along with a high-band, multiple-redundancy satellite feed. Downstairs, there was a parlor where Rob kept his small book collection in an alcove by the fire—I was surprised to see that it was almost entirely poetry; a scatter of Larkin, Eliot, Frost, Dickinson, Pope, Yeats and Donne, beside a few Asimovs, Le Guins, and Clarkes—with a low tartan divan where he sat to read these works. Which, I supposed, might also serve as a second bed, although he hadn't yet made it up.

He took me out on his launch. Showed me his scallop beds and the glorious views of this ragged land with its impossibly wide and empty beaches. And there, just around the headland, was the stretch of bay where both Rob's parents had been found, and I could almost hear the Blue Men of the Minch calling to us over the sigh of the sea. There were standing stones on the horizon, and an old whaling station at the head of a loch, and a hill topped by a medieval church filled with the bodies of the chieftains who had given these islands such a savage reputation through their bloody feuds. And meanwhile, the vast cosmic shudder of the collision of two black holes was travelling toward us at lightspeed.

There were scallops, of course, for dinner. Mixed in with some fried dab and chopped mushroom, bacon and a few leaves of wild garlic, all washed down with malt whisky, and with whey-buttered soda bread on the side, which was the Highland way. Then, up in humming shrine of his parents' old bedroom, Rob checked on the status of his precious sources again.

The black hole binaries had been spiraling toward each other for tens of thousands of years, and observed here on Earth for decades. In many ways, and despite their supposed mystery, black holes were apparently simple objects—nothing but sheer mass—and even though their collision was so far off it had actually happened when we humans were still learning how to use tools, it was possible to predict within hours, if not minutes, when the effects of this event would finally reach Earth.

There were gravitational observatories, vast-array laser interferometers, in deep space, and underground in terrestrial sites, all waiting to record this moment, and Rob was tapping into them. All everyone else expected to see—in fact, all the various institutes and faculties had tuned their devices to look for—was this.... Leaning over me, Rob called up a display to show a sharp spike, a huge peak in the data, as the black holes swallowed each other and the shock of their collision flooded out in the asymmetrical pulse of a gravitational wave.

"But this isn't what I want, Lita. Incredibly faint though that signal is—a mere ripple deep in the fabric of the cosmos—I'm looking to combine and filter all those results, and find something even fainter.

"This...." He dragged up another screen, "is what I expect to see." There was the same central peak, but this time it was surrounded by a fan of smaller, ever-decreasing, ripples eerily reminiscent of the display Rob had once shown me of the ghost-flicker of those photons all those years ago in Leeds. "These are echoes of the black hole collision in other universes."

I reached out to touch the floating screen. Felt the incredible presence of the dark matter of other worlds.

"And all of this will happen tonight?"

He smiled.

8.

There was nothing else left to be done—the observatories Rob was tapping into were all remote, independent, autonomous devices—so we took out chairs into the dark, and drank some more whisky, and collected driftwood, and lit a fire on the shore.

We talked about books. Nothing new, but some shared favorites. Poe and Pasternak and Fitzgerald. And Rob confessed that he hadn't got on anything like as well as he'd pretended with his first forays into literature. How he'd found the antique language and odd punctuation got in the way. It was even a while before he understood the obvious need for a physical bookmark. He'd have given up with the whole concept if it hadn't been for my shining, evident faith.

"You know, it was *Gulliver's Travels* that finally really turned it around for me. Swift was so clever and rude and funny and angry, yet he could also tell a great story. That bit about those Laputan astronomers studying the stars from down in their cave, and trying to harvest sunbeams from marrows. Well, that's us right here, isn't it?"

The fire settled. We poured ourselves some more whisky. And Rob recited a poem by Li Po about drinking with the Moon's shadow, and then we remembered those days back in Leeds when we'd gone out onto the moors, and drank and ingested far more than was good for us, and danced like savages and, yes, there had even been that time he and I had gazed up at the stars.

We stood up now, and Rob led me away from the settling fire. The stars were so bright here, and the night sky was so black, that it felt like falling merely to look up. Over there in the west, Lita, is the Taurus Constellation. It's where the Crab Nebula lies, the remains of a supernova the Chinese recorded back in 1054, and it's in part of the Milky Way known as the Perseus Arm, which is where our dark binaries would soon end their fatal dance. I was leaning into him as he held his arms around me, and perhaps both of us were breathing a little faster than was entirely due to the wonders of the cosmos.

"What time is it now, Rob?"

"It's...." He checked his watch. "Just after midnight."

"So there's still time."

"Time for what?"

We kissed, then crossed the shore and climbed the stairs to Rob's single bed. It was sweet, and somewhat drunken, and quickly over. The Earth, the Universe, didn't exactly move. But it felt far more like making love than merely having sex, and I curled up against Rob afterward, and breathed his cinnamon scent, and fell into a well of star-seeing contentment.

"Rob?"

The sky beyond the window was showing the first traces of dawn as I got up, telling myself that he'd be next door in his parents' old room, or walking the shore as he and his avatar strove to deal with a torrent of interview requests. But I already sensed that something was wrong.

It wasn't hard for me to pull up the right screen amid the humming machines in his parents' room, proficient at mek as I now was. The event, the collision, had definitely occurred. The spike of its gravitational wave had been recorded by every observatory. But the next screen, the one where Rob had combined, filtered, and refined all the data, displayed no ripples, echoes, from other worlds.

I ran outside shouting Rob's name. I checked the house feeds. I paced back and forth. I got my avatar to contact the authorities. I did all the things you do when someone you love suddenly goes missing, but a large part of me already knew it was far too late.

Helicopters chattered. Drones circled. Locals gathered. Fishermen arrived in trawlers and skiffs. Then came the bother of newsfeeds, all the publicity I could ever have wished for. But not like this.

I ended up sitting on the rocks of that bay around the headland from Creagach as the day progressed, waiting for the currents to bear Rob's body to this place, where he could join his parents.

I'm still waiting.

9.

Few people actually remember Rob Holm these days, and if they do, it's as that good-looking guy who used to present those slightly weird nature—or was it science?—feeds, and didn't he die in some odd, sad kind of way? But I still remember him, and I still miss him, and I still often wonder what really happened on that night when he left the bed we briefly shared. The explanation given by the authorities, that he'd seen his theory dashed and then walked out into the freezing waters of the Minch, still isn't something I can bring myself to accept. So maybe he really was like the Visitor from Taured and simply vanished from a universe which couldn't support what he believed.

I read few novels or short stories now. The plots, the pages, seem over-involved. Murals rather than elegant miniatures. Rough-hewn rocks instead of jewels. But the funny thing is that, as my interest in them has dwindled, books have become popular again. There are new publishers, even new writers, and you'll find pop-up bookstores in every city. Thousands now flock to my library in Seoul every year, and I upset the conservators by allowing them to take my precious volumes down from their shelves. After all, isn't that exactly what books are for? But I rarely go there myself. In fact, I hardly ever leave the Isle of Harris, or even Creagach, which Rob, with typical consideration and foresight, left me in his will. I do my best to keep the scallop farm going, pottering about in the launch and trying to keep the crabs and the starfish at bay, although the business barely turns a profit, and probably never did.

What I do keep returning to is Rob's small collection of poetry. I have lingered with Eliot's Prufrock amid the chains of the sea, wondered with Hardy what might have happened if he and that woman had sheltered from the rain a minute more, and watched as Sylvia Plath's children burst those final balloons. I just wish that Rob was here to share these precious words and moments with me. But all that's left is you and I, dear, faithful reader, and the Blue Men of the Minch calling to the waves.

The Seventh Gamer

Gwyneth Jones

The Anthropologist Returns to Eden

SHE INTRODUCED HERSELF by firelight, while the calm breakers on the shore kept up a background music—like the purring breath of a great sleepy animal. It was warm, the air felt damp; the night sky was thick with cloud. The group inspected her silently. Seven pairs of eyes, gleaming out of shadowed faces. Seven adult strangers, armed and dangerous; to whom she appeared a helpless, ignorant infant. Chloe tried not to look at the belongings that had been taken from her, and now lay at the feet of a woman with long black hair, who was dressed in an oiled leather tunic and tight, broken-kneed jeans; a state-of-the-art crossbow slung at her back, a long knife in a sheath at her belt.

Chloe wanted to laugh, to jump up and down and wave her arms; or possibly just run away and quit this whole idea. But her sponsor was smiling encouragingly.

"Tell us about yourself, Chloe Hensen. Who are you?"

"I'm a hunter." she said. "That's my trade."

"Really." The crossbow woman sounded as if she doubted it. "And how are you aligned?"

"I'm not. I travel alone, seeking what fascinates me. I hunt the white wolf on the tundra and the jaguar in the rainforest, and I desire not to kill, but to know."

Someone chuckled. "That's a problem. Darkening World is a war game, girly. Didn't you realize?" It was the other woman in the group, the short, sturdy redhead: breaching etiquette.

"I'm not a pacifist. I'll fight. But killing is not my purpose. I wish to share your path for a while, and I commit to serving faithfully as a comrade, in peace and war. But I pursue my own cause. That is the way of my kind."

"Stay where you are," said her sponsor. "We need to speak privately. We'll be back."

Six of them withdrew into the trees that lined the shore. One pair of eyes, one shadowy figure remained: Chloe was under guard. The watcher didn't move or speak; she thought she'd better not speak to him, either. She looked away, toward the glimmer of the breakers: controlling her intense curiosity. There shouldn't be a seventh person, besides herself. There were only six guys in the game house team—

They reappeared and sat in a circle round her: Reuel, Lete, Matt, Kardish, Sol and Beat. (She *must* get their game names and real names properly sorted out.) Silently they raised their hands in a ritual gesture, open palms cupping either side of their heads, like the hear-no-evil monkey protecting itself from scandal. Chloe's sponsor gestured for her to do the same.

She removed her headset, in unison with the others, and the potent illusion vanished. No shore, no weapons, no fancy dress, no synesthetic. Chloe and the Darkening World team—recognizable but less imposing—sat around a table in a large, tidy kitchen: The Meeting Boxes piled like a heap of skulls in front of them.

"Okay," said Reuel, the "manager" of this game house, who was also her sponsor. "This is what we've got. You can stay, but you're on probation. We haven't made up our minds."

"Is she always going to talk like that?" asked the woman with the long black hair, of nobody in particular. (She was Lete the Whisperer, the group's shaman. Also known as Josie Nicks, one of DW's renowned rogue programmers.)

"Give her a break," said Reuel. "She was getting in character. What's wrong with that?"

Reuel was tall and lanky, with glowing skin like polished mahogany and fine, strong features. He'd be very attractive, Chloe thought, were it not for his geeky habit of keeping a pen, or two or three, stuck in his springy hair. Red, green and blue feathers, or beads:

Okay, but pens looked like a neurological quirk. The nerd who mistook his hair for a shirt pocket.

He was Reuel in the game too. Convenience must be a high priority.

"Who wants bedtime tea?" Sol, with the far-receded hairline, whose game name she didn't recall, jumped up and busied about, setting mugs by the kettle. "Name your poisons! For the record, Chloe, I was in favor." He winked at her. "You're cute. And pleasantly screwy."

Reuel scowled. "Keep your paws off, Bear Man."

"I don't like the idea," grumbled Beat, the redhead. "I don't care if she's a jumped-up social scientist or a dirty, lying media-hound. Fine, she stays a day or two. Then we take her stuff, throw her out, and make sure we strip her brain of all data first."

Sol beamed. "Aileen's the mercurial type. She'll be your greatest fan by morning."

Jun, whose game identity was Kardish the Assassin, and Markus of the Wasteland (real name Matt Warks) dropped their chosen teabags into their personal mugs and stood together watching the kettle boil, without a word.

Thankfully Chloe's bunk was a single bedroom, so she could write up her notes without hiding in the bathroom. She was eager to record her first impressions. The many layered, feedback-looped reality of that meeting. Seven people sitting in a kitchen, Boxes on their heads, typing their dialogue. Seven corresponding avatars in post-apocalyptic fancy-dress *speaking* that dialogue, on the dark lonely shore. A third layer where the plasticity of human consciousness, combined with a fabulously detailed 3-D video-montage, created a sensory illusion that the first two layers were one. A *fourth* layer of exchanges, in a sidebar on the helmet screens (which Chloe knew was there, but as a stranger, she couldn't see it); that might include live comments from the other side of the world. And the mysterious seventh, who maybe had a human controller somewhere; or maybe not. That's evolution for you. It's an engine of complexity, not succession.

Chloe had got involved in video gaming (other than as a casual user) on a fieldwork trip to Honduras. She was living with the urban poor, studying their cultural innovations, in statistically the most deadly violent country in the world—outside of active warzones. Everyone in "her" community was obsessed with an open source online role-playing game called *Copan*. Everyone played.

Grandmothers tinkered with the programming: Of course, Chloe had to join in. While documenting this vital, absorbing cultural sandbox she'd become fascinated by the role of Non-Player Characters (NPCs)—and the simple trick, common to all video games, that allows "the game" to participate in itself.

A video game is a world where there's always somebody who knows your business. In a nuclear-disaster wasteland or a candy-colored flowery meadow; on board an ominously deserted space freighter or in the back room of a dangerous dive in Post-Apocalypse City, without fail you're going to meet someone who says something like *Hi, you must be looking for the Great Amulet of Power so you can get into the Haunted Fall Out Shelter! I can help!* Typically, you'll then be given fiendishly puzzling instructions, but fortunately you are not alone. A higher-order NPC will provide advice and interpretation.

In any big modern game the complex NPCs were driven by sophisticated AI algorithms, enriched by feedback from real humans. Players might choose them as challenging opponents, or empathic allies, in preference to human partners. But Chloe wasn't so interested in imaginary friends (or imaginary enemies!). She wanted to study the mediators—the NPCs "whose" role was to explain the game.

She'd told her *Copan* friends what she was looking for, and they had recommended she get in touch with Darkening World.

Darkening World (DW) was a small to medium Post-Apocalyptic Type, Massive Multiuser Online Role Playing Game (MMORPG) with a big footprint for its subscriber numbers. There were televised tournaments; there was gambling in which (allegedly) serious money changed hands. Pro-players stayed together in teams, honing their physical and mental skills. They sometimes lived together, which made a convenient set-up for studying their culture. But the game house tradition wasn't unique to DW, and that wasn't why Chloe was here. Her *Copan* friends had told her about the internet myth that some of Darkening World's NPCs were sentient aliens. The idea had grown on her—until she'd just had to find out what the hell this meant.

Reuel and his team were hardcore. They didn't merely *believe* that aliens were accessing the DW environment (through the many dimensions of the information universe). They knew it. Reuel's "Spirit Guide," his NPC partner in the game, was an alien.

Elbows on her desk, chin on her fists, Chloe reviewed her shorthand notes. (Nothing digital that might be compromising! This house was the most wired-up, saturated, Wi-Fi location she'd ever entered!) She liked Reuel, her sponsor. He was a nice guy, and sexy despite those pens. Was she putting him in a false position? She had not lied. She'd told him she was interested in Darkening World's NPCs; that she knew about his beliefs, and that she had an open mind. Was this true enough to be okay?

One thing she was sure of. *People who believe in barbarians, find barbarians.* If she came to this situation looking for crazy, stupid deluded neo-primitives: crazy, stupid deluded neo-primitives was all that she would find—

But what a thrill it had been to arrive on that beach! Like Malinowski in Melanesia, long ago: "alone on a tropical beach close to a native village, while the launch or dinghy which has brought you sails away out of sight...." *And then screwing up completely,* she recalled with a grin, *when I tried to speak the language.* In Honduras she'd often felt like a Gap Year kid, embarrassed by the kindness of people whose lives were so compromised. In the unreal world of this game she could *play,* without shame, at the romance of being an old-school adventurer, seeking ancient cultural truths among dangerous "natives."

Although of course she'd be doing real work too.

But what if the "natives" decided she wasn't playing fair? Gamers could be rough. There was that time, in World of Warcraft, when a funeral for a player who'd died in the real world was savagely ambushed. Mourners slaughtered, and a video of the atrocity posted online—

How do people habituated to extreme, unreal physical violence punish betrayal?

Like a player whose avatar, whose eye; whose *I* stands on the brink of a dreadful abyss, about to step onto the miniscule tightrope that crosses it, Chloe was truly frightened.

She was summoned to breakfast by a clear chime and a sexless disembodied voice. The gamer she'd liked least, on a very cursory assessment, was alone in the kitchen.

"Hi," he said. "I'm Warks, you're Chloe. Don't ever call me Matt, you don't know me. You ready for your initiation?"

"Of course."

"Get yourself rationed up." He sat and watched; his big soft arms folded, while Chloe, trying to look cool about it, wrangled an unfamiliar coffee machine, identified food sources, and put together cereal, milk, toast, butter, honey....

"You do know that's a two-way screen in your room, don't you? Like Orwell."

"Oh, wow," said Chloe. "Thank God I just didn't happen to stand in front of it naked!"

"Hey, set your visibility to whatever level you like. The controls are intuitive."

"Thanks." Chloe gave him her best bright-student gaze. "Now what happens?"

"Finish your toast, go back to your room. Review your costume, armor and weaponry options, which you'll find pretty basic. Unless maybe you've brought some DW grey-market collateral you plan to install? On the sly?"

She shook her head, earnestly. "Not me!"

Warks smirked. "Yeah, I know. I'm house security. I've deep-scanned your devices, and checked behind your eyes and between your ears also: You're clean. Make your choices, don't be too ambitious, and we'll be waiting in the Rumpus Room."

He then vanished. Literally.

Chloe wished she'd spotted she was talking to a hologram, and hoped she'd managed not to look startled. She wondered if Matt, er, *Warks*'s bullying was him getting in character, or was she being officially hazed by her new housemates? *They will challenge me*, she thought. *They have a belief that they know is unbelievable, and whatever I say they think I'm planning to make them look like fools. I'll need to win their trust.*

The Rumpus Room was in the basement. The hardware was out of sight, except for a different set of Boxes, and a carton of well-worn foam batons. The gamers sat around a table again: long and squared this time, not circular. A wonderful, paper-architecture 3-D map covered almost the whole surface. It was beautiful and detailed: a city at the heart of a knot of sprawling roads; a wasteland that spread around it over low hills: complete with debased housing, derelict industrial tract; scuzzy tangled woodland—

"We need to correct your ideas," said Josie Nicks, the black-haired woman. "I'm Lete in there, called the Whisperer, I'm a shaman. This is *not* a 'Post-Apocalyptic' game. Or a 'Futuristic Dystopia.' Darkening World is set now. It's fictional, but completely realistic."

But you have zombies, thought Chloe. Luckily she remembered in time that modern "zombies" had started life, so to speak, as a satirical trope about blind, dumb, brain-dead consumerism, and kept her mouth shut.

"Second thing," said Sol, the gamer with no hair in front, and a skinny pigtail down his back. "They call me Artos, it means The Bear. You know we have a karma system?"

"Er, yeah. Players can choose to be good or evil, and each has its advantages?"

"*Wrong.* In DW we have reality karma. Choose to be good, you get *no* reward—"

"Okay, I do remember, it was in your wiki. But I thought if you choose good, every time, and you complete the game, you can come back with godlike powers?"

"I was speaking. Choose good: no reward. Choose evil, be better off, but you've degraded the Q, the *quality of life*, for the whole game. Keep that up and get rich and powerful: But you'll do real damage. Everyone feels the hurt, they'll know it was you, and you'll be hated."

"Thanks for warning me about that."

"The godlike power is a joke. Never happens. Play again, you start naked again. If you ever actually *complete* this game, please tell someone. It'll be a first."

"In *battle*, you're okay," Lete reassured her. "Anything goes, total immunity—"

"Another thing," broke in the redhead. "I'm Aileen, as you know: Beat when you meet me in there. You can't be unaligned. In battle you can be Military, Non-Com or Frag. You're automatically Frag; it means outcasts, dead to our past lives, because you're on our team. We mend trouble, but we sell our swords. Everyone in the Frag has an origin story, and you need to sort that out."

"You can adapt your real world background," suggested Reuel, "Since you're not a gamer. It'll be easier to remember."

"There is no kill limit—" said Jun, a.k.a. Kardish the Assassin, suddenly.

Chloe waited, but apparently that was it. The team's official murderer must be the laconic type. Which made sense, if you thought about it.

"Non-battlefield estates are Corporate, Political and Media," resumed Sol. "They merge into each other, and infiltrate everybody. They're hated as inveterate traitors, but courted as sources of supply. So tell us. Who paid your wages, Chloe?"

Seven pairs of eyes studied her implacably. Darkening World attracted all shades of politics, but this "Frag" house, Chloe knew, was solidly anti-Establishment. Clearly they'd been digging into her CV. "Okay, er, Corporate and Political." A flush of unease rose in her cheeks, she looked at the table to hide it. "But not *directly*—"

"Oh, for God's sake!" groaned Warks. "When you meet me in there call me Markus, noob.... You guys sound as if you've swallowed a handbook. You don't need to know all that, Chloe. Kill whatever moves, if you can, that's the entire rules. It's only a *game*."

"Just don't kill me," advised Reuel, wryly. "As I'm you're only friend."

Warks thumped the beautiful map, crushing a suburb. "Let's GO!"

Chloe knew what to expect. She'd trained for this. You don the padding on your limbs and body. Box on your head, baton in hand and you're in a different world. The illusion that you are "in the map" is extraordinary. A Battle Box does things to your sense of space and balance, as well as to your sensory perceptions. You see the enemy; you see your teammates: You can speak to them; they can speak to you. The rest is too much to take in, but you get instructions on your sidebar from the team leader and then, let battle be joined—

It was overwhelming. Karma issues didn't arise, they had no chance to arise, there was only one law. Kill everything that moves and doesn't have a green glowing outline (the green glow of her housemates)—

Who she was fighting or why, she *had no idea*—

HEY! HEY! CHLOE!

Everything went black, then grey. She felt no pain: She must be dead. She stood in the Rumpus Room, empty-handed, a pounding in her ears. The gamers were staring at her. Someone must have taken the Box off her head: She didn't remember.

She screamed at them, panting in fury—

"Anyone who says *it's only a game* right now! Will get *killed, killed, KILLED!*"

"Hayzoos!" exclaimed Warks. "What a sicko! Shame that wasn't live!"

The others looked at him, and stared at Chloe, and shook their heads.

"Maybe...." suggested Aileen, slowly. "Maybe that *sidequest—?*"

Chloe stayed in her room, exhausted, for the rest of the day. Two hours (by the Game Clock) of rampageous, extreme unreal violence had wiped her out. Her notes on the session were shamefully sparse. When she emerged, summoned for "evening chow" by that sexless voice, she was greeted as she entered the kitchen with an ironic cheer.

"The mighty sicko packs a mean battle-axe!"

At least sicko (or psycho) was a positive term; according to her DW glossary.

"Many big strong guys, first time, come out shaking after they see the first head sliced off. DW's neural hook-up is *that* good. Are you *sure* you never played before?"

"Never." Chloe hung her head, well aware she was being hazed again. "I've never been on a battlefield. I've only slain a few zombies, and er, other monsters—"

"You took to it like a natural," said Reuel. "Congratulations."

But there was a strange vibe, and it wasn't merely that the compliments rang hollow. The gamers had been discussing her future, and the outcome didn't feel good.

The Skate and the South Wind

Next morning the chime-voice directed her to go to Reuel's office after breakfast. Nobody was about. She ate alone, feeling ritually excluded, in the wired-up and Wi-Fi saturated kitchen: surrounded by invisible beings who watched her every move, and who would punish or reward her according to their own secret rules.

An abject victim of the tech-mediated magical worldview, she crept to the manager's office—as cowed as if somebody had pointed a bone at her. The door was shut; she knocked. A voice she didn't know invited her to enter.

Reuel was not present. A young man with blue, metallic skin, wearing only a kilt of iridescent feathers, plus an assortment of amulets and weapons, sat by her sponsor's desk. His eyes were a striking shade of purple, his lips plum-colored and beautifully full. His hair, braided with more feathers, was the shimmering emerald of a peacock's tail. He was smiling calmly, and he was slightly transparent.

"Oh," she said. "Who are you?"

Three particularly fine feathers adorned his brow: blue, red and grass-green.

"I am Reuel's friend, Pevay. You are Chloe. I am to be your Spirit Guide."

"That's great," said Chloe, looking at the three fine feathers. "Thanks."

"You're wondering how I can be seen 'in the real world?' It's simple. The house is Wi-Fi'd for DW holos." Pevay spread his gleaming hands. "I am in the game right here."

"I'm not getting thrown out?"

"Having proved yourself in battle, you are detailed to seek the legendary 56 Enamels; a task few have attempted. These are jewels, highly prized; said by some to possess magical powers. I could tell you their history, *Chloe*."

The hologram person waited, impassive, until she realized she had to cue him.

"I'd love to know. Please tell."

"They were cut from the heart of the Great Meteorite by an ancient people, whose skills are lost. Each of the 56 has a story, which you will learn in time, *Chloe*."

This time she recognized the prompt. "Okay. Where are they now?"

"Scattered over the world-map. Do you accept the quest, *Chloe*?"

Chloe hadn't *emphasized* her interest in the alien. She'd talked about sharing the whole game house experience. But she wasn't sure she believed her luck. *I'm looking at Reuel*, she thought, glumly. *The whole secret is that Reuel likes to dress up in NPC drag, and he's going to keep me busy on a sidequest so I can't ruin the team's gameplay.* Then she remembered the seventh shadowy character, at the meeting on the shore.

Her heart leapt and her spine tingled.

"I accept. But I don't know if I'm staying, and it sounds like this could take forever?"

"Not so. I know all the cheats." Pevay grinned. His teeth were silvery white, and pointed. He had a lot of them. "With me by your side you'll be picking them up in handfuls."

She went down to the Rumpus Room alone. The basement was poorly lit, drably decorated and smelled of old sweat. Thick cork flooring swallowed her footsteps. Her return to anthropology's Eden had morphed into a frat-house horror movie or, (looking on the bright side) a sub-standard episode of *Buffy*. The map was gone. The Battle Boxes lay on the table, all personalized except for one. Glaring headlamp eyes, a Day of the Dead Mexican Skull. A Jabba the Hutt toad, a Giger Alien with Hello Kitty ears. A dinosaur crest, and a spike from which trailed a lady's (rather grubby) crimson samite sleeve.

Invisible beings watched her. Elders, or ancestors. Scared and thrilled, the initiate donned the padding, lifted the unadorned Box and settled it on her head. She tried not to make these actions look solemn and hieratic, but probably failed—

She stood in an alley between high dark dirty walls. She heard traffic. As the synesthetic kicked in, she could even *smell* the filthy litter. Pevay was there in his scanty peacock regalia: looking as if he'd been cut and pasted onto the darkness.

Who are you, really? she wondered. *Reuel? Or some other gamer in NPC drag, who's been messing with Reuel and his friends?* But she wasn't going to ask any questions that implied disbelief; not yet, anyway. Chloe sought not to spoil the fun.

"Are you ready, *Chloe*?"

"Yes."

"Good. All cities in the Darkening World are hostile to the Frag except one, which you won't visit for a long time. To pass through them unseen we use what's called the Leopard Skill, in the Greater Southern Continent where your people were formed. Here we call it fox-walking. You have observed urban foxes?"

"Er, no."

"You'll soon pick it up. Follow me."

To her relief, *fox-walking* was a game skill she'd met before. She leapt up absurdly high walls and scampered along impossibly narrow gutters, liberated by the certainty that she couldn't break her neck, or even sprain an ankle. Crouching on rooftops she stared down at CGI crowds of citizens, rushing about. The city was *stuffed* with people, who apparently all had frenetically busy night-lives. She was delighted when she made it to the top of a seventy story tower: though not too clear how this helped them to "cross the city unseen."

Her Box sidebar told her she'd won a new skill.

Pevay was waiting by a tall metal gantry. The glitzy lights and displays that had painted even the zenith of the night sky were fading. Mountains took shape on the horizon. "That's where we're going," he said. "Meteorite Peak is the highest summit."

"How do we get there?" She hoped he'd say *learn to fly.*

"Swiftly and in luxury; most of the way. But now we take the zip-wire."

The Jet Lift Terminal was heaving with beautiful people, even at dawn. Chloe stared, admiring the sheen and glow of wealth: Until one of them suddenly stared back. A klaxon blared, armed guards appeared. Chloe was grabbed, and thrown out of the building.

<Free-running only requires a cool head> said Pevay's voice in her ear, as if over a radio link. <Now you must learn the skill 'unseen in

plain sight.' Step quietly and don't look at them. Give no sign of curiosity or attention.>

Apparently her guide had no cheat for humans with idiotic reflexes. It took her a while to reach the departure lounge, where he was waiting at the gate. A woman in uniform demanded her travel documents. Chloe didn't know what to do, and Pevay offered no suggestions.

"*Guards!*" shrieked the woman. Pevay reached over and drew her towards him. He seemed to kiss her on the mouth. She shriveled, fell to the red carpet and disappeared.

Hey, thought Chloe, slightly creeped out. What happened to *fictional but completely realistic?* But she hurried after her guide, while the armed-security figures just stood there.

"Was I supposed to have obtained the papers?"

<Yes, but it's a tiresome minigame. Sometimes we'll miss those out.>

The Jet Lift took them to a viewpoint café near the summit of Meteorite Peak. They stole mountaineering gear, evaded more guards and set out across the screes. Far below, the beautiful people swarmed over their designer-snowfield resort. The cold was biting.

<Take care> whispered her guide. <There are Military about.>

Chloe reached for her weapons, but found herself equipping *camouflage* instead.

"I didn't know I was slaved to you," she grumbled.

"Not always. I'm detailed to keep you away from combat. Your enthusiasm is excessive."

They reached the foot of a crag: a near-vertical face of shattered, reddish rock, booby-trapped with a slick of ice. "This stage," said Pevay "requires the advanced skill *Snow Leopard*. You'll soon pick it up, just follow me."

The correct hand and footholds were warm to the touch: She should have been fine. But she hadn't thought to consume rations or equip extra clothing. The cold had been draining her health. She felt weak, and slipped often: wasting more health. When she reached the ledge where Pevay was waiting, and saw the cliff above them, she nearly cried. She was finished.

"You missed a trick," said Pevay, sternly. "Remember the lesson."
He gave her a tablet from one of his amulet-boxes, and they climbed on.

The ascent was exhilarating, terrifying; mesmeric. She watched her guide lead the final pitch, and could almost follow the tiny clues that revealed the route to him; found by trial and error if you saw only the rock: obvious if you were immune to the game's illusions—

High above the clouds they reached a rent in the cliff face: One last traverse and Chloe stepped into a cave. A chunk of different rock stood in a niche: adorned with tattered prayer flags and faded sacred paintings; a radiant jewel embedded in its surface—

"This is a shard of the meteorite," said Pevay. "The ancient people fired their first Enamel here without detaching it from the matrix. Take it, *Chloe*."

The jewel lay in her hand, shining with a thousand colors.

"You have won the first Enamel. Save your game, *Chloe*!"

No, she thought. *I'll do better*. She replaced the prize, stepped backwards, and fell.

She stood with her guide in the icy wind, at the foot of the crag: an attack-helicopter squadron clattering across the sky behind them.

"Are you crazy?" yelled Pevay, above the din. "You just blew the whole thing!"

"You helped me when I went wrong and I'm grateful, but I want to do it *right*."

He seemed at a loss for words, but she thought he was pleased.

"Save your rations. I'll give you another rocket fuel pill."

She accepted his medicine humbly. "Thanks. Now cut the dual controls and I'll lead." When she took the jewel again, she felt as if her whole body had turned to light. "That was *amazing!*"

Pevay laughed. "Now you're getting the juice, new kid!" A spring had risen from the cavity where the jewel had been. He bent to drink, grinning at her with all his silvery teeth.

"Oh, yeah! That's some *good* stuff!"

DW had a warp system that would take you around the world map instantly, but Chloe hadn't earned access to it. She was glad Pevay didn't offer her a free ride. She didn't feel cold as they walked down: Just slightly mad; euphoria bubbling in her brain like video game altitude sickness. The contours of this high desert, even its vast open-cast mines, seemed as rich and wonderful; as colorful and varied as any natural environment—

"It was fantastic to watch you climb! You're an NPC, I suppose you can see in binary, the way insects see ultraviolet. I was thinking about a myth called *The Skate and the South Wind* that I read about in Lévi-Strauss. He's an ancient shaman of my trade: hard to understand, heavy on theory; kind of wild, but truly great. A skate, the fish, is thin one way, wide if you flip it another way. Dark on the top surface, light on the underside. The skate story is about binary alternation. Lévi-Strauss said so-called 'primitive' peoples build mental structures, and formulate abstract ideas, like 'binary code,' from their observation of nature. All you need is your environment and you can develop complex cognition from scratch—"

"You need food, Chloe. I'd better give you another rocket fuel pill."

"No, I'm fine. Just babbling. Do you really come from another planet?"

He seemed to ponder, gazing at her. His pupils were opaque black gems. Her own avatar probably looked just as uncanny-valley: But who looked out from *Pevay*'s unreal eyes?

"They say you're an anthropologist. Tell me about that, *Chloe*."

"I study aspects of human society by immersing myself in different social worlds—"

"You collect societies? Like a beetle collector!"

If a complex NPC can tease Pevay's tone was mocking. But if truth be known, Chloe saw nothing wrong with being a beetle collector. People expected more, a big idea, a revelation: But she was a hunter. She just liked finding things out; tracking things down. She'd be happy to go on doing that forever.

"I started out in Neuroscience. I was halfway through my doctorate when I decided to change course—"

"The eternal student. And you finance your hobby by working for whoever will pay?"

Chloe shrugged. "You can't always choose your funding partners. The same goes for DW, doesn't it? I try not to do anything harmful. Are you going to answer my question?"

"What was your question, *Chloe*?"

"Do you really come from another planet?"

"I don't know."

She sighed. "Okay, fine. You don't want to answer, no problem."

"I have answered. *I don't know*. I don't remember a life outside the game. Are you here to decide whether the gamers' belief is true or false?"

"No! Nothing like that. Most people's cultural beliefs aren't fact or evidence based, even if the facts can be checked or the evidence is there. I'm interested in how an extraordinary belief fits into the game house's social model."

"Then the team should have no quarrel with you. You don't seem fatigued. Shall we collect the second Enamel now, *Chloe*?"

"I thought you'd never ask."

The gamers weren't around when she returned, but she must have done something right. That evening she found she'd been given access to the transcripts, playback and neuro-data for the three sessions she'd shared. The material was somewhat redacted; but that was okay. What people consider private they have a right to withhold. But what *mountains* of this stuff DW must generate! And *all* the records just a fleeting reflection of the huge, fermenting mass of raw computation that underpinned the wonderful world she'd visited; and all powered by the *juggernaut* economic engine of the video game industry—

No neuro-stream for Pevay, of course…. *But why not?* she wondered. Maybe he's a mass of tentacles or an intelligent gas cloud in his natural habitat. He's still supposed to be interfacing with the game, some way. Shouldn't he show up, in some kind of strange traces? Anomalies in the NPC data? She'd have to ask Reuel. He'd have an answer. People take a great deal of trouble justifying extraordinary beliefs. They're ready for anything you ask. Still, it would be worth finding out.

If Pevay *wasn't* being sneakily controlled by a human gamer he was an impressive software artefact: able to simulate convincing conversation, and a convincing presence. Chloe wasn't fooled by these effects. People got "natural" replies from the crudest forms of AI by cueing responses without realizing it. They were doing most of the work themselves. *People*, she thought, *are only too eager to respond emotionally to dumb objects, never mind state-of-the-art illusions. A favorite* hat *will fire up the same neurons as the face of a dear friend. (Making nonsense of that famous Turing Test!)* But the quality of the neuro was amazing. If she couldn't examine Pevay's data, why not try some reverse engineering?

Mirror neurons, predictive neurons, decision-making cells in the anterior cingulate…. All kinds of fun. She worked late into the night, running her own neuro-data through statistical filters, just to see what came out; while tapping her stylus on her smiling lips. (A habit she had when the hunt was up.) *Start from the position that the gamers aren't "primitives" and they aren't deluded. They're trying to make sense of something.*

A Fox in the City

Chloe was summoned to a second meeting on the beach, and told that she could stay, as long as she was pursuing her sidequest, and as long as Pevay was willing to be her guide. She could also publish her research, subject to the approval of all and any DW gamers involved— but only if she collected all 56 Enamels. While living in the house she must not communicate Darkening World's business to outsiders, and this would be policed. Interviews and shared gameplay sessions were at the discretion of individual team members.

Chloe was ecstatic. The Enamels quest was so labyrinthine it could last forever, and publication so distant that she wasn't even thinking about it. She eagerly signed the contract that was presented to her, back in Reuel's office; a DW lawyer in digital attendance. Reuel told her she'd find the spare Battle Box in her room. She was to log on from that location in the future. The team needed the Rumpus Room to themselves.

She sent a general message to friends and family, and another to her supervisor, saying she wouldn't be reachable. She didn't fancy having her private life policed by Matt Warks, and nobody would be concerned. It was typical Chloe behavior, when on the hunting trail.

Chloe had envisaged working *with* a team of DW gamers: observing their interaction with the "alien NPC" in gameplay; talking to them afterwards. Comparing what they told her, and how they behaved, with her observations, and with the neuro.... She soon realized this was never going to happen. The gamers had their sessions, of which she knew nothing. She had her sessions with Pevay. Otherwise— except for trips to a morose little park, which she jogged around for exercise—she was alone in her room, processing such a flood of data she hardly had time to sleep. Game logs; transcripts; neuro. "Alien sentient" fan mail. Global DW content. She even saw some of the house's internal messaging.

Nobody knocked on her door. Once or twice she wandered about after dark looking for company. All she found was a neglected, empty-feeling house, and a blur of sound from behind forbidding closed doors. She felt like Snow White, bewildered; waiting for the Seven Dwarves to come home.

Only Aileen and Reuel agreed to be interviewed face to face. The others insisted on talking over a video link, and behaved like freshly captured prisoners of war: stone-faced, defiant and defensive. Needless to say they all protected the consensus belief, in this forced examination. Josie evaded the topic by talking about her own career. Sol, the friendliest gamer (except for Reuel), confided that he'd pinpointed Pevay's home system, and it was no more than 4.3 light years away. Then he got anxious, and retracted this statement, concerned that he'd "said something out of line".... Warks smugly refused to discuss Pevay, as Chloe didn't understand Information Universe Science. Aileen, who was Reuel's girlfriend (sad to say), believed implicitly, *implicitly*, that Pevay came from a very distant star system. Jun, the silent one, had the most interesting response: muttering that *"the alien thing was the best explanation,"* but then he clammed up completely, so she had to cut the interview short. But Reuel was the only player, apparently, who'd had sustained contact. Spirit Guides rarely appeared on the field of battle. They had no place there. Not much of a warrior, her sponsor was the acquisitions man, embarking on quests with Pevay when the team needed a new piece of kit; a map; a secret file. Or lootable artworks they could sell, like the 56 Enamels—

Chloe had not realized she was doing Reuel's job. She was as thrilled as an old school adventurer; allowed to decorate his own trading canoe. The "natives" had awarded her a place in their social model!

Maintaining any extraordinary belief, in a world of unbelievers, becomes a conspiracy. She hadn't expected anyone to break ranks (although Jun had come close). But she was all the more puzzled that she'd been accepted by the team at all. Why had they let her in?

She resigned herself to the isolation. Documenting her own interaction with Pevay was a fascinating challenge, in itself. By day (gaming outside daylight hours was against house rules) they went hunting. By night she worked on the data, which was no longer one-sided. Somebody had quietly decided to give her access to the house's DW NPC files: A privilege Chloe equally quietly accepted. She analyzed the material obsessively; she invented new filters, and still she wasn't sure. Was she being hazed by these cunning IT freaks? Or was what she saw real? She couldn't decide. But she was *loving* the investigation.

Apart from once, when she was detailed to join a groceries run in Matt Warks's van, she only encountered the gamers if she happened to be in the kitchen when someone else came foraging. Aileen met her by the coffee machine, and congratulated her on settling in so well. Chloe remembered what Sol had said about Aileen becoming her greatest fan. "It's like you've always been here. You *understand* us, and it's great."

Soon after this vestigial conversation she was invited to join a live sortie. She'd been hoping this might happen, having noticed the "any DW gamers" catch-all clause in her permission to publish: But she went to the Rumpus Room feeling nervous as all hell.

Reuel, Aileen and Sol shook her warmly by the hand.

Warks, Jun and Josie nodded, keeping their distance.

Then Aileen gave Chloe a hug, and presented her with the spare Box (which had disappeared from Chloe's room the night before, when she was absent foraging for supper). It was newly embellished with a pattern of coiling leafy fronds.

"Chloe means *green shoots*," explained Aileen, shyly. "D'you like it?"

"I love it," said Chloe. And she truly was thrilled.

"Be cool," said Reuel, uneasily. "Real soldiers try to stay alive."

Chloe didn't get a chance to embarrass the team with her excess enthusiasm. The mission went horribly wrong, almost at once. They were in the Amazon Basin, with a Frag and Military combined force called "The Allies": defending the land rights of an Indigenous People. Plans had been leaked, The Allies were overwhelmed. The Empire raiders counted enormous coup and vacated the scene; it was all over inside an hour.

Her brain still numbed by the *hammer, hammer, hammer* of artillery fire, Chloe blundered about, in the silence after battle, without having fired a shot: unable to make sense of the torrent of recriminations on her sidebar. She ran into someone escorting a roped-up straggle of Indigenous Non-Combatants—and recognized the jousting spike and the samite sleeve. She'd been sure that romantic helm was Reuel's, but it was the Battle ID of Josie Nicks; or "Lete the Shaman."

"What are you doing with the Non-Coms, Lete?" asked Chloe.

"Taking them to the Allied Commander for questioning. They might know something."

"Don't do that!"

"Nah, you're right. I can't be bothered. Someone else can pick them up." Methodically, Josie shot the non-combatants' knees out, and walked away. Chloe stared at the screaming heap of limbs and blood. Josie's victims all had the glowing outline. They were the avatars of human gamers, and seemed to be in real agony.

She ran after Josie. "Hey! Did you know they were *real people?*"

"'Course I did. Non-Coms can be sneaky bastards, prisoners are a nuisance, and it was fun. What's your problem?" Josie flopped down by a giant broken stump. "You know who I am, Chloe. You interviewed me. A female geek making a name in the industry is judged all the time. I need to be seen to be nasty: And this is the way I relax. Okay?"

She took out her bag of bones and tossed them idly.

"Was it you who convinced the team to let me stay?" asked Chloe. "I've been wondering. I know it wasn't Reuel, and you're the shaman—"

Josie, looking so furious Chloe feared for her own kneecaps, swept up the bones and jumped to her feet. "No, it wasn't." she snarled. "You're breaching etiquette, Corporate spook. Leave me alone. Find the quick way home and I hope it's messy."

Chloe didn't find the quick way home. There was nobody around to kill her, and suicide, she knew, was frowned upon. She drifted on, avoiding unexploded ordnance, heaped bodies and random severed limbs, until Reuel found her. His helmet decoration was the dinosaur crest. Which made sense; sort of. Minimum effort. He offered her a fat green stogie.

"Lete told me you were upset. Don't be, Greenshoot. Guys who take the Non-Com option know what they want from the game, and they do us all a favor. I admire them."

"I don't understand," said Chloe. "The whole thing. Look at this, this *awful* place—"

"Yeah," sighed Reuel. "Non-fantastic war-gaming is hell. It's kind of an expiation. Like, we play the bad stuff, but we don't sugar it." He'd said the same in his interview. "But hey, I have *incredible* good news. I was waiting for a chance to tell you in the map, because this is special. Pevay's going to open a portal!"

"A *portal?*"

"Into his home world dimension. And I'm going to pass through it!"

The Second Law

The house felt sullen. If the team was celebrating Reuel's news they were very quiet about it, and Chloe wasn't invited to share. Maybe she was thought to have jinxed the Amazon Basin event? Or maybe she was being paranoid. She once caught Jun in the kitchen and he silently, poker-faced, made her a cup of tea, but she didn't dare to ask him how he felt. She finally asked Aileen, who had started messaging her, calling her *Greenshoot*.

<Scared. So scared. Really afraid for him.>

<For *Pevay?*> Chloe messaged back, astonished.

<NO! FOR REUEL. What if he can't get back? What if he doesn't get converted into game-avatar form and he explodes in the other dimension or he can't breathe or his skin boils off. I'm BEGGING him not to go. PLEASE help!>

<Maybe it won't work?> suggested Chloe. <Maybe nothing will happen?>

A wounded silence was the only answer.

Chloe started prowling at night again: no longer looking for company, just desperate for a change from her four walls. She couldn't leave the building in case she missed something, but she needed to think, and pacing helped.

The Darkening World subculture was going crazy. Offers from fans and fruitcakes eager to take Reuel's place were pouring in. A South Korean woman insisted her son, suffering from an incurable motor neuron disease, would be cured by a trip to another dimension, and pleaded for Reuel to make way (and pay their airfares). DW sceptics jeered in abusive glee: hoping Reuel would come back as a heap of bloody, inside-out guts. True believers who hadn't been singled out for glory insisted *their* alien NPCs knew nothing about this "portal," and Reuel was a fantasizing, attention-seeking loser—

Chloe had no terms for comparison. She'd had no contact with any "alien NPC" other than Pevay. She hadn't interviewed anyone except her housemates—an exercise that had not been a great success. Her choices had been limited from the start. She'd had to find a game house within reach: She was partly financing herself and couldn't pay huge airfares. And the players had to speak either English or Spanish—

But how would you know, anyway? How could you tell if you were talking to a "different" DW alien? An NPC is an avatar controlled by the game: code on a server. Anyone who controlled Pevay could have a whole wardrobe of DW avatars. All over the world, interacting with multiple gamers, yet all with the same "alien sentient" source—

It made her head spin.

The Darkening World house was haunted. The hunter's prey had become the hunter. Ancestors and elders looked on; offering no protection.... She spun around and there was Pevay, cut and pasted on the shadows. He turned and led her, his footfalls making no sound, to a dark corner opposite the door to Reuel's office.

Fox-walking again, she thought. "Why are you following me?" she asked.

"Why do you walk around the house at night?"

"I'm ... uneasy. Someone's betraying them, you know. Is it Josie?"

"No, it's Matt Warks."

His eyes gleamed. She thought of the eighth person on the beach. Her persistent illusion (recorded in her notes) that there were *seven* players, not six, living in this game house—

"Oh, right. I decided he was too obvious."

"Gamers can be obtuse. They tend to believe what they're told, and ignore what they are not told. It's a trait many kinds of people share, *Chloe*."

"Since we're talking, what do players call this game, where you come from?"

"Darkening World, of course."

She noticed he'd dropped the story that he didn't remember his other life. "But how do they understand what that means? On your planet?"

"Easily, I assure you. Any sufficiently advanced technology—"

"Is indistinguishable from magic. Yeah, I know that one. Arthur C. Clarke's Third Law."

"I was speaking. Any sufficiently advanced technology destroys its environment."

Chloe's spine had started tingling all the way up to her ears.

"There is a Second Law," added Pevay. "About heat. The same problem, same limits, for my world and yours."

"Always about heat," whispered Chloe. "I know that one too. Our peoples should get together."

The silence that followed was electric. Chloe had *no idea* where this was going—

"Chloe, when next we meet in the map, we're going after Enamel 27."

Fine, she thought. *Back to the gameplay. Enough heavy lifting for now.*

"Twenty-seven," she repeated. This notorious Enamel was rated practically impossible to obtain, on the DW message boards. "Okay, if you say so. Am I ready?"

"With me beside you, yes."

"Fantastic. Pevay, are you really going to 'open a portal?' What does that even *mean*?"

But he'd gone.

She was back in her room before she realized he'd led her to one of the few and tiny blind spots in house security's surveillance. Their conversation had been off the Warks record.

The Bar-Headed Geese

Logging on from her bunk had worried Chloe at first. She was afraid she'd break something, or run into walls and knock herself unconscious. She was used to it now: She could set the Box to limit her range of real movement. She stood on the shore of a lake, a vast silver puddle, shimmering on a dry plain among huge, naked hills. Her Box told her Pevay was near, but all she could see was a whole lot of birds. All she could hear was a *gaggle, gaggle, gaggle* of convivial honking. Her eye level was strange, and she'd been deprived of audible speech: She only had her radio link.

    <Pevay? Where are we?>

    <On the High Desert Plateau, about fifteen hundred kilometers from Meteorite Peak.>

    <My body feels weird. What am I?>

    <You're a bar-headed goose, *Chloe.*>

The birds must be geese. They were pearly grey, with an elegant pattern of black stripes on their neat little heads. They seemed friendly: not about to attack her for being an outsider, like the vicious troupe of langur monkeys she'd been forced to join, to get the eighteenth jewel—

    <We're going to hide ourselves in their Southern Migration. Very, very few gamers have hit on this solution, although the clues are there. This is, in fact, the only possible way to reach the twenty-seventh Enamel alive, and the timing is tight. Are you ready, *Chloe*?>

    <Yes.>

    <When the flock rises, rise with them. You must gain altitude very quickly. *Push* on the downthrust; fold your wings inward on the upstroke. You have been in battle twice?>

    <Not really,> confessed Chloe. <Once in the sandbox, and a live sortie that was sort of screwed up. But you must know about that.>

    <Be prepared for the noise. We are rare, and there are many hunters who have paid good money to count coup on us. Keep a cool head and push on that downstroke. You'll soon pick it up. Just follow me.>

The geese rose, in one massed storm of wings. Chloe pushed on the downstroke: tumbled, struggled and found her rhythm in a cacophony of high-powered gunshot. She pushed and pushed until the desert was far below; and her success was glorious.

Her Box told her she'd attained the advanced skill Migrating Goose.

    <Well done,> said Pevay's calm voice in her ear. <Now, conserve energy. Stay in formation; keep well behind the leaders and away from the edges. Fly low along valleys, where the air is richer. Push to rise

above the high passes. You must keep your wings beating, never falter, and you will not fail.>

The twenty-seventh Enamel was the back-breaker. You got one shot. If you made a second attempt the jewel wouldn't be there. Chloe'd had plenty of time to regret her eager signing of that contract, but really it made no difference. If she failed to collect all 56 Enamels, and the gamers insisted she couldn't publish, she'd still have learned a lot. Actually she was glad she was trying for the twenty-seventh. It would be so *amazing* if she made it, and she had nothing to fear. After many hours of absurd daring and insane patience, she'd won thirteen Enamels so far. There were plenty more. She could go on pursuing her sidequest for months; for another year, for *as long as Pevay was willing to be her guide.* That dratted contract said so! Living in the moment, she pushed on the downstroke, folded on the upstroke, and the crumpled map of the high desert flew away beneath her.

Halfway across the ravaged Himalaya; maybe somewhere close to the eroded, ruined valley of Shangri-La, Pevay prompted her to lose altitude. She followed him, spiraling down. Her Box cut out for a moment: Then they stood on turf in their human forms, on a precarious spur of rock, surrounded by staggering, naked, snow-streaked heights; like two window-cleaners on a tiny raft above Manhattan. A small grey stupa sat on the green spur.

The flight had been a physical feat of endurance, not just a game-feat. Chloe's health was nearly spent and her head was spinning. The crucial questions she'd planned to ask on this trip, which might be the last before the portal, had slipped out of her grasp—

"Pevay. *You* told the team to let me stay, didn't you? *You* advised them to give me a sidequest?"

"My role is to offer advice, *Chloe.*"

"I think you wanted to talk—to someone other than a gamer. You could be anyone, couldn't you? You could be an animal. You can take any shape, can't you?"

"Of course, in the game. So can you; *Chloe.*"

"If Africa's the *Greater Southern Continent*, what do you call South America, in Darkening World?"

"The *Lesser Southern Continent*?" suggested Pevay, patiently.

Some of Chloe's dearest friends were Colombian, including two of her grandparents. She took offense. "Huh. That's garbage. That's insulting. On what grounds, '*Lesser*'?"

"Land area? Population? Number of nations? Of major cities? It's only a game, Chloe."

"Oh yeah, dodging responsibility. I think you should say '*I'm* only a game!' "

"Take the jewel."

Pevay was smiling. There'd be time to discuss what she'd just let slip when she wasn't dizzy with fatigue. The twenty-seventh Enamel shone in the cupped palms of a cross-legged stone goddess, atop of the stupa mound. She had no idea what kind of final challenge she faced: might as well just go for it. Armed and dangerous, worn out and not nearly dangerous enough, she bowed to the stupa, and claimed the jewel. Immediately all hell broke loose.

She was knee-deep in Enamels. They poured out of the sky.

"No!" yelled Chloe, appalled. "NO!!! PEVAY! You sneaky BASTARD!"

"The great hero who secures Enamel 27," said her guide. "Has earned all the rest. Congratulations. Your quest is complete and my work is done."

He vanished. He'd warned her she'd be picking up the jewels in handfuls.

Chloe took off the Box and returned to her shabby bunk: exultant and heartbroken. The Enamels quest was over too soon and she had *loved* it. She didn't realize the full horror of what Pevay had done until the next day, when the team told her her stay was over.

The portal would be opened without her.

The 56 Enamels

A year later, long before she'd finished working on her Darkening World paper, Reuel messaged Chloe out of the blue. He was in town, and wanted to talk about old times. They met in a coffee bar, in the city where Chloe had a job at a decent university. Reuel was looking well. He didn't have pens in his hair. He wore a suit; he was working as an actuary.

"So what happened in the end?" said Chloe. "I mean, obviously I know you didn't end up stranded on Planet Zog. You came home safe. But what was it like, on the great day?"

Aileen had kept in touch, but Chloe had never had a full account. Recently, when she'd checked the Darkening World message boards, the "alien NPCs" strand seemed to have faded away.

"It's so cool that you followed the story," said Reuel. "You were a great guest. Okay, what happened was this." He frowned, as if trying to recall the details of something he'd left far behind; just for Chloe's sake.

"Pevay opened the portal. I passed through; I returned. I don't remember a thing about the other place."

"You don't remember. Wow. Just like Pevay. He didn't remember either."

Reuel shrugged. "I went to wherever Pevay comes from and I came back. My Box hadn't recorded anything. I didn't remember: And that's all."

"Were you really disappointed?"

"No," he said firmly. "It's how things were meant to be."

"What about Pevay? How did *he* think it went?"

"I never knew. Never saw him again. We had a different Spirit Guide after that. Looked like Pevay, but it wasn't the same guy. I think opening the portal cost him; maybe got him into trouble, and now he has to stay at home. Anyway, I've quit pro-gaming. I don't have the time. I also broke up with Aileen, by the way." He smiled, hopefully.

"That's sad," said Chloe. "Would you like another coffee? And then I have to dash."

The romance was gone.

Where do you find a leaf? In a forest.

Where do you find a new species? *In a rainforest* would be a good bet. Or any dynamic environment, rich in niches for life; where conditions conspire to create a hotbed of diversity.

Chloe had become interested in AI sentience when she was still an undergraduate. She'd taken a course in Artificial Intelligence; out of idle curiosity. She'd been at a lecture one day, watching a robot video (probably it was iCub) and a thought popped into her head, a random thought that would, eventually, change her career path.

No. This is not the way it happens.

Life is random, she wrote, in the secretive shorthand notebook she started using at this time. *(Nothing digital that might be compromising!) I bet mind is the same. Mind isn't about building cuter and cuter dolls. Or crippled slaves. Mind is a smolder that ignites, in its own sweet time, in a hot compost heap of inflammable material. We'll never build real AI sentience: It will be born. It will emerge from us; from what we are.*

Magic begins where technology ends.... When they feel competent people don't need magic. They only resort to extraordinary beliefs, rituals and words of power when they're out of their depth. That's what Malinowski had observed in Melanesia long ago, and it was still true; a truth about the human condition (like many of the traits once patronizingly called "Primitive!"). The gamers were extremely competent, but they'd known that Pevay was beyond them: So they called him an alien because the alternative was too scary. Chloe understood all that. She even understood why Pevay had vanished the way he did. By "opening a portal" he'd given the gamers closure, and covered his own tracks. But why had her Spirit Guide double-crossed her? Maybe she'd never know.

A datastick had arrived in the post, soon after her banishment. It held the 56 Enamels: They were hers to keep. Chloe had been touched at the gesture; *astounded* when she looked up the monetized value of her digital treasure online. After she'd met with Reuel she uploaded the jewels, and looked at them again. She would never sell. She would keep the Enamels forever, if only to remind her that in Darkening World *she had lived*.

Was Pevay scared of taking the final step? He and his kind were very far from helpless! But she had visions of the "human zoos" where Congo pygmies had been caged, with the connivance of her own people, in the bad old days. For this reason she'd kept quiet, and always would keep quiet. No decent anthropologist exploits her collaborators.

But the Enamels gave her hope.

Chloe published an interesting paper on the culture of online gaming teams. It was approved by the DW community, and well-received by her peers. And she waited.

One day an email arrived. The source was anonymized. Untraceable. The message was short. It said "You are cleared for publication, *Chloe*." It was signed DW.

And so Chloe Hensen embarked on the great adventure of her life. The rest is history.

Fieldwork

Shariann Lewitt

"GRANDMA, DO YOU think Ada Lovelace baked cookies?" We were in her kitchen and the scent of the cookies in the oven had nearly overwhelmed my childhood sensibilities.

"I don't think so sweetie," Grandma Fritzie replied. "She was English."

"Oh. Mama doesn't bake either."

Grandma Fritzie shook her head. "There wasn't any good food when she was young."

"Did her Mama bake?"

"Maybe. But not after they left Earth. They only had packaged food on Europa, and no ovens or hot cookies or anything good. That's why your Mama is so tiny. We're going to make sure you get plenty of good things to eat so you grow up big and strong."

Grandma Fritzie sneered when she said "packaged food." She was the head of the Mayor's Council on Children and Family Health, and I lived with her while Mama was in the hospital.

My mother won the Fields Medal when I was eight. That might not have presaged another breakdown if the press had reported it as "Irene Taylor, Russian-born American mathematician working in algebra" etc. etc. But of course they did not. Some reporter even asked me, "So what was it like, being Kolninskaya's granddaughter? You never knew your grandmother, of course...."

To which I replied that I knew my grandmother very well, that she lived all of three subway stops away in Brooklyn just like me and would tell me not to open the door to strangers. Then I slammed the door in the reporters' faces. I went to live with Grandma Fritzie and Grandpa George three days later when Mama went to the hospital.

The press couldn't just leave her alone. She'd been a hero, done something amazing and brave when she'd only been a bit older than me, and now she'd only been the fourth woman to win a Fields Medal, and the media had to be horrible to her.

Even when I was eight I knew she wasn't like other people's mothers, was fragile in some way I didn't understand, and I swore that I wasn't going to be like her. I was going to be like Daddy and Grandma Fritzie and Grandpa George.

And maybe even, though I wouldn't admit it, like Tatyana Kolninskaya, the famous grandmother I had never met. The one who had died and who my mother never talked about. Because at least Kolninskaya had gone out and explored, left her room, left our planet even. Unlike Mama, who never wanted to leave our brownstone in Park Slope except to go to her office, and even then didn't like to take the subway. *Too many people*, she said, which confused me. I thought she'd feel better with lots of people around. But, as Grandma Fritzie said, I was a sensible child and my mother's neuroses were not comprehensible to me then. I don't understand them now, either, but at least I understand where they came from and I'm pretty impressed that she's managed to function at all. Let alone become one of the leading mathematicians of her generation. Besides, everyone knows that mathematicians are a bit strange, even those who grew up on Earth with loving parents and all the fresh food they could ingest.

None of the Europa survivors returned to anything close to normal. Most accepted implants to mitigate the worst of their nightmares, but Mama was afraid that it would interfere with the part of her brain that saw into math the way she does. So she uses drugs to lessen the bouts of PTSD that even the Minos Station orphans who took the implants suffer to a lesser extent.

Now that I've been there, now that I've seen the ice and what remains of Minos Base, and flown that journey and have some idea of what she went through, finally, now I can forgive her. For her fears and her craziness but also for the way she disappeared into her work for so much of my life.

There is only forever the ice. It expands to the dull greenish horizon flat and grayish green, as if it teases at being alive.

Only of course it is not. Underneath is the sea, pulsing and alive. Maybe alive.

But the sea never fascinated my mother the way it did everyone else. She only cared for the ice.

The ice spoke to her. She loved the cores she pulled from it. Here a dusting of dark material that possibly came from an asteroid strike, and on another layer a slight change in color that indicated a change in chemical composition. She couldn't wait to get it back to the lab and see what had happened in that place, back then.

She loved the ice and it killed her. It killed all of them, and then we were trapped and there was the horror of the return I dare not remember. Therapy and meds forever keep me almost safe for moments, but then I drift and I can't quite understand with the clarity I have when I forego the chemical equilibrium. So I try to keep away from memories of the ice. Aunt Olga in Moscow has never been kind about it, but she is not the one who wakes up screaming from dreams about the long trip home, the pressure of navigation and celestial mechanics on the shoulders of a thirteen year old because almost all the grownups had died.

I read my mother's memoir on the way out. She had given it to me, me alone, not my brother or my father. And even though I had known that she was Tatyana Kolninskaya's daughter, that she had lived for more than two years on Europa and that it had formed her and destroyed her together, I had never really thought of her as a young girl living in that environment. I had only wanted to see her as a mother, as my mother. I didn't want to have to recognize her as a person apart from my need for her.

But then, I had asked far more of her and I knew it. And I was curious to know what Minos Base, and the great Tatyana Kolninskaya, had been like.

Tatyana Kolninskaya did foundational work on the preconditions for life on other planets, which had been a fundamental question for science. Kolninskaya, like many others, believed Europa the most likely body to host that life. Warm seas lurked under that ice, seas and oceans both, heated by friction.

According to the reports they sent back, they had discovered at least virus-like fragments of DNA. Not quite full animals, which was disappointing, but viruses could survive even hard vacuum. Had they come from asteroids or comets? Or were they the result of some previous contamination?

But the samples never made it back and until our mission no one had been able to corroborate the finding. We were going to sample and survey and see if they had made a mistake. We knew there was a possibility of contamination from their trip, or even possibly earlier robotic vehicles, but our PI had worked out a program to compare the DNA so that we'd be able to tell if some virus had hitched a ride and flourished here. Or confirm, finally, whether there was, in fact, life in the oceans beneath the ice.

> *I was always sure she loved the ice more than she loved me, but she was so happy at Minos. She sang with me in the evening when she got in. All of us kids got a skewed education. Surrounded by scientists and engineers in a narrow range of specialties, we did learn a fair bit about planetary geology and evolutionary biology, a smattering of useful mathematics, and how to play the clarinet. We all spoke the four mission languages (Russian, English, Mandarin, and Spanish) and, while we had no inkling of human history we had a firm grasp of the politics of getting grants (which I later realized mapped onto all human history with painful accuracy).*

Mama was acknowledged a genius of getting funding, as well as math. Not only for herself, but for her grad students and half the department. "I learned from my mother. It is the only talent we shared."

Somehow, I doubted that.

> *Apart from the sciences, our education had been— idiosyncratic. We studied the poetry of Neruda, Li Bai, Li Qingzhao, Luo Binwang, and Jorge Luis Borges formally. Otherwise literature was left to whatever random selections we made from the central computer library, which included the complete work of Isaac Asimov, Alice Munro and Tolstoy. The full works of Nabokov and Henry Miller were also there but barred to those under sixteen, but little of F. Scott Fitzgerald, George Bernard Shaw or Federico Garcia Lorca had been included. Nor were any French or German language writers represented. I didn't realize that people who were not from the Mission language groups ever wrote anything of note, though I am grateful for escaping* Moby Dick.*
> Theater and music formed most of our evening entertainment. Carlos' mother was a magical guitarist and my*

father played the violin, so sometimes we had impromptu concerts in the dining hall. We learned to play the clarinet because that was the only instrument available that the adults would let us children touch. Their own were too precious for beginners. Sometimes we would perform plays by Shakespeare, Chekhov, and Gilbert and Sullivan. I got into a nasty hair pulling fight with Wang YeFei when I was cast as Helena to her Hermia in A Midsummer Night's Dream. *Well, we were supposed to fight in that scene after all, but the adults stopped the production and both of us were not permitted to perform for three months. Which was especially painful for the audience of* Pirates of Penzance *since YeFei had the best voice of us all.*

We were celebrities of a sort, the Minos children, the Minos survivors. I was thirteen when I was placed in an elite Planetary Educational Foundation Center under yet another grant for the children of explorers with the rest.

There we learned that our greatest deficiency was table manners. We had none. My mother's sister's family in Moscow, who took me in for those first holidays after our return, was aghast at my inability to behave like a civilized person. They did not make any allowance for the trauma, and when I started screaming the morning we woke to an ice covered world, they returned me posthaste to the Center. I was never invited to return, and I have never seen them again, not even when I have visited Moscow as an adult.

The other Minos orphans had had much the same experiences, except Martin who had gone to LA where there was no ice. But she shrieked and dove under the dining table whenever jets flew by or trucks rumbled on the street, and so his family reacted just like all the rest. So the nine of us, who had lived together on the ice, bonded even more firmly. There were too many strangers. The food tasted wrong. We wore little clothing, and that all disposable. And the place was dangerous in all the wrong ways.

We could breathe the air and walk out without a suit. We wouldn't freeze or asphyxiate or die in explosive decompression (which made up many of our scary childhood stories), but we dared not speak to people we didn't know.

At least all the children had made it home. One of the two grownups who had survived and returned with us, flown the ship that I had navigated, never left a supervised facility again.

☼ ☼ ☼

"Mom's doing serious math," my big brother Sergei said when I got home to make the announcement.

Bad news. That meant she was off her meds. Which meant do not tell her anything important and most of all do not ever mention Europa. Just the word once set her off in a fit where she threw dishes out the window of our Park Slope brownstone. They hit the sidewalk when Mrs. Coombs was walking Tyrus and she told the entire neighborhood that Irene Taylor was off her head. Again.

I was only ten at the time and still in school in the neighborhood and the other kids looked at me like I was some kind of freak show. As usual, I went to live with my grandma when mom went crazy.

I have a perfectly good grandmother who is nothing like Tatyana Kolninskaya. Grandma Fritzie bakes the best chocolate chip cookies ever, is five foot ten with skin the color of milk chocolate and laugh lines around her mouth. She's a family physician, now head of the Mayor's staff specializing in children's services, and she works with domestic abuse victims on Thursday nights. Grandpa George is a dentist. He disapproves of cookies on principle and always tried to get us to eat apples instead. I don't need to tell you how well that went.

Tatyana Kolninskaya was a name in a textbook until I became advanced enough that I read her original work. And yeah, it was that brilliant. Really that brilliant. Of all the Minos team, she was the one who made the conceptual leaps about the possibilities for Europa.

But I never felt any particular connection with her. I knew the history and I couldn't avoid my mother's neuroses, but Kolninskaya had been dead for decades before I was born. No one looking at coffee-with-an-extra-cream skin and nappy haired me would ever guess I was half blond Russian. And I kind of like to keep it that way.

I'm just plain Anna Taylor and if anyone makes the connection to my Dad, well, okay. Dad insisted that they give me Kolninskaya as a middle name but I don't acknowledge it. No K on my degrees anywhere. No one has made any big deal that Paul Taylor, the jazz pianist, is married to Irina Maslova, who is the daughter of Tatyana Kolninskaya. Mom has gone by Irene Taylor ever since they married when she was a grad student, and all her degrees and publications and awards are under that sanitized, Anglicized name. As if changing her name could erase the Irina who had lived through Minos Station and navigated that ship back to Earth when she was just a kid.

Grandma Fritzie did not want me to go. "Honey, you'll be gone how long? It'll be years, and dark, and it's dangerous. I remember when Minos Station was lost in the ice. And think of the malnutrition. That's why your mother is so tiny. They didn't have any decent food out there on Europa. All those Minos children grew up undersized. What if you get pregnant and you have some tiny undernourished baby?"

I shrugged. "Mama isn't the only person in the world under five-ten." Grandma Fritzie and I are the shortest people in the family, excepting Mama, who is barely five-two. "And I'm not getting pregnant. After Minos, children aren't allowed on exploratory expeditions anymore. Besides, I'm not even dating anyone.

"We're not staying. We're just doing a prelim survey to confirm the findings from Minos, and it's a job and I'll get a ton of papers out of it. We just need a few samples to bring back. They didn't bring anything back, you know, so no one could verify their results."

"You're not dating anyone?" Grandpa George said. "What happened to that nice boy we met at Thanksgiving?"

"He didn't want kids. Besides, this is an amazing opportunity for me, especially right out of grad school. No matter what we find, there's so much to discover that there are going to be a zillion journal articles and I've got to publish my ass off to get myself a nice academic...."

"Language, young lady."

"Sorry Grandma."

"But she can't tell Mom," Sergei interrupted. "Mom's doing serious math." Which is why we were all huddled in Grandma and Grandpa's huge living room in Grand Army Plaza instead of Park Slope, even with Sergei visiting from Paris with his French wife and their new French baby.

"Honey, I don't know how she'd tell your mother even if Irene were taking her meds and then some," Grandma Fritzie said. "I'm not even sure that I approve."

"I certainly don't, that's for sure. I don't approve of any grandchild of mine leaving this planet," Grandpa George said. "Bad enough you have to study something as dangerous as volcanoes. I don't see why you couldn't study something safe like computers and stay right here on Earth. Humans belong on Earth, not traipsing around the solar system getting themselves killed or starved or abandoned on ice."

I sighed. They knew perfectly well that I had to do fieldwork. I love fieldwork. That's why I fell in love with geology, actually. How could I explain it? Everyone else except Mom was into things to do with people. Even Sergei, the bad boy, went off to Paris and became a chef. Though maybe after my announcement I'll be the bad one and

Sergei, with his new daughter and new restaurant, will have joined the ranks of respectability.

Only Mom really understood that things that have nothing to do with people could be just—fascinating. All by themselves.

I did not become a geologist because of my famous grandmother. I became a geologist because when I was ten we went to Hawaii and I saw a volcano erupt. It was all very proper, in a helicopter over Volcano National Park, but I had never seen anything ever so thrilling or so beautiful.

I became obsessed by volcanoes. I read about them, watched them, studied them constantly. When other tween girls had pictures of teen dream movie stars or boy bands up in their rooms, I had pictures of exploding mountains and lava floes. I became a volcanologist.

Then the Europa project appeared. I fell in love with the possibilities. And I understood Tatyana Kolninskaya, understood what had driven her off Earth and onto the ice.

The project manager had been one of her graduate students, but hadn't qualified for the Europa mission because he had a heart condition. He hadn't realized that I was her granddaughter and I've kept it that way. Just Anna Taylor from Brooklyn, you know. Forget that K. Doesn't stand for anything. But he quivered with excitement when he talked about the waters of Europa, about the seas trapped in the ice, separate from the oceans beneath them, and the friction that kept them warm. With explosive plumes very much like volcanoes—one of which had killed most of the Minos team.

There may be volcanoes beneath Europa. They wanted a volcanologist who could study the ice plumes and the tides, and also possibly locate volcanic vents.

I'd done my dissertation on underwater vents on Ganymede, Europa and Enceladus. Volcanoes presage life. Life needs heat, and heat can come from the planet's core or star, or tidal friction as with Europa, or any combination. But unique life forms have evolved around oceanic volcanic vents on Earth. If it happened on Earth it could happen elsewhere.

I was hooked, and I was hired. My dissertation had been grounded in the observations we had from flybys and robot landers, but the Minos material had more depth. How could I pass up the opportunity to go there myself?

"I want to go. I need the publications and this could make my career. It's not my fault my mother is crazy."

"No, it's not your fault. But we don't have to like it just the same," Grandpa George said, and Grandma Fritzie nodded in agreement.

Sergei ignored me, but then he was in the kitchen preparing something intricate. I set the table, which at least gave me something to do. The starched linen cloth was so old it was wearing thin in places, the fine china with the gold scroll pattern along the edges that Grandma Fritzie had gotten from her grandma and the heavy silver that had come from Grandpa George's family connected me with my own history. The serving spoon engraved with the elaborate B for "Browne" came from Ruth Browne, who had been Grandpa's great-grandmother's in Syracuse. She had been a nurse and had been a little girl during school desegregation. I'd grown up on the stories of Great-great-grandmother Browne being bussed to a white school district and how grown women had screamed nasty words at her and thrown eggs. But that hadn't bothered her so much as the kids in her class wouldn't ever pick her for the dodge ball team. And she was always in the last reading group, every single year, although she tested at a ninth grade reading level in fourth grade.

I hoped she would have been proud of me, and I felt her courage as I laid the heavy serving spoon on the table. I loved my family. I loved my work. I never wanted to hurt anyone, ever. But no matter what, I was going.

I wondered, for the first time, whether Tatyana Kolninskaya had faced resistance as well, whether my Great-Aunt Olga and their parents had been afraid and tried to talk her out of it. Mama had said that Aunt Olga had been elegant and stern and disapproving. But Tatyana was taking along a child, my mother. I, at least, was going alone.

Ice. So many many colors of ice. And so abnormally flat, as well. Europa is the flattest body in the solar system. I was standing on a great body of water. More water was frozen right here on the surface of Europa than existed in all the oceans of Earth.

And I was here. Standing. On. Europa.

Like my mother and my grandmother before me. They too, had seen the colors of Jupiter with its rings above the horizon and the endless smooth ice. As I looked at the gas giant above it didn't seem so strange, suddenly, the ice and the stranger in the sky. I felt as if my mother were with me, as if I saw it through her eyes as well as my own. And Tatyana Kolninskaya was there too, watching. Silliness, I knew, but this was a place they had known and now I had come, the third generation.

We had set down ninety minutes previously and gone through a meticulous systems check before we suited up and started hauling equipment from the outer hatches. We would use the lander as our indoor base—we'd already been sleeping there and had our few personal items comfortably stowed.

More importantly, it had an efficiently designed lab that we could access from outside, including an airlock with a built-in laser spectrometer, scanning microscopes, sequencers and all requisite instruments so that we could run the basics without contamination. But we had to haul the larger equipment out to the sites, drill out cores, and survey *in situ*.

The lander had been designed so that we had to lift and carry as little as possible. After five months in zero gee, even with all the mandatory exercise, we were weak. I was not looking forward to dragging all that apparatus anywhere, even if it was just to the power sledge.

I only weighed a hair over twenty-one pounds on Europa. After five months in space, it felt like a ton. Our equipment, fortunately, only weighed about six hundred pounds on Europa, and there were six of us to haul it out and secure it to the sledge. Back home it would have been a joke.

We'd trained for the physical challenges of the mission. We'd worn the bulky suits in saline tanks and practiced securing the power pack ties to the sledge frames and getting the drill tripods set up, but nothing could simulate what happens to the body after five months of zero gee. We all worked out on the trip out here and geologists are a pretty fit crowd to start with. Even I, the city kid, was an avid camper and thought nothing beat a white water canoe trip or an afternoon of snowshoeing for a great time. When we ran the drills back home I never broke a sweat. Now I was breathing hard just getting the panels detached.

By the time we set up and returned to the lander I felt like I'd been run over by a tanker. The only reason I peeled out of that cumbersome, overstuffed suit was that I thought maybe I would hurt less without the constant pressure of the tubing across my aching shoulders and the steel rings restricting my movements. My teammates looked every bit as exhausted as I felt. None of us were good for one more step, not even Richard, the hydrologist post-doc who had been an alternate on the US men's Olympic speed skating team once upon a time.

"Anyone want dinner?" Ilsa Grieg, our chief organizational martinet (whose official position was aeronautical engineer and not

Boss of Everyone) asked, but I was too tired to eat. All I wanted was to fall asleep, and I barely made it to my bag before I did.

The first week went by in a blur of agony and exhaustion punctuated by awful food. Grandma Fritzie was right, there was nothing good to eat out here. Not that I noticed; I was too tired to pay attention to anything except the fact that my shoulders felt like they were tearing apart and my legs were constantly sore. And we all stank. The recirculated air in the lander smelled of unwashed bodies. We showered for a timed five minutes in lukewarm water on a three day rotation and used dry shampoo on our hair. Whoever had masterminded supplies had probably thought scientists wear white lab coats and sit at benches all day. But drilling ice cores at minus one hundred sixty Celsius, while wearing a suit, is not exactly sitting in front of a screen eating Doritos and wearing a tee shirt. No, we knew the real reason was because water is heavy and hard to haul, and drinking takes precedence over bathing. But still, yuck.

My mother had grown up here? I could barely imagine surviving more than our three weeks of data collection. My grandmother and mother had lived here for twenty-seven months, and would have stayed much longer. I could not imagine how someone could be a child here, how to play and run in suits, how to get away from the grownups in the cramped quarters of Minos Base. And yet my mother had written about it in her memoir as if it had been normal. I suppose for her it had.

In that thin atmosphere and low gravity, we could almost fly and our games always involved long jumps and chases. We were not heavily supervised as the adults went about their work, so we learned to take care of the suits ourselves.

The day of the accident Victor and Madison had lab time, and so were in charge of watching us. We kids had a kind of pact with Victor and Madison. They were two of the younger expedition members and not parents themselves, so they didn't have the same fears for us as the other adults. Like all children, we wanted independence and to be away from the eyes of grownups. Victor and Madison were both willing to be very lenient so long as we gave them the quiet they desired to concentrate on their work.

In the second week things began to change. We broke into three teams of four, and I had lab time as well as fieldwork. For several shifts a week I did stare at a screen as the sensors processed samples we'd retrieved. My body had adjusted to the hard work and the minor gravity and I was no longer so utterly spent. I could pay attention to the ice formations and the view of Jupiter overhead.

Ice.

I am a volcanologist, but first I am a geologist and the ice on Europa holds such promise, teases with such secrets. Under all that ice burns a hot core, heated by constant friction of the tide as it is pulled by Jupiter. Some astronomers have conjectured that Jupiter is a proto-star, a dwarf that, had it developed fully, would have been a binary for our Sun. Instead it remained a gaseous smudge above us, duller than the surface of this moon. Though to be fair, Europa has the highest albedo in the system.

And deep in its heart, at the bottom of those liquid oceans under the ice are volcanoes. Very probably in those oceans is some form of primitive life as well, though the narrow band of atmosphere would not support much on the surface.

We drilled. We took measurements. We compared them with the Minos readings and found that they agreed. The only uncertainty was—had we brought it ourselves?

The partial DNA we found in what we thought was a virus matched a set of readings that Minos Base had recorded and sent back. It was rare and it seemed to be distributed far more densely in the area close to where Minos had been located.

"So is it spontaneous, or did it come with the first mission?" Michael Liang asked over what passed for our seventeenth dinner on site. Michael, being the top evolutionary biologist and one of the mission PIs, was in charge of the gooey stuff. Like looking for life.

"I don't know how Minos could have contaminated the environment," Ilsa Grieg answered. "They kept strict protocols on containment of all biological material, including waste from meals...."

"If you call that swill biological," I muttered.

"As I said, they kept strict protocols," Grieg was not about to be interrupted by a mere post-doc.

"They were killed in an ice plume. That means dead bodies," I interrupted again, the image so much more clear in my mind now that I knew the ice. The flat, brilliant surface reflected a billion shades of white and red rust trapped in the upper layers. Sometimes the rust lay on top, as if a comet had dusted the surface with cinnamon, and we'd run spectroscopy on every sample we could lay gloves on and I could tell them half the specific comets that had left deposits. Had the bodies truly been captured by the Jovian gravitational field, or had they been ripped apart and some pieces pulled back to the surface of Europa?

"Those bodies were encased in suits," Grieg said. "They should not have been breeched, even in an ice plume."

"Suits can be breeched," Liang said. "And those bodies were thrown out of Europa's gravity by the plume. But it's possible that some—debris—from the accident came back down. All the surfaces of the lander and our equipment were blasted with radiation, but it's still possible some virus survived. Contamination has always been a consideration. Back in the old days, they deliberately crashed a probe into Jupiter rather than take the chance it would crash here and contaminate any possible life on Europa. But that was before we started getting more robust readings and had to come in and take samples ... and the samples pass the protocol that compares them to known sequences."

"And our sterile precautions are much improved," Grieg had to get in her point. "We are far more advanced about such things now. Between the radiation sterilization and the other precautions we should no longer be a danger. The tests show that even dropped into a full volcano the suits remain intact."

"And I am Marie of Romania," I muttered under my breath. Richard shook his head at me.

"So what have you found?" Richard changed the subject.

Liang smiled. "We've confirmed the virus. The rest is—speculative. But promising. Very promising. Tests so far appear to confirm that this is not contamination."

"So we did it. We found extraterrestrial life. Proof that life exists on places other than Earth. It's here, around us, in this ocean," Richard said like a prayer in the stillness of the tiny lander common space.

We didn't jump up and down, congratulate each other, yell, break out champagne. We didn't have champagne. And this was bigger than a boisterous celebration, this was momentous, this was awe.

Had Minos hung on this moment too? Had my grandmother known this indrawn breath of the last of the old knowledge before the new universe broke around us? We are not and never have been alone. We had confirmed life on Europa.

"Viruses can survive almost anything," Liang said as if this were a perfectly normal conversation. "Anna, we need to find that volcanic vent you proved in the mathematical models, we need to find real warmth to see if there are native animals here and make sure they are not contaminated by the earlier mission. We have to go on the assumption that we can screen for contaminated material. We've only got four days left and a lot of work to do."

So we turned things over to Team Two. Since Europa keeps the same face toward Jupiter, we had light to work and had split into groups to maximize the time. Also to minimize the use of resources, like sleeping bags and heaters. I was in Team One and should be going off shift, but I was too excited to sleep, so I went back to my charts, looking for seismic activity to see if I could identify any possible volcanic activity in our survey region. Not that I hadn't run the data before, but this time I tightened the grid and used the ice plume indicators. I was not convinced that the ice plumes had anything to do with subsurface volcanic activity. Richard and I had spent the first week here, when we weren't drilling or sleeping, looking for ice plumes and what created them. I considered this a safety issue as well as scientifically interesting. My grandmother had died because they had been taken unaware. But the more I looked the more I was convinced that the plumes were the result of interaction between the weak magnetic field of Europa and the strong one of Jupiter which creates some very strange phenomena.

In any event, I started a much finer search from the vibration receptors we had placed at the collection sites. The next morning, over something that the supplies had labeled coffee but resembled that dearly missed beverage only in color and some degree of bitter kick, I showed Michael and Richard what I'd done. "If we can set up a deep heat sensor here, maybe in a few hours even we can have some idea whether it would be worth drilling." I indicated a spot deep in a crevasse. I'd specifically looked at crevasse areas to minimize the drilling—hard, heavy work with sixty-five klicks of ice to go through before you hit liquid water. And the heat vent would be far below that.

"You didn't sleep all night, did you?" Liang looked at me like my advisor used to when I'd made a particularly stupid mistake.

I shrugged. "It was interesting. I couldn't sleep."

He grunted. Richard crossed his eyes at me. "Hit the bag. We'll probably go place the sensor, but you're not doing anything until you get some sleep."

He was right. I was seriously sleep deprived and not making the best decisions, which meant I argued that I had to go with them to position the sensors. He wasn't a geologist and Richard was a hydrologist who didn't know squat about volcanic vents, and I ended up spilling imitation coffee all over my pants, which didn't make my case any stronger. But I'm stubborn, and when I'm tired I'm worse, and Liang was a decent PI so he figured it was easier to give in than to fight. We were only placing a sensor. Besides, who would go with him? Liang? Or Grieg, who wasn't a geologist either? Richard couldn't go alone.

This was not heavy work, but rules were that no one went out on the surface alone. No one, never, not for any reason. I'd never thought about the rule because all my previous forays had been drilling, or placing sensor arrays, which took as many able bodies in the field as we could muster. This though? This weighed less than one pound under Europa gravity and I knew exactly where it went, and I was cranky from being up my whole sleep cycle. We took the scooter, since the site was nearly ninety klicks off. I tried to set the coordinates for the area but my hands were clumsy from exhaustion and too much caffeine. I'd say I could do the sequence in my sleep, but I was just about doing that and it wasn't working. Finally Richard took the navigator from me and keyed the sequence while I suited up.

The scooter had barely room for two adults and a sample kit. The sensor rode on top of the sample case and the rope ladder secured below as we skimmed over the slick surface. Like flying, my mother had said, and she was right. At this velocity, if I just added a light hop I would be sailing overhead—almost like paragliding but without the sail since Europa's atmosphere wouldn't support us. But velocity and muscle would still make for quite a ride.

And then we were at the crevasse. We unloaded the rope ladder and secured it to the edge and started down. I hoped it would be long enough. We'd used it to explore several of the crevasses before, though it hadn't reached close to bottom on some others and we'd lowered equipment deep into them and waited to get readings back from deep inside. What made those deep grooves that laced the surface of Europa? That was Richard's question and he could talk about the crevasses endlessly. Richard strapped the sensor on his back after a brief argument (I insisted that it was my equipment, he insisted that I was too tired. I tried to take it but my hands were jittery and I lost the argument right there).

Climbing into the depths is like climbing back into time. Or it would be on Earth, where we know that ice has formed in layers. On Europa? Kolninskaya's main theory stated that it is not, that all the ice formed at once. Certainly it appears that way, without the striation that one sees on Earth. Cloudy white-gray with hints of blue and reddish brown, lots of reddish brown that always made me think of cinnamon sprinkled over and swirled through.

We didn't know what made the crevasses on the surface. Before Kolninskaya, geologists debated whether they had been caused by liquid ocean responding to tidal forces, or earthquakes, or even volcanic activity. Kolninskaya settled that one—the readings had made it clear that the lines followed the moving magnetic field of the moon.

The rust is iron and the salt water beneath the surface responds as Europa moved in and out of Jupiter's powerful magnetic field. Ice shifts and cracks appeared.

Richard had studied the patterns of the surface crazing, hoping to identify older and younger stress lines and trace the action across the surface. Only now I saw the red as blood frozen from—debris. Or perhaps the red of a rag of suit.

Climbing down is always harder than climbing up. I didn't like looking down into what looks like forever, even when I weighed less than thirty pounds. The thin polymer struts that make up the rungs of the ladder didn't look like they can support the massive boots, though of course they did quite well even under full Earth gravity. But on Earth I only wore hiking boots to set sensors. On Earth I could feel the rope with my hands, I could feel the breeze, I could smell the air and enjoy the warmth of the sunlight.

The joy and wonder of an alien environment is balanced by the hard truth that you can't get out of it. There is no warmth, nowhere to run, none of the comforts of home. I still felt awe every time my sterile glove touched Europa ice, but I knew that when it came time to leave, I would be more than ready to go. Twenty-seven months? How had they remained sane?

"You coming?"

I shook myself from my reverie and continued down. We only had a kilometer of ladder. Who knew how deep the crevasse went? But I was fortunate this time and we had let out only three quarters of the ladder before we hit the bottom.

Richard stepped carefully, aware that the ice was not even. He used a probe before taking any step to judge the solidity and texture beneath. Minos teams had gone down into several crevasses, but we had done only sensor readings for the survey. From the previous mission we knew the bottoms of these cracks did not follow the pattern above, but that the ice itself could be broken and even soft. In a few areas Minos Team had found sections that appeared to be near the consistency of slush on the surface. That had been the most exciting finding of all, surface water, proving the existence of at least one of the lakes earlier scientists had theorized. But with the destruction of Minos Base and the emergency evacuation, no samples had returned for us to study. One of our first mission objectives had been to head to those coordinates and pick up samples of the slush, both to analyze in our own lab and to take home for others to study.

I followed in Richard's footsteps since he had the probe. We only needed to go a few steps to find a good stable platform to anchor the sensor. Even working with the thick gloves, between the two of us it was easy going. Though the temperature plummeted this deep, we were not blinded by the surface albedo. And then we started the long climb back.

We were perhaps two thirds of the way up—far enough at least that I could see the brilliant light of the surface—when the shriek of the alarm tore through me. "Suit breech, suit breech," it cycled through in the mechanical voice.

My suit had torn and might be leaking, but the only possibility was to keep climbing. The suits have multiple redundancies built in for every system. A mere outer breech would not endanger me, certainly not until we were able to reach the scooter. There would be supplies there to patch it up until we got back to the lander.

"Alarm noted," I told the system to shut off the racket.

"You get that?" Richard asked once my ears stopped ringing.

"Yeah."

"It'll hold. Keep climbing."

Climb. Just climb. Hand, hand, boot, boot. Look up, never down. Redundant systems. The suit is not depressurizing. There is plenty of air. I'm fine. Richard is fine. We'll get back to base. Just climb.

My mind shut down so that I saw only the next rung and then the next. I refused to think about anything else, though the ghost of Kolninskaya crept through. I could hear her in my mind. *Yes, child, one at a time. Slowly. The suit will hold. You will go home. I will not let you die.*

The fear froze like the ice around me. Cold, unfeeling, I felt distant from my body, and it seemed as if something helped me up.

And then I was over the top and Richard had his thick glove down to offer me a hand up. I stood on the brilliant white ice crusted with cinnamon rust.

My suit had a snag near the left elbow. There was duct tape on the scooter. Dear old duct tape, good for everything, everywhere. Even on Europa. Richard tore off large swathes of it and ran it around the outer layer of my suit. "You're good to go," he said.

When we got back to the lander and peeled out of the suits, I took mine into the common space and started to pick off the silver gray tape.

"I wouldn't look," Richard said.

I had to look. The tape stuck fast and it took more work than I anticipated to tease the stuff off, but I was trained to be patient. Anyone who has had to use a paintbrush to dust down layers of sediment knows that slow and steady eventually gets you there.

At minus two hundred thirty Celsius, ice is magnificently solid. Shorn apart, it is crystal sharp, like obsidian. The suit held well enough, though, with the duct tape. Which only proved that duct tape is the one of the great forces of the universe.

Which also proved that the suit was not impregnable.

Not that it mattered in terms of contamination, I reminded myself. The third layer had closed. Nothing had gotten in or out. As for the Minos Team's deaths, eyewitness accounts and sensor recordings agreed that the bodies in the ice plume were jetted away from the surface and Europa's weak gravitational field. They had plummeted toward Jupiter and had most likely burned on entry to the gas giant's atmosphere.

I wondered again if my mother had seen them. The witnesses who testified later were the two adults who had been observing the party. The children—well, Victor and Madison hadn't paid too much attention to them that day. My mother said that those two had generally tried to shirk any teaching responsibilities. She didn't mind—when they did give lessons they were neither interesting nor rigorous. She preferred lessons with the more senior team members, who often forgot these were not even university students. Mama had managed to convince Professor Chiang to teach her naïve set theory before she had started high school.

We felt it blow more powerfully than we had ever felt anything blast since we'd left Earth. The ground shook us all so we tumbled; no one could stand through the violence of the tremor. But only Carlos looked up. The rest of us started to run as soon as we felt the first shock.

I don't remember how I got back to Minos Base. One of the older kids, I guess, probably Martin, got us back. We hadn't wandered so far.

The base remained untouched. Victor and Madison looked at the sky and held each other, sobbing. Then they said we had to leave. Now.

We asked where our parents were, and Madison said carefully that they had all been killed in an ice plume. That we had to get back to Earth immediately. That we had to prioritize and pack, food and water, suits and tanks first, then records and samples, whatever we could salvage.

Victor sank to his knees, wrapped his arms around himself and started to rock back and forth. He said nothing intelligible for months. I understood much later that they would have heard our parents die.

We hauled what we could to the transport, food packs and water. Our parents had been strong people, large and powerful, but we were all small for our ages. Stunted by the lack of food, by the lack of gravity to work our muscles, we tired easily and had trouble getting even the barest necessities stowed away. Paul Song, the smallest of us, though not the youngest, downloaded the records, or as many as he could get over.

The ground shook at times and reminded us that we were not on solid ice, that we could be blasted out to Jupiter or churned into ice. We went too fast in our fear, we ran as fast as we could, as we dared. We wanted to finish and be gone from this place that had become a nightmare.

I am not so sure we even cared so much about remaining alive, but getting away was something to fix our minds on rather than the fear. Better to go through checklists, to calculate escape velocity and fuel reserves than think about the body of my mother hurled toward Jupiter, cremated in its atmosphere.

I took navigation; even before we left Earth my talent for mathematics had been clear. Aunt Olga had offered to keep me home so I could attend the best math schools in the country, maybe the world. How many times on Europa did I wish I were back on Earth instead of far away? I had wondered constantly why my mother had insisted on dragging me off when I could have remained in Moscow and won school prizes and worn dresses and shoes and not a vacuum suit whenever I left the enclosure. Where people would have praised me and paid attention the way they always had and said what a prodigy I was instead of having only this pack of unevenly educated kids as friends. Didn't she know my life was horrible?

And then she was dead. Gone forever. I did not mourn so much at first, but later, later....

I had to navigate. Madison stepped in as pilot and she was barely qualified. Her training was in evolutionary biology and she'd only completed the required safety training for any crewmember. All she knew were the basics of how to fly. Victor, who had been one of Mama's graduate students, was no better trained, and less help. Paul took care of the onboard computer systems and little YeFei turned out to be quite good at mechanics. Every hour I worried about asteroids, gravitation and fuel requirement and how to get home. I had constant nightmares of getting the reentry angle wrong and burning us all alive. To this day I wake up in panic thinking that I am burning, burning, dying inside the Rosalyn Yalow.

The only way I could remain sane was to focus on the math. Trajectories, geometries moving through space, distant, abstract equations that had nothing to do with life or death, that comforted me in their stillness, were my safety. They whispered to me and I could see into them, see the next movement and the one after as if it were a thing done. So I moved into that space in my mind, where only the equations existed. Nothing threatened me there. Nothing hurt and no one died. Here in the equations only truth existed, and the deeper I went into the truth the more clearly I could see it. Why would I ever want to leave that place for the real world of hurt and fear and lies?

We were so very close to Earth by then and I believed Earth would be my salvation. I was wrong. Earth is full of nightmares. Only in the world of mathematics am I safe.

I read my mother's private memoir during the months we flew out, and I was surprised by how deeply I felt for her. I was amazed at her courage. What had appeared as fragility all my life attested to a kind of nerve beyond anything I had ever imagined. She never spoke of her time on Europa or her mother's death. Only when I told her I was going, in the dining room of my grandparents' apartment, she surprised us all.

Dad brought Mama in. As always, she was the only blond porcelain skinned person in the room, and she was a good four inches shorter than anyone else at the gathering (Sergei's French wife being the next smallest and fairest member of the family). She looked delicate, her wide blue eyes haunted, still so thin that one might think that she had never seen a decent dinner since her return to Earth. We gathered around the same table where we had every Thanksgiving and Christmas dinner and birthday and graduation party in my life. Sergei served some fancy concoction and Grandpa George stood up. "I believe we are here because our brand new Dr. Anna has an announcement."

I stood up to general applause, though they'd called me "doctor" to death a month earlier at my graduation.

"I've got an amazing opportunity for my post-doc," I started, not daring to look at my parents. "I'm one of the geologists for Michael Liang's expedition and we'll be leaving in eighteen months." I took a deep breath. "For Europa."

Dead silence. Then I glanced under my lashes to see my mother smiling slightly. She nodded. "Yes, I always knew you'd go," she said as everyone else held their breath. "You are just like her, you know. My mother. Tatyana Kolninskaya. You are her very image."

Which I found very hard to believe since Kolninskaya had been all the colors of ice, white skin and pale blue eyes and platinum hair.

"And now," she said with a quiver to her voice, "let us enjoy this wonderful meal Sergei has made. It will be a long time before I have my children together again."

She even tried to smile. Was this the mother I had known as a child? I was in awe of her courage.

I was right about the vent. We drilled and took samples and this time it was Liang who didn't sleep. We had to make our re-entry window, but he wanted to make every minute count. On our twentieth dinner he announced that he had confirmed an actual cell sample from the vent area. True extraterrestrial life.

"I'll still have to run more screens for contamination," he said when he made the announcement. "But the first pass looks like no match to anything of Earth origin."

I spent the week before we left for Europa in Brooklyn. The day before I had to leave, Mama took me for a walk around the Japanese garden in the Brooklyn Botanical Gardens. We wandered around the reflecting pond with the azaleas and cherry trees and drifting willows, all as serene as my mother appeared. We sat for a while on one of the benches in silence, just appreciating the scene.

Then she pressed a chip into my hand. "My memoir," she said. "Of Europa. I've never shown anyone, not even your father. But you are so much like my mother, and you're going there."

But as she pressed it into my hand, she did not let go of my palm and we sat together, her tiny bird fingers strong, grasping my much larger hand.

"What do you mean that I'm like your mother?" I had to ask. The whole idea confused me. I thought of myself as much more like Grandma Fritzie and perhaps Dad.

She smiled softly. "You need so deeply to know things. You are so passionate. You are strong and single minded. But also, you love. That is the gift you gave me. I wondered why my mother took me to Europa, why she did not leave me in Moscow with Aunt Olga."

"Aunt Olga is a twit," I couldn't help but respond.

Mama laughed. "Agreed. But more, I realized, I realized for myself when you children were born, and the more I knew you, that she took me because she wanted me with her. We believed it was safe then, after the Lunar colony established protocols for children living in space communities. She enjoyed my company. She told me what she did in the day, what interested her, why she loved the ice. I think she was sad because I did not love it, too."

"So it's okay."

She smiled. "We're surrounded by these cherry trees. You know what the Japanese say about the cherry blossoms and their beauty. I think that is true of all life, of all of us. Come back to me, my Anna. You are so like my mother, so unafraid, so sure about your great adventure. Come back."

Growing up I thought Mama was weak and afraid of everything. This woman before me was something different, some person I had never seen before. I held her very hard against my chest and if I cried on her shoulder, no one saw.

Our return trip was fairly uneventful. I started writing up the papers that I would submit on my return and Richard and I started talking about more than just geology. Okay, yeah, I'd noticed when we first started working together that he was cute. But after nearly two years we had both begun to admit that we were—interested. We had another year to go on the post-doc, and then there was job hunting and the two-body problem, and it's not exactly like there are a million jobs screaming out there for geologists and planetary scientists. But both of us decided not to think about it until after we finished our post-docs. After all, a thousand other things could go wrong in the meantime. He might not want children. He might not want to settle on the East Coast. He might leave his dirty socks in the living room or not like basketball. Or he could be a Lakers fan.

Mom and Dad had come down to Houston to spend some time with me while I did the de-comp and re-established my wobbly Earth legs. I knew it was a big deal for Mom especially, but she was smiling, normal, even when everybody in the flight center tried not to stare at her too much (though one of the interns did ask for her autograph on one of her books, which she granted graciously, and even let him snap a selfie with her and said book). Though most of the time it was both my parents with me and Richard, Mom and I did ditch the guys to get our nails done, and so that Mom could talk to me alone. But she didn't want to talk about Richard, or even about Europa.

"You remind me so much of her that sometimes it frightens me. Did you read what I gave you?"

I nodded.

She bit her lip and the two little lines between her blue eyes stood out hard. "I don't know, Annushka, if you can tell me, but you are like her. What do you think? Why do you think she took me with her to that place? Why didn't she leave me safe in Moscow?"

"Mom, Mama," I took my one dry hand and touched the back of her arm. "She took you because she couldn't bear to be away from you. Don't you see it? And when you say I'm like her, I'm like you. I'm just like you. But maybe not as brave."

"But I am not brave and I hate the ice," she said.

"Mama, you're the bravest person I know. But look at this."

I showed her my first article from the Europa mission right there in *Geology*. With me as first author. Anna Kolninskaya Taylor. "And I've been offered a more senior position on the Enceladus team as well."

Mama blinked and swallowed hard. "You will go out again?"

I smiled. "No Mom, it's a robot mission." I sighed with frustration "Maybe if this turns up enough to warrant it." I shrugged. "Funding. You know."

And Mama laughed. Not a little giggle or sad smile, but a full out laugh. "Oh, yes, Anna, you have a lot to learn. Not only about your volcanoes, but the process of getting grants. I will help you. I am very good at this, you know."

.

Made in the USA
Monee, IL
25 June 2022

98615571R00132